The Sojourner's Tale

Evans Bissonette

DEDICATION

To my wife Sue and to my family for their constant support and encouragement.

CONTENTS

ACKNOWLEDGMENTS

The Sojourner's Tale would not be the book it is, had it not been for the support I received from all the members of both the *Troy-Birmingham Writers* and *The Writers Connection*. Special recognition goes to Martha Hale (*Russ and Holly: A Midwest Country Odyssey*), Martha Shoopman (*Dancing with Devils*), and Maria Taormina (*Divine Plates, Three Lives in One*) for having freely provided their feedback and encouragement.

Sojourner - *(Noun: sojurn, so jurn er)*
A temporary inhabitant, a newcomer lacking inherited rights;
to stay or reside in a place temporarily.

Chapter 1: The Journey Begins

Howling Wolf stood in the shade of a tree and watched the last of Tigal's[1] caravan disappear around the bend and into the forest. A slight rustle behind him interrupted his thoughts. He turned to find Bright Moon, the village Shaman watching him. He suspected her dark eyes had been locked on him, studying him from afar, long before she made her presence known. Nodding, he greeted her, "What brings you here?"

Bright Moon stepped forward, a slight smile crossing her lips. She knew that he would be at this place, away from the crowds, and away from prying eyes. She also suspected his son, Red Deer, would want to march off with dignity. Even as chief, Howling Wolf would not interfere with his wish.

---

[1] Tigal – He is a merchant chief and the leader of a traveling caravan as well as a friend of Howling Wolf and the Narwikin peoples.

"Did you get a chance to see your son off before the caravan left?" She asked.

Howling Wolf grunted something unintelligible, leaving his reply open to interpretation.

Bright Moon decided to change her line of questioning. "There are many boys beginning their Sojourn this season, how did you get Tigal to agree to take all of them?"

She and Howling Wolf had been friends long before he rose to become chief. In their youth, after he slew a pair of tigers, she found him, treated his wounds, and nursed him back to health. How long ago was that? She had to think about it. *Three hands[2] worth of summers had past. No, three hands worth of summers was when her mate, Kaliska, began the long sleep[3]. Two hands worth of summers is when Howling Wolf's mate, Yellow Flower, went into the-sleep-from-which-no-one-wakes after Red Deer, her second child, was born. I know it wasn't one hand's worth of summers. That was when . . . when . . . when the great bear came and destroyed my life. No, it wasn't then. It must have been four hands worth of summers. Yes, that's right; four hands worth of summers had come and gone. Yes, they were young then those many summers ago, but not so now.*

Howling Wolf stared out across the valley, still watching the place where he last saw Tigal's caravan. "Tigal can always use a few extra bodies," he finally said. "It works out for all of us."

Waiting for him to continue, Bright Moon remained silent and met his words with a solemn gaze.

---

[2]Counting - In this culture, the people count on their fingers. Accumulated counts are in sets of five and are referred to as one hand's worth since "one hand's worth" is a count of five and two hand's worth, a count of ten. Individual numbers are Da (1); Jar (2); Cha (3); Tug (4); and Mux (5). For numbers six through ten, Pra plus the count, as Pra-Da (6), Pra-Jar (7), etc.

[3]The long sleep/The-sleep-from-which-no-one-wakes - Death was associated with sleep, and is referred to as "the-sleep-from-which-no-one-wakes" as well as "the-long-sleep"

Howling Wolf didn't know what he could tell her that she didn't already know, but continued anyway, "Before the caravan returns here, its travels will allow them to visit several villages along the way. Because each village will have developed their own skills—their own way of doing common tasks—Tigal and his people will observe each boy and decide the best location to leave them that they may learn. Later, when the caravan returns, if the lads have gained wisdom and new skills, they can rejoin his cavalcade and return home."

"So you're saying the Narwikin peoples willingly turn their young boys over to the caravan. Remind me again why they send them off like this." She knew the answer, knew it as well as he did, but she wanted her chief to remind himself that he was not the only father that was making a sacrifice.

"By the time they've seen two hands' worth of summers, they've seen everything in the village, have done everything in the village, and get to think that they are the mightiest being under the stars. This sojourn lets them—forces them—to go out into the world where they find out they don't know everything. They leave here as boys, but return as men."

"Red Deer wasn't like that, was he?" Again, having experienced some of his escapades, Bright Moon was familiar with the answer and didn't work too hard at hiding her smirk.

Howling Wolf scoffed. "Red Deer was born headstrong and stubborn. Rambunctious from the start, he searched for adventure. He was a real handful that tested everyone's patience every moment of the day. While he needed to make this trip . . . I needed him to make this trip even more. Lucky for us, our grandfathers' grandfathers discovered that sending boys out to claim their manhood worked best for everyone."

"Ahhh . . . and what about those who don't come back?"

Howling Wolf was quiet for a long moment before he spoke. "It . . . it works out best for everyone."

Bright Moon studied her friend's face. It spoke the words that his lips did not, so she asked, "What troubles you?"

Howling Wolf stared off into the distance for a few moments, and then returned his gaze to Bright Moon. "It's the things that were last said . . . or not said. It's the uncertainty . . . the wondering if I'll ever see him again . . . to have a chance to . . . ."

"Do you want to know if you'll ever see him again?"

Howling Wolf dropped his gaze and scanned the ground near his feet as if looking for lost treasure while he thought about her question. *Unlike the Shaman, I am not burdened with being able to glimpse the future. I do not have a trace of doubt in her answers even though I know they could bring great pain or great joy. Am I brave enough to hear her words? Am I brave enough to live with the truth, whatever it is?* Making his decision, he took a deep breath and let it out slowly. Along with it came his reply. "Yes."

Bright Moon had foreseen his response. She tightened her grip on her walking stick[4], nodded, closed her eyes, and was silent for a few moments before she began to speak. "Some of those that left today will never return; some will come back after the flowers of the next spring; the others will return by the end of two summers . . . except for the one you cherish. Red Deer will return, but—unlike the rest—his absence will be longer. One hands' worth of summers will have come and gone before we see him again. He will have had great adventures and have faced great challenges. When he returns, he will bring people with him. Later, others will follow—one of those will become your wife—but the turmoil they faced will follow them like the dark follows the day."

"Wait!" Howling Wolf cried out. "No more . . . I can take no more."

---

[4] Walking Stick - A device used by many people to facilitate balance while walking. Walking sticks can come in many shapes and sizes and were used by their owners for three purposes: One was to help balance them especially when carrying heavy loads over rough ground; at night, they were used as center poles for construction of a temporary sleep-shelter; lastly, a walking stick was for protection as each stick could act as a club and had at least one sharp end.

She opened her eyes and saw Howling Wolf watching her, stunned by her revelation.

"I know you still mourn Yellow Flower[5], but she sleeps the-sleep-from-which-no-one-wakes" Bright Moon said. "You are young and need to take a new mate. She will help carry the burden of leadership. You need her . . . and she needs you."

Strong visions created by her words flooded Howling Wolf's mind, forcing out all but the most basic thoughts. He staggered under the shock of her words. "This cannot be. I . . . I cannot let this happen. I will go after him." It was all he could do, to take a few stumbling steps toward the caravan's dust still hanging in the air beyond the first clump of trees.

Bright Moon seized his arm, halting him. "No matter what you do, you cannot stop this. No matter what you do, he will go . . . and he will return. Those that he brings with him will need our help. Those that come after will join with us to fight the turmoil they had already faced. Red Deer will have to rely on what he has learned and the skills you have taught him. While he is gone, you should spend more time with your grandson, Crooked Foot. He needs to learn these lessons and develop these same skills."

Howling Wolf's shoulders slumped. "The question I asked . . . if I were braver, I would ask for more, but I know too much now. You should not have answered me."

Deep in thought, Bright Moon bit her lip, "No one can un-shoot an arrow, not even I, nor can I un-speak the words you have heard."

---

[5] Yellow Flower - Now deceased, she was Howling Wolf's mate (wife) and Red Deer's mother.

Yet another day on this endless trail. Red Deer plodded along, each step putting distance between him and home. Tigal set a fast pace, not a full run, more like a brisk walk. Every member had to watch their step, make good use of their walking sticks and be surefooted[6].

After two moons of doing this, Red Deer began to think the issues he had faced at home weren't so bad after all. His musing woke that little voice inside his head and it began to prod him . . . no, actually made fun of him and his situation. Like a knife, that inner voice slashed away at his confidence. Wrapped in contempt, it seemed to sneer each statement it seemed to speak. *Hey, you longed to go.* It said. *You longed for travel and adventure. Aren't you getting what you longed for? Let's make a list so you can compare what you wanted and what you got.*

Let's see, you wanted a change of scenery, and that's what you got. Sure it's a choice between the back of the person in front of you or the rough ground you tread over. Either way you're getting a change in scenery.

A chance to camp out. Well, yes, you have that every time you stop for the night. In the village, you'd have the same old sleeping place in your family's shelter. On the trail, you get a new place to sleep every night. Of course, if you want a shelter, you'll have to build your own. Or you could choose to go without and show everyone how tough you are to sleep out in the weather. In a shelter or out, either way, you'll have all the comforts of home. With your precious pack of trade goods, the one they gave you to carry when you joined the caravan, as your pillow and the animal hide robe your mother made you becomes your blanket.

Don't forget the wonderful meals you get on the trail. Every morning you get your fill of gruel[7] and an issue of jerky[8] or pemmican[9]

---

[6] Surefooted - Not likely to stumble, slip, or fall.

[7] Gruel - Depending on availability, they boiled cereal meal (oats, rice, semolina, etc.) in water, milk, or both. This may also be referred to as porridge.

[8] Jerky - A meat cut into strips, trimmed of fat, marinated in a spicy, salty, or sweet rub or liquid, and dried or smoked with low heat (usually under 70°C/160°F) or is occasionally just salted and sun-dried. The result is a

to munch on throughout the day, followed by a delightful thin stew each night.

Enough, Red Deer mentally barked the command to himself. I admit the trip is not what I expected and it does not contain any of the comforts of home, but it will get better. Meantime, I will not allow myself the luxury of complaining. After all, I wanted this and I will make it work. Now, leave me in peace and let me think about something else.

Red Deer used his walking stick to balance himself as he picked his way along this endless trail on this boring day. Unconsciously, he shifted his pack. Maybe he could entertain himself recalling the steps that led him here. Mentally, he began recounting the events.

Three moons earlier he, and two others, had stood before the tribal council. It was time for the ceremony, he had both longed for and dreaded. Longed for, because it would mean he would be free to travel, to see the world beyond his tribe's lands and meet new people. At the same time, these opportunities were the things he had dreaded.

As the village shaman, Bright Moon stood behind the three lads as she presented them to the council. The villagers, particularly those youngsters not yet old enough to be sent off, sat nearby in rapt attention.

As Council-Chief, Howling Wolf sat in the middle of the row of elders, and faced the three boys before them. They listened to Bright

---

salty, savory, or semisweet snack that can be stored for a long time without refrigeration. The word "jerky" comes from the Quechua term charqui, which means to burn (meat). Jerked meat was one of the first human-made products and is derived from this crucially important food preservation technique. It was essential for survival.

[9]Pemmican - A concentrated mixture of fat and protein (usually meat) used as a nutritious food as a mainstay while on the trail or as a supplement when other food was available. Traditionally pemmican was prepared from the lean meat of large game such as buffalo, elk, or deer. The meat was cut in thin slices and dried over a slow fire or in the hot sun until it was hard and brittle. Then, using stones, it was pounded into very small pieces, almost powder-like in consistency. This was mixed with an equal amount of fat. When available, nuts and dried fruits were pounded into powder and then added to the meat/fat mixture. The resulting mixture could be packed into rawhide pouches for storage until needed.

Moon speak of the tests given the boys, both individually and as a group, and told of how each lad had performed.

With her final words, she raised her hands high in the air and in a clear voice spoke for all to hear. "Oh, great Chief Howling Wolf, it is my belief the ones standing before you are ready to face the final test. To show they are willing to become men, they ask to go into the world, to meet new people, gather new ideas, and return to share their knowledge. What say you?"

The silence did not last long. For show, the elders put their heads together and a low undertow of murmurs rose as if they were discussing what they had been told. In reality, when they were approaching this age, the eligible boys in the village were secretly under observation. Based on the collected information, the discussions had already taken place and the council's decisions had been made.

When quiet returned, Howling Wolf looked to his left and his right, nodded, and stood to address the community in general and these youths specifically. "Tigal, the Caravan Master, has sent out his runners to announce that he expects to be here by the next full moon. We sent word back that we have goods to trade and ask that he take you lads into the world, leaving each of you at a different village along his route. That way, you may learn new crafts and grow into men. Until now, you were boys. You lived as boys, played as boys, thought as boys. Now is the time for you to put away these traits and prepare yourselves to become men."

The caravan came to a halt. Taking advantage of this short break, footsore porters dropped their packs and sprawled out on any soft spot they found. Lost deep in his own thoughts, Red Deer, oblivious to the change, tripped over a loose pack.

"Hey, watch where you're going," the pack owner barked.

"Sorry," Red Deer said. "I wasn't watching."

"Well, next time you should keep a better eye out, or I'll have to teach you a lesson."

"Really? Would that be a lesson in how to run my mouth?"

The pack owner, a youth who appeared to be a little older and taller than Red Deer, jumped to his feet. Fists clenched, he rushed forward. Red Deer let him get close before quickly slipped off his own pack, spinning around, and slinging it at the charging youth. Unable to stop, the youth collided with the pack and went down. Others in the immediate area perked up. If this developed into a fight, it would be an entertaining break from the boredom of the trail. Jeers and taunts erupted from the crowd. Onlookers started to choose sides; some wagering on the outcome.

Walking stick still in hand, Red Deer strode past his adversary and picked up his bundle. "I am Red Deer. Thanks for stopping my pack."

His adversary sprung back to his feet. "Red Deer, ha! When I, Great Buffalo, get through with you, your name will be Whimpering Dog." He lunged at Red Deer, who quickly danced out of his pursuer's reach.

Great Buffalo lunged again. Red Deer slipped the tip of his walking stick between his adversary's feet and twisted. Once more, Great Buffalo found himself in the dirt. Getting up again, he approached Red Deer with more caution. Not wanting to end in the dirt a third time, he watched Red Deer's every move. More people had joined those already gathered. They grew noisier when Great Buffalo grabbed Red Deer in a bear hug and picked him up off the ground.

Red Deer drew his head back and brought it sharply forward. Their heads collided. The head-butt broke Great Buffalo's hold. Shocked, he dropped Red Deer and stumbled back. Freed from his adversary's grip, Red Deer landed on his butt. Realizing what had happened, Great Buffalo fell on his opponent before Red Deer had a chance to regain his feet.

The pair rolled around in the dirt until Great Buffalo managed to settle atop a bucking Red Deer. Acting fast, but not fast enough, Great Buffalo attempted to pin his opponent's arms. Red Deer clawed the ground around them, looking for something he could use. He came up with a handful of sand and flung it toward the face that loomed over him, leering. Temporarily blinded, Great Buffalo lost his grip for a moment. That was the break Red Deer needed. He pushed again, forcing Great Buffalo to roll off. Red Deer jumped onto his opponent, knocking the wind out of him and grabbed a nearby limb. Laying it over Great Buffalo's throat, he pressed down enough to restrict the young man's airflow.

"Hold, you two," Tigal's booming baritone cut through the noise. The crowd grew quiet.

"I think I've seen enough." The caravan master pointed to Great Buffalo, "You. You've been with my caravan the longest, tell me what happened."

"This lout wasn't watching where he was going and tripped over my pack," Great Buffalo said. "Then he started a fight by hitting me with his pack."

The Caravan Master turned to Red Deer. "You, new boy, is this true? What do you say?"

"Well, yes sir . . . sort of . . . I wasn't watching where I was going and I tripped over his pack. Then he," Red Deer pointed at the other youth, "offered to teach me something, but ran into my pack. I think that's when you arrived." He gave the caravan master an innocent look. Had the man accepted any part of his story?

Tigal, recalling his own impetuous youth, attempted to remain stone faced while he thought about a resolution to the situation. He motioned to Aditsan[10], his second-in-command, who stepped forward. "These two lads seem to have a lot of energy. They can help us out by putting it to use," Tigal said. "Tie them together... so they'll learn to cooperate. See that each of them have an extra pack to carry and some nights of guard duty." Tigal paused for a moment

---

[10] Aditsan - Navajo name meaning "Listener"

and then added, "When they've been tamed, bring them back to me."

Chapter 2: Work Together

"Kill each other if you must, but the packs entrusted to you belong to Chief Tigal." Aditsan watched his men finish tying a cord—about two man-lengths in length—from Great Buffalo's left wrist to Red Deer's right wrist. He turned his attention back to the two boys. "Since you two appear to have so much energy, Chief Tigal asks that you carry additional packs. You are to protect everything given you with your lives... or you can deal with me," he threatened. For emphasis, if any were needed, he continued to give them a cold stare before finally adding, "The caravan is ready to move on. Gather your packs and join the others." Having other business, Aditsan left them standing there to work out any details.

Once Aditsan was out of range, Great Buffalo began issuing orders. "Since I have been with the caravan three summers, I am obviously the most experienced, the oldest, the wisest, and the strongest." He picked up his original packs and added the new baggage Aditsan had assigned him. Staggering forward under the load, he added, "Therefore, it is only right I take the lead." He punctuated this decision by smugly adding a final insult, "You can follow me, but be careful not to trip over your own feet again."

Red Deer burned with revenge as he gathered his packs and gear. Poisonous thoughts ran through his head. I would not be in this predicament if Great Buffalo-Dung hadn't sprawled out, spreading his lanky frame all over, I would not be carrying extra goods. I would not be tied to this clumsy dolt[11].

---

[11] Dolt - A person who is stupid and entirely tedious at the same time. Many times they are oblivious to their own mental incapacity.

This litany of thoughts continued while he eyed the rope that tied them together, following it all the way up to his rival's wrist. Ahead of them, the path through the forest went from level ground to a small incline. It presented a perfect place to exact some punishment for this scrawny lunk's[12] ill deeds.

Quickening his pace, Red Deer caught up with his nemesis. "Hurry up; we're falling behind the others. Aditsan will be upset if you don't move faster."

Not wanting to taste any more of Aditsan's wrath, Great Buffalo picked up his pace unaware that Red Deer looped the cord around a convenient tree stump.

Stopping short, Red Deer added, "Hurry now, here comes Aditsan."

Nearly in a panic at the idea, Great Buffalo quickened his pace just as he started up the rise. The slack in the rope between him and the stump ran out and jerked him to a halt. Under the burden of his unfamiliar load, the jolt pulled him sharply backwards. Great Buffalo found himself on the ground looking up at the sky and then at Red Deer peering down at him.

"Good thing you were in the lead, wise one," Red Deer jeered.

Shedding his pack, Great Buffalo forgot everything as he pounced on his enemy. The pair locked in combat, rolled around on the ground and only became aware of Aditsan's presence when blows from his walking stick began raining down on them.

"You two again!" An unhappy Aditsan roared. "No more of this child's play. I have more important tasks to tend to than the likes of either of you. Now, straighten up and fall in line."

Humiliated, the pair joined the end of the line of marchers and was greeted with snickers and catcalls. The procession started forward without further incident. That

---

[12] Lunk – (noun) short for lunkhead; a slow-witted person

lasted until the convoy reached a spot where the trail split. The path went on either side of a tree, creating a narrow island and a definite obstacle before they merged into one again.

Both boys stumbled along under their loads without looking ahead farther than the ground in front of them. Without thinking, Great Buffalo took the path to the left; Red Deer, the path to the right. The cord that connected them snagged the tree and brought them up short. Each glared at the other, knowing, just knowing, that the other individual had taken the wrong path on purpose.

Great Buffalo yanked, nearly pulling Red Deer over. Digging in his feet, Red Deer came to a halt, and a tug-of-war began. Forgetting everything else, even Aditsan's warnings, they dropped their loads and began wrestling. Pitching around in the dirt, the pair rolled in the brush and grass surrounding the tree. Their efforts carried them onto a hive of ground bees that let it be known they were not happy about the invasion and quickly broke up the fight.

Attempting to outrun the bees, the pair fled the area, tripping and falling as they ran. Neither could outrun the other because the rope between them kept them together. When one went down, the other was hauled up short. Every incident became a lesson in cooperation as each soon learned that they could not run from this new adversary while attempting to drag their companion.

Breathless, covered in welts, mementos freely provided by the bees, they reached the tail end of Tigal's caravan . . . and Aditsan. "Go back and get your packs . . . now!"

Meekly, the pair turned and started back down the path they had just fled... not quite hand-in-hand.

###

The second day went a little better than the first, partially because their stint of night guard-duty cut into their sleep. Shouldering their loads, the pair staggered along the trail.

They were crossing the lowlands where the air, already hot and heavy, was filled with pesky insects. Conditions would change, the older members told them. Soon, they would begin winding their way through the foothills. They would exchange the hot, muggy, bug-filled air for cooler temperatures, but a steeper climb.

Neither the bugs nor the steeper climb appealed to the lads, but what could they do? The weariness they felt seemed bone deep, but there would be no rest. They had to move with the caravan at the same quick pace they had experienced from the beginning. Step-by-step through the day until mid-afternoon, Finally, Red Deer called a halt. "Stop, I need to catch my breath," he said.

Great Buffalo halted and turned to Red Deer. His partner leaned on a tree to steady himself while he vomited. Great Buffalo sneered, "If you drank more water, you wouldn't be puking your guts out now. It's time to move." He took two steps toward Red Deer, creating some slack on the constant tie between them and then gave it a sudden jerk. The effort wrenched Red Deer off balance. Stumbling, the lad let go of the tree and the pair started for the caravan. To Great Buffalo's surprise, the other lad came along without a fight.

While the pair had dallied, the caravan had continued its quick pace up the trail, and the boys had to run to shorten the distance between the caravan and themselves. Up to now, both boys had been quiet, and the trek continued without incident... but not for long.

"Wait," Red Deer said.

Great Buffalo made a face as he halted. "What now?"

"I have to pee."

Disgusted, Great Buffalo let out a long sigh, "What next? Well, go ahead; I can't wait here all day."

"I'm shy," Red Deer confessed, "so turn your back."

Great Buffalo shook his head as he turned away. *This kid is so lame*, he thought, *but we're behind and if it will hurry him along, then I'll turn my back.* A moment or two passed before he heard the trickle of water—the sound he expected. Satisfied, he relaxed only to be surprised by Red Deer, restricted only by his packs, quickly run past bumping Great Buffalo hard enough it knocked the astonished lad to the ground. He scrambled to his feet in time to see Red Deer disappear around a bend up the trail.

Shocked, Great Buffalo turned around to find that Red Deer had managed to slip out of the cord that bound them together and then tie it around a small sapling. After knotting it several times, he finished by fixing his water pouch to drain on the knots making them difficult to untie.

It would be dark soon. Not bothering to try to undo the knot, Great Buffalo began yanking on the tree, working the roots free. He would free himself and catch up with the caravan and this young upstart. When he did, he hoped to have plotted an appropriate revenge.

###

Great Buffalo caught up with the caravan just as it stopped for the night. Even in the fading light, he found Red Deer smugly leaning on his walking stick. Great Buffalo unceremoniously dropped his packs and struck out with his own walking stick. Red Deer expected the move and parried the blow then ducked and rolled to the side before rising to one knee. Great Buffalo turned to continue the attack.

Aditsan, on an inspection walk, came on the lads just as the fight broke out. Walking sticks could act as a club and had at least one sharp end. If the boys were carried away by their anger, they could go from delivering welt-raising whacks to delivering damaging, even fatal, blows. "Enough!" He roared.

Caught, the boys stopped their fight. Red Deer, realized he was free of his restraint. If Aditsan found him like that, he would not be happy. Tigal's Second-in-Command, his back turned to Red Deer, did not see the lad snag the end of the rope with his walking stick and pull it within reach. By the time he turned around, Red Deer had the loose cord wrapped around his wrist, hoping the dim light would let him pass inspection.

Aditsan eyed the pair. "How come you're late?"

Before Great Buffalo could open his mouth, Red Deer blurted out, "He had to stop and pee."

The remark elicited peals of laughter from those within earshot; even Aditsan had to suppress a grin. Recovering, he said, "Hurry and build your night shelter. You've got guard duty later tonight. Don't be late, again."

As instructed, the boys turned to the task. Great Buffalo sullen and humiliated; Red Deer elated, but on the lookout for any sign of retaliation from his rival.

The third day began with a light drizzle. It saw the sun rise and dart in and out behind thinning clouds. Despite the rain, the caravan broke camp after their morning gruel and took up their quick pace. Great Buffalo and Red Deer, having experienced night-guard duty again, moved as if in a daze, their decisions slow as they labored under a fog of exhaustion.

The trail they followed was not in continuous use, and in many places was close to being overgrown. Ahead, a shoulder-high branch stuck out, ending near the middle of the path. This gave Great Buffalo an idea. In the lead, he slowed down as he neared the spot, giving Red Deer time to close the gap between them. Reaching the branch, Great Buffalo grabbed it and began to race forward. The branch,

17

firmly held in his grip, bent back. Unaware of the branch, Red Deer, connected by the rope, had to move quickly to keep up. When Great Buffalo felt the branch had reached the limit of its ability to bend, he let it go. Released, the branch sprung backwards toward its original point. The fog of near-exhaustion clouded Red Deer's mind and slowed his reflexes. The branch surprised him and he was on his back before he realized what hit him.

Great Buffalo, just a few feet ahead, was bent over busily filling the air with laughter. Red Deer grabbed the cord that connected them and yanked, pulling the unsuspecting Great Buffalo toward him. Red Deer attempted to get to his feet, but slipped on the wet grass. The two lads collided and ended in a heap. Punch-drunk[13], both broke into laughter.

Aditsan popped out of the brush ahead. "Hey, you two, you're falling behind. Get on your feet and catch up. . . . Now!" He didn't wait for them to respond. To him, it was never a question whether they would.

Both boys got to their feet, made sure they had all their gear, and trotted up the trail with only a minimal amount of jostling. Their pace, which began as an easy trot, soon became a race, with each trying to outrun the other. Bumping and nudging their way along, the pair failed to consider that the route they followed narrowed and soon would not be wide enough for side-by-side travel. More importantly, the trail hung on the side of a hill where it carved a path through the tall, wet grass and brush, which hid the gully it skirted.

Side-by-side in their race, the boys continued their competition. Red Deer nudged Great Buffalo, who shoved back. On the outside, Red Deer was swallowed by the brush. Great Buffalo, happy with his success, chuckled to himself. Push me, kid, he thought, and you'll end up in the brambles.

Thrown off balance by Great Buffalo, Red Deer disappeared through the brush to find there was only open air beneath him. Before he could cry out, his weight pulled the

---

[13] Punch-drunk – A state of being slaphappy due to exhaustion

cord that bound them taunt, yanking a surprised Great Buffalo off his feet and through the brush. Unable to stop their fall, they tumbled down the steep bank. The tangle of packs, uprooted shrubs, and boys finally coming to a stop in an ankle-deep puddle at the bottom.

Recovering from the shock of this latest adventure, the mud-covered youths looked up at the indicators left by their impromptu trip. Their downward path was clearly marked by a trail of broken branches and ripped up shrubs.

Scrambling to their feet, they tried to climb back the way they came but could get no more than a few feet up the slick side before sliding back into the silt-filled creek.

On the way down, the brush they grabbed at, pulled out slowing their fall and cushioning their stop. What worked for them then, now worked against them by pulling loose at the slightest tug. Out of breath, they sat down and looked at each other.

Red Deer was the first to ask the question on both of their minds. "What do we do now?" He used water from the tiny creek to wash away some of the mud as he considered this dilemma and waited for his partner to respond.

Great Buffalo looked around. "We're not going to be able to climb out of here. The sides are too steep, the rain has made them slick, and the brush pulls out at the slightest tug. Lucky for us, the rain only produced this tiny stream or we'd be trying to swim out of here."

Red Deer snorted in disgust. *Great Buffalo's been with the caravan for three summers and all that he can tell me is what I already know.* Suppressing the urge to say what he really thought, Red Deer suggested, "Maybe, if we yell for help, someone will hear us and…."

Great Buffalo shook his head. "We are too far behind. They wouldn't hear us. Anyway, I don't think I want to have Aditsan find me down here." He shrugged. "The gully hugs the trail they are traveling. I think we should follow it until we can find a way up and out."

Red Deer nodded his agreement. He thought about the possibility of facing an angry Aditsan and quickly added, "Yes, before they miss us." They picked up their gear and walking sticks and began picking their way down the gully.

The humid air clung to them. On the hillside, the air had moved freely, but here in the depths of the gully there was no breeze. Red Deer needed something to draw his thoughts away from their condition. "How did you get here?" He asked.

Caught off-guard, Great Buffalo turned and stared. "I slid down the side of the hill right after you." He grew worried. *Did my companion land on his head?*

"No, I mean you said... well. I was sent out to learn and I expect to be with the caravan for a one summer, but you said that you've been with the caravan for three summers. How did that happen?"

Great Buffalo grew silent for a moment and then spoke softly. "We...my mother and father... they sleep-the-sleep-from-which-no-one-wakes." After that revelation, he withdrew back into his silence for a time. Red Deer put a comforting hand on his companion's shoulder, but said nothing. This was not the time for his words.

They continued in silence before Great Buffalo spoke again. "I grew up in a fishing village. From the time I was very young, I worked with my father and we built many fine ships. To find fish, my people sailed up and down the coast. When they were not fishing, the men of my village hunted. Life was good, but then things changed." He let out a long sigh.

"Changed?" Red Deer prompted. "What happened?"

"There were many storms. The ships could not get out. When they did, they came back with empty nets."

"But, your people could still go hunting."

"The Long Cold[14] came. My people said it was worse than any they remembered. The herds left. My people were starving. The cold winds came. Many grew sick... and then they entered the-long-sleep ... my mother and father among them." Great Buffalo's voice became hoarse and quiet resumed once again. Some time passed before he started his narration again. "Tigal's caravan arrived when I was trying to sew them into their burial shrouds. He took me in and told me I could stay with him until I found a place I liked. I've been with the caravan ever since."

Great Buffalo shook off his glum feelings, signaling that he no longer wanted to talk about it. "Luck is on our side," he said with forced cheerfulness. "The rain continues, but at the same pace, meaning the caravan should go slower and be easier to catch."

Red Deer, also eager to change the subject, added, "The descent of the gully flattens. Judging from the fringe of bushes lining the trail's edge, the path they travel also drops lower so we should be getting close to a place where we can climb out."

Elated at seeing this, the boys hurried forward. They hoped to find the point where the path and gully was close enough they would be free to rejoin the procession before they were missed. This is where their luck ran out.

Excited, Great Buffalo pointed ahead of them. "I see the caravan. It's winding its way toward the top of that ridge. When it comes down the other side, I think it will go into the forest. If we hurry, we can catch them before they disappear into the woods."

The boys picked up the pace and made good time until they ran into the next problem. The gully, still too steep to let them reach the trail, ended at the curve of a previously unseen creek. Swollen by the morning's rains, it had changed

---

[14] The Long Cold - Winter. Seasons occurred even in the Ice Age with winter longer while spring and summer were shorter.

from a sleepy stream to a sprawling river which skirted the low side of a hill and then disappeared around another bend.

Red Deer looked at this new obstacle. "Do you know how to swim?"

Great Buffalo nodded. The boys scampered to the water's edge. Scanning the surface from one side to the other, they could see rocks, or the telltale white froth indicating submerged rocks. "Good," they chorused, "the ground here is flat so the water spreads out and should be shallow."

They waded their way through the river, stopping now and then to splash the cool water over their faces. Rushes and brush separated them from the woods, and the place where they expected to catch the caravan. Reaching the other bank, they started forward, happy and excited only to come to a sudden halt.

The air filled with high-pitched squeals and the sound of crashing brush. The boys dropped their packs, making a barricade. They stood shoulder-to-shoulder, behind this makeshift wall with their walking sticks—the closest thing they had to spears—now at the ready.

Exploding out of the brush, came a wild hog—a sow to be exact—one that must have recently delivered a litter of piglets. Normally shy unless provoked, hogs are slung low to the ground, unusually quick, they can be extremely vicious. A foursome of scrawny wild dogs, the reason for the hog's flight, followed right behind her, nipping at her feet and looking for an opportunity to close in for the kill.

Slowly, Great Buffalo leaned toward his companion. "They haven't seen us. Maybe they'll carry their combat past without noticing, and we can slip away."

Red Deer nodded, but added, "Or, maybe we could wait and see who wins, then take the prize away from them."

Bug-eyed, Great Buffalo said, "Four dogs . . . an angry sow . . . and us! Have you lost your mind?"

Red Deer shrugged. "At least we won't be returning empty-handed to face Aditsan."

Wheeling around, skidding to a halt in front of the boy's packs, the sow robbed Great Buffalo of any reply. Bent on making a stand, she had not noticed the boys; intent on making a kill neither had the dogs.

The four dogs, barking continuously, lined up in a shallow half-circle facing their prey. Searching for her weak spots, the dogs feigned attacks, lunged and backed away. The pair of dogs in the center charged in, one from the left and one from the right. At the same time, the sow lunged at the dog on her left. It stopped and quickly backed away. In a flash, the sow veered right, caught the dog there, and opened its side with its razor sharp tusks. It flung the wounded carcass[15] aside. The dog on the far left took this opportunity to charge. It caught the sow under the neck. The animal squealed and shook its head vigorously, tearing open the wound. The dog lost its grip and dropped off. Before it could get away, the sow attacked, eliminating the attacker as a threat.

Blood spewed from the sow's wound. She turned to face the other two dogs. They closed in for the kill. She was mortally wounded, but they should not have counted her out just yet. The first dog led the charge; the second one was right on its heels. The sow flipped its head, and the closest felt her tusks. It was the last thing it felt. The second darted under the sow's chin, hoping to strike another blow at this vulnerable area, but it found itself pinned to the ground when its adversary collapsed and breathed its last.

"Come on," Red Deer said. "We need to put them out of their misery." Great Buffalo, still bound to Red Deer, understood their obligation, and joined in the process.

Great Buffalo surveyed the bodies lying around them. "What should we do now? The caravan will be here soon."

---

[15] Carcass/Carcasses - The body of a dead animal, especially one slaughtered for food.

Red Deer looked toward the hill's summit expecting to see the caravan. "We need to take turns hauling our packs and gear over to the trail the caravan will use."

"Why take turns? Why not just grab all our gear and packs and carry it over there?"

Red Deer shrugged. "There are probably others interested in our prizes. We risked our lives staying here. If the fight between the dogs and the sow had turned out differently, we would have had a real problem on our hands." He worked the cord's loop off his wrist.

Great Buffalo thought about what Red Deer told him. "So, while one of us makes the trip, the other one waits here to protect our kills." Following Red Deer's example, he freed himself. "When we get the dog's bodies over to the trail, we can tie one to another by their hind feet and suspend them over a branch. If we need to, we can use the cord or our belts to hang the sow's carcass. That will be the easy part."

"What do you mean?" Confused, Red Deer looked at the lanky youth.

Great Buffalo pointed at the animal. "Take another look at the size of this hog. Moving the dogs are one thing, but moving the sow that distance would be another challenge. I think it's going to take some thought to come up with a solution."

"You got it." Red Deer said. "But, if we want something to show Aditsan, that's what we'll have to do."

Each made a trip hauling gear and packs over to the trail while the other waited at the fight scene. It took four trips to get the dogs moved and hung and two more trips to haul all the packs.

Red Deer looked at the sow's carcass. "I've never moved anything this big. Have you?"

Great Buffalo squatted down and tugged at the animal's head. "When the hunters from my village would return from the hunt, they carried their game on a long pole. I don't think that will work for us, but do we have any of the cord that Aditsan used to tie us together?"

Red Deer helped Great Buffalo find the rope. He tied it to the animal's hind legs near the ankles and tried pulling the carcass. It moved slowly, but it was difficult for both lads to get a good purchase on the cord.

Red Deer dropped the cord. "I got an idea. Help me find a long branch. We can put it through the free end of the rope, and each of us will have something to grab as we pull."

In the lead, Aditsan held up a hand, halting the caravan. The strange sight ahead caused him to call a halt. Porters took advantage of the pause, to drop their packs and find a resting spot.

Chief Tigal came forward to find the reason for the delay. Aditsan pointed up the trail, past the pile of gear and the dog carcasses that hung in nearby trees, to the two troublesome young men hitched to a crossbar straining to drag an enormous wild hog carcass behind them.

The second-in-command smiled. "Would you say they've finally learned to work together?"

Tigal nodded and then looked at the sun peering down at them through a thin layer of clouds. It was early, but they could use the time to carve up the animals. Dying, the animals had made the ultimate sacrifice, and nothing would be wasted. Fresh meat would be welcome.

"It is early," he said, "but let's make camp here. The sow shows signs of having a litter. Check with our new young hunters to see which direction she and the dogs came from then send a small scouting party out to search the area. If the sow has young they will not be able to survive on their own. If they're found and are large enough, save them as trade goods; otherwise, they can go into the stew pots."

He looked over the animals hanging in front of him. "Tell the clan leaders to have these carcasses harvested. See that everything is distributed evenly." He paused and looked around before continuing. "If you feel that hunting together has changed our two trouble-makers into a useful tool, then have them brought to me. I have another task for them."

Chapter 3: A New Task

In many ways, a caravan is like any other village. It's a tribe made of family units within clans, but this village is always on the move, and this way of life presents both opportunities and challenges not found in regular villages.

Clan chiefs supervise each family's activities. As caravan leaders, Tigal and Aditsan's jobs are to oversee the clan chiefs, settle disputes, insure discipline, and manage the business portion of their venture.

In the circle of events, a celebration may occur when the caravan arrives at a settlement, after which the caravan puts their goods on display. Then the villagers bring out their wares, and the bargaining begins. When agreements are reached, exchanges are made. The business of trade over, the caravan readies itself for departure. That is when their greatest challenges occur.

A caravan has to carry everything needed for survival on the move. Each family unit packs their own belongings. They also must carry food and water for themselves and any animals they have—enough to last until they reach their next destination. Finally, they bundle up the trade goods—newly acquired items along with those items not exchanged—and then they move on to their next location.

###

After three hard days and two long nights, Aditsan recognized that Great Buffalo and Red Deer had finally learned that their greatest success came when they worked together. Satisfied with the results, he felt they would no longer present a problem. He could finally deliver a pair of tired, but wiser, lads to Tigal at his campfire and be done with them.

Responding to Tigal request, Aditsan and the two boys found the Caravan Master locked in negotiations with his clan chiefs, so the trio waited quietly nearby. As second-in-command, Aditsan didn't mind the delay. It provided a respite from his other duties as well as a chance to watch Tigal skillfully negotiate a disagreement between the clan leaders.

Negotiations completed, the clan chiefs disbursed and the caravan master went back to examining a pelt that had been left with him. Aditsan cleared his throat. Tigal looked up, saw his lieutenant with his two charges, and summoned them over.

Aditsan indicated the lads should take a seat opposite the caravan master while he chose a spot halfway around the fire between them and Tigal.

The boys plopped down and Tigal set aside the pelt he was examining. "I might be mistaken, but it seems you two are carrying more bumps and bruises than last time I saw you."

The lads, eyes downcast, sat quietly and waited for Tigal to continue. They did not have to wait long. Directing his attention to Aditsan, the Caravan Master asked, "For the sake of the caravan, have they learned to be more cooperative?"

"It appears so, Great Chief," Aditsan said. "At first, it did not appear they would learn anything, but that changed. By the end of the second day, they appeared to have acquired the ability to talk to each other. Judging from today's results, I'd say they understand that cooperation works better, especially when they encounter obstacles."

Tigal nodded and turned his attention back to the boys. "Do you agree with him?"

In the last three days, the pair had learned many lessons, the greatest of which was that it was never prudent to question Aditsan's assessment. Both boys nodded, but said nothing.

Tigal looked from one to the other, giving them a chance to speak if they needed. They remained silent. "Good!" Tigal shifted his position and then leaned in closer. "Since you have learned to work together, I have a special task for the two of you—one that is very important to our caravan; not only will it require you to think, you will be required to be secretive and cunning. To be successful, you will have to work together. Are you willing to accept this new duty?"

This unknown task, whatever it is, would be better than the duties the boys had been faced with, even discounting the last three days. The pair, acting as one, smiled and nodded enthusiastically.

"As we travel," Tigal said, "I send runners ahead. They carry a message to the villages along our route to let them know when we should arrive."

This wasn't news. The fact that he let the next village know of their pending arrival was his common practice. He knew it gave the villagers time to prepare. Alerted to his schedule, the village would send runners to smaller settlements in their vicinity, places too small for the caravan to bother searching out, but willing to bring their trade goods for barter. In this manner, everyone—the host village, the caravan, the outlying settlements—benefitted. Both boys knew such a practice meant there would be plenty of goods trading hands. They also suspected what the caravan chief was telling them was a prelude to something more important. They were right.

At a nod from Tigal, Aditsan handed him a small wooden bowl. The caravan chief held it out and leaned in closer for the boys to inspect its contents. "Take a taste and tell me what you think," he said.

Reaching into the bowl, each boy took a pinch of the coarse, off-white crystals, looked at it, and then put a smidgen on the tip of their tongue. "Salt," Great Buffalo said. Red Deer nodded.

It is well known that all villages prize salt. It is something caravans carry as trade goods. No mystery there. They knew there had to be more. Mystified, their interest at its peak, both boys looked at Tigal and waited for him to explain.

"There is one village, a very special village, where we trade our goods for their salt and then use the salt to trade with others."

"We have done that for years. It is a good plan," Aditsan said.

"Good, yes…." The caravan master interrupted his narrative to scold two men staggering under a bag of grain. "An animal or a porter can only carry what one of you can carry. Split the load up or we'll lose both the load and the carrier."

The men stumbled off to adjust the cargo. Satisfied, Tigal started his narrative again. "Are you familiar with the Sea People?"

The lads looked at each other. Great Buffalo shook his head. If he had passed through this village on previous trips, it was just one of many meaningless, look-alike villages. Red Deer could offer nothing. He had not heard of this group. Even though this was his first caravan trip, his travels had become so mundane; he could not tell you the name of the last village they visited.

"Would you like to learn something new?" The caravan chief, a master of persuasion, watched the boys, measuring their reaction.

The lads' faces lit up at the opportunity. "Yes sir. That would be good."

"The Sea People have been harvesting salt for as long as anyone can remember. They have the knowledge. They are the only ones we know of that have it. Their knowledge costs us dearly."

The caravan master, emotionless, stopped to fill and light his pipe while the pair of boys thought about his words. Their curiosity would get the better of them, and they would be caught in his web.

Why was Tigal telling them this? Neither one knew what they could offer. There was only one way to find out. Red Deer looked Tigal in the eye and asked, "How can we help?"

The caravan chief paused. "I need you two to go in and learn how they get their salt. Knowing that, maybe we can be in a better position to negotiate with them. Barring that, if we learn the secret, we might find another tribe with which we can trade."

The boys looked at each other. This was a task like no other they had faced. Tigal watched them for a moment before he continued. "My caravan will follow our regular route and make several stops along the way, but we should reach the village in two moon's time. Aditsan will arrange for a small party to take you directly there. It will be a two-day trip. That will give you time to find out about their salt before I arrive." Tigal leaned in as close as the campfire would allow, dropped his voice, and said, "Here's what I need you to do...."

###

For this trip, Aditsan replaced the boys' walking sticks with spears especially selected by him. To make sure the lads were not looked at as inexperienced, Aditsan made sure the spears did not have the sheen that outsiders would recognize as new, nor did they look like castoffs that no one wanted. Rather, they had the look of a device that had been around long enough to see some action. The boys, having grown up using clubs and spears not only in mock-combat but also on real hunts, were able to demonstrate their skills for him. Aditsan, always prepared, felt the spears would speak to the bearer's experience. A pretense, but if played right, it would be one not called, or if called, it would be one the pair would be able to back up.

Aditsan and two of his scouts led the way to the Sea Peoples' village. They did not go directly in, but camped in the nearby woods, hidden from the villager's view. The grove became their observation post. For the next two days they watched the village and studied the terrain. From their location, they could see the inlet across which stood a bluff and the village they needed to enter.

Beyond their camp, thick forest on the lee side of the ridge abruptly gave way to scrub on the windward. In turn, wild grasses replaced scrub in the dunes near the water's edge. A similar pattern of trees, grass, and dunes was repeated across the inlet.

Backed by higher cliffs, the rugged banks of the bluff sheltered a cove where the Sea People made their home. Homes like none other. Generations back, these people had taken advantage of this natural amphitheater high up on the bluff's face.

Climbing the rock walls, they built shelters in crevasses and crannies until those places filled. As the village expanded, new shelters spilled over onto narrow ledges. Late arrivals were forced to shelter behind a heavy stockade. It was constructed across the open mouth of the stadium. A narrow path led down from the plateau to the stockade where a small gate provided the only entrance. From there, the path meandered across the face of the bluff, dipping lower until it reached the dunes at the sea's edge. Beyond the dunes, above the tide level, lay a beached vessel. Nearby, women and children worked on the hull of the overturned craft.

While the two scouts stood watch, Aditsan and the boys stood in the shade and peered through the foliage. "Tell me what you see, "he commanded.

Red Deer shrugged. "People are coming and going."

"You'll have to do better than that," Aditsan challenge. He turned to Great Buffalo. "What do you see?"

"In the morning, a procession—mostly women, children, and old men—come out of the stockade and move down to the beach. In the evening, a drum sounds and the same group returns."

"Good." He pointed to Red Deer. "What can you add to that?"

"Coming or going, the procession moves very slowly as if there is a great drought and they lack food. There aren't many men. The few we've seen are old. The village does not send out hunting parties, perhaps because there are no young men around. People at the beach appear to be working on the boat, but it doesn't look like it will ever see water again." Red Deer looked at Aditsan. Was that what he was looking for? Was that enough?"

Aditsan turned back to Great Buffalo. "What else?" Hands out, the boy shrugged. He had nothing to add; neither did Red Deer.

Aditsan pointed to the bluff across the way. "Look closely, and you will see the path from the plain down to the village is a scant trail, hardly wide enough for two people to pass comfortably." He paused, and the two boys jumped in. It was all the opening they needed.

Great Buffalo, the first to speak, said, "It snakes downward from the ridge, disappearing behind hillocks, as it descends."

Red Deer joined in as if it were a sport. "Sure, while it hugs the bluff in some places, the trail skirts the stockade walls and meanders past the gate before it drops down toward the rolling dunes and the shore."

Great Buffalo closed his observations with, "The trail is well-worn. This means that it's the only way in or out of the village. They feel they are secure from attack because the ridge that meets the plain is too high and rugged, while the trail is too narrow to allow an army to pass."

Aditsan smiled but just slightly. He was pleased that his protégés were coming along satisfactorily. "Yes, you're both right, except for one point."

Mystified, both boys looked at him and waited for an explanation.

"Tomorrow, the narrow path that will keep out an army is going to be your way in." He laughed as he watched their jaws drop.

###

Red Deer leaned against a gnarled tree and waited. Since midday, they were at the place where the trail left the plain and began its descent toward the stockade gate. Nearby, Great Buffalo, one hand shading his eyes, watched the path from the beach. From within the village a drum sounded three loud beats. Hearing this signal, the group on the beach gathered their belongings into bundles and began a slow trudge through the sand hills and up the trail toward the stockade. The boys had watched the same routine every day since they arrived, but today was different. Today, this event would get them into the village.

Great Buffalo and Red Deer shifted their packs, grabbed their spears, and began a quick descent along the winding trail. If they reached the gate after the group from the beach, they would be locked out overnight. However, if they timed it right and were the first to reach the gate, they could block the way and make the procession a bargaining token for their gaining entrance. The two boys moved swiftly along the twisting path, but descending, they lost sight of the beach and the group working its way up from there.

Compared to the path they were on, the trail widened—but not much—as it reached the village, then narrowed once again as it curved around and dropped toward the dunes. The stockade's heavy timbers, pierced by a narrow gate, bridged the gap between the opposite walls. Flat and rocky, the ground outside showed no sign the others had entered.

Great Buffalo and Red Deer walked past the gate and stopped near the mouth of the trail to the beach. Still within hailing distance, Great Buffalo cupped his hands and called out, "Shelter for a couple of wanderers?"

The guard, an old man, had been napping in the shaded tower. Irritated by the interruption that awoke him so abruptly, he gave a surly reply. "Eh? Who are you and what's your business?"

Red Deer chuckled to himself. "We come from afar and bring news of a caravan. Is this of interest to you?"

"Maybe, maybe not," was the ill-tempered answer. "Move on and don't waste my time."

The sound of chattering voices interrupted their negotiations. The group from the beach, mostly women and children, came around the bend in the trail confirming that the boys had arrived first. They could breathe easier now. The old men and the women in the procession, seeing that two armed youths barred further passage, dropped their bundles and sat down to wait. Both boys struggled out of their pack and, following the example the procession had set, they also sat.

Comfortable, Great Buffalo called back to the guard, "I invoke the *Wanderers' Right*."

"What? What's this you say?" The guard was taken aback by this demand.

"The Wanderers' Right binds you provide us with food and shelter for three days before you can turn us out."

"I know of no such thing. Be gone! Away with you I say!"

Back on his feet, Great Buffalo tried a different approach. "Is Running Wolf still your chief? Remind him of his duties under the *Wanderers' Right*."

Red Deer also stood up and added, "Oh, and tell him a Narwikin is here with a present from our Caravan Master, Chief Tigal."

The guard made no reply. From within the stockade, sounds of a commotion, punctuated by voices in heated debate, indicated something was happening. Deciding this stalemate could take a while; Red Deer made a comfortable seat of his pack and waited. Great Buffalo shrugged and joined him.

Casually they scanned the area, appearing to take interest in the village built into the bluffs or the stockade. Their real interest lay in the condition of the women and children in the procession.

Sad-faced, these poor souls spoke in low voices and paid little attention to them. The children's movements were lethargic. Everyone had a gaunt look. Their clothing hung on emaciated frames.

Finally, a scraping noise from inside signaled the bar on the gate being raised. It swung open silhouetting a man. Slowly, he hobbled toward the two boys. Seeing this, the women stood, picked up their packs, gathered the children, and began filing past Red Deer and into the stockade. Both boys got to their feet slowly, allowing them time to inspect the approaching emissary.

An old man, as frail looking as the others, stopped a short distance away. "Narwikin, what do you have for Running Wolf?"

"Something we'd like to put in his hands so we may see the joy in his face." Red Deer tried not to make it apparent that he noticed the man's ill-fitting clothes.

The old man made a noise, a grunt or scoff, Red Deer wasn't sure which, and replied, "Running Wolf is very busy these days. Few get an audience with him."

Stone-faced, the old man looked at the pair in silence for a short time.

Great Buffalo shrugged and finally broke the stillness saying, "Well, I guess we'll just gather our things and be on our way then."

Shocked, the old man blinked. "Wait!"

"Wait? Wait for what?" The boys acted surprised, but continued to slip on their packs. Red Deer looked at his partner. "I see no reason to wait, do you? We've done as Chief Tigal instructed and might as well go back now."

Great Buffalo pursed his lips, as if deep in thought. "Yes, we've met our part of the bargain. If we leave now we should be able to get through the forest before nightfall."

The old man's stone-face disappeared as he tried to rescue the situation. "I am White Hawk, his advisor. I could take…"

"No. Thank you anyway," Great Buffalo said. "We'd like to see him ourselves. So, if we can't do that, then we don't want to trouble you." Making a final adjustment to his pack, he turned to Red Deer. "Are you ready?"

"Wait!" The old man commanded.

"What now?" Red Deer tried to sound exasperated.

"If you don't give me the gift, I… my men will take your packs from you."

Red Deer turned back and took a step forward. Putting a hand on the scruff of the old man's neck, he pulled him forward until their noses were but a finger's width apart. Great Buffalo spear in hand, moved to cover Red Deer's back.

Red Deer didn't glare, but he didn't smile as he said, "Yes, they could, but we both know what would happen then, don't we?"

Eyes wide, the old man spoke quickly. "If your people attack, we could just hole up in our village. It's easy to defend. The path isn't wide enough to let more than a couple of people…"

Red Deer cut him off. "Oh, yes. It's not what I meant, but I agree. You could hole up there… but for how long? Eventually, you'd run out of what little food and water you have, and then what would you do?"

"Not… not what you meant?" White Hawk was baffled. "I don't understand. What did you mean?"

Releasing him, Red Deer drew back a little, "You steal from us and word gets out. No matter what you do, no matter how you try to hide it, word always gets out, and when it does, traders, caravans, everyone will stop coming. Your salt will pile up. You'll have to pack up and move on. Is that what you want?"

Panic in his eyes, White Hawk stammered out, "N . . . n . . . no! Not at all."

Putting a hand on the old man's shoulder, Red Deer spun him around. Great Buffalo took up a position on his other side. Arms wrapped around White Hawk as if they were old friends, the trio strode toward the gate, "Good. Neither do we. So let's go see Running Wolf."

A youth on either side of him, White Hawk was propelled through the gate before he could regain his wits.

Running Wolf ran a withered hand over the beaver pelts again. "These are very nice."

"The best," Red Deer agreed.

Great Buffalo chimed in, "Chief Tigal asked us to bring something to repay you for all you have done for him."

The old chief grunted and took a long draw on his pipe, "You are both so young to be entrusted with such a task." He handed the pelts to White Hawk.

White Hawk, more interested in the hides than the conversation, volunteered, "We were all younger once. It's the way of life."

Running Wolf stared at the small cook fire without speaking, hypnotized by the dancing flames. Their movement accentuated the depth of the lines in his face but did little to eliminate the darkness. With some reluctance, White Hawk passed the pelts on to Running Wolf's son, Little Wolf. Agitated, the furs didn't interest the chief's son.

Red Deer could see that they, like the other villagers he'd come in contact with, looked tired, underfed, and worried. Directing his attention to the chief, Red Deer said, "You are troubled?"

After another puff on his pipe, the old chief spoke. "Long ago, in the days of my grandfather's grandfather, the Sea People learned how to harvest salt. They used it to trade for the goods they needed. Because of salt, they prospered and grew."

White Hawk added, "Yes, life was easy so they put aside the ways of their forefathers."

Attempting to draw another puff on his pipe, Running Wolf flashed a bitter smile before continuing. "Now we have grown too much. We are too many. Sadly, we've forgotten the old ways."

He stopped, knocked the ashes from his pipe, and then refilled it.

"Our best hunters are gone," White Hawk added bitterly. "Those left behind, the older ones have forgotten how to fish and hunt and are not up to the challenges these tasks offer. The younger ones never bothered to learn."

Little Wolf, shook his head in dismay as he explained, "Before you came, another stranger arrived. He offered us his hand in friendship, saying his people would trade for our salt. He also asked us for our peoples' help to carry the goods back to his village, a place he called Kam Na Udo. He promised to load them up with many wonderful items to bring back. Some of our people—those old enough to leave home up to those too old to travel—went to see this new place. My brothers and their wives, and our best hunters and their wives, went with him. They never returned. We don't know why."

Taking a firebrand from the fire, Running Wolf lit his pipe and blew out a great cloud of smoke. "In two moons, the caravan you spoke of will be here."

Great Buffalo nodded. "Chief Tigal asks us to bring word ahead that his caravan should be here by then."

Not to be left out, Red Deer added, "He has many goods to trade and would like much salt in return. That'll be good for you."

The old man grimaced but said nothing.

Little Wolf snorted. "It would be good if we had lots of salt, but the stranger took most of it and gave us little in return."

White Hawk shook his head in dismay. "Our village is left with those too young or too old to hunt. Our boat ran onto the rocks. We cannot fish. Our people are starving. They have grown too weak to hunt or fish, even too weak to harvest the salt. Without it, we'll have nothing to trade. "

Great Buffalo and Red Deer fell silent while they watched the dancing flames. The silence that had fallen was made deeper by the crackling of the small fire.

The chief, his advisor, and his son, stared aimlessly at the flames. Their hopelessness, like a pungent odor, hung in the air. Red Deer looked the old man in the eye. "You have been a good friend to Chief Tigal. He had us bring these pelts to you. I think he would want to show his friendship by having us stay and help you."

Startled, the three looked at him. Shocked, Running Wolf asked the question on all of their minds, "How… how can the two of you help?"

Great Buffalo was quick to answer. "Your people need food. We will go hunting."

Red Deer nodded. "Fresh meat should prove our value, don't you agree?"

Chapter 4: Hunting

The stranger that had visited the Sea People not only took their salt, he also the bulk of the men along with the men's wives. For the most part, the village was left with a population made up of the old, the infirmed, and those too young to leave home. Stripped of this valuable resource, both Red Deer and Great Buffalo knew the village was on the verge of disaster and they needed to do what they could to prevent that from happening.

"The herd... we were wondering, do you think they'll be there in the morning?" Running Elk ventured.

It was as Great Buffalo and Red Deer had witnessed. The other youngsters—mere boys and girls called on to act older and wiser than they actually were—saw Little Wolf in a position of authority and not as a confidant. They saw Running Elk as one of them and made him their spokesperson. In Great Buffalo and Red Deer's estimation, the group had made a good choice. Little Wolf would need someone that demonstrated the willingness and determination that Running Elk was showing, and the pair were sure they would make use of this trait before the hunt was over.

Great Buffalo's attention remained focused on watching a young girl—not quite a woman, but older than those around her—turn the spit slowly over the hot coals while he tested the Running Elk's resolve by not answering immediately. A short distance away, his back to a tree, Red Deer feigned sleep while he eavesdropped on the conversation.

Running Elk persisted. "When the darkness came, they grazed on the slope up ahead...."

Great Buffalo broke off his observation to look the lanky youth in the eye. It had been a hard day with little rest. The youth appeared near exhaustion, yet there was so much more to accomplish before this adventure was over. Great Buffalo put a confident hand on the lad's shoulder. "Tell the others that the animals are resting and they should do the same."

Hearing those words brought a smile to Running Elk's face. Satisfied, he returned to the campfire. Both Great Buffalo and Red Deer hoped these few words would allow everyone to relax. It had been a long day and it would be a long night with many challenges.

That morning, before the sun crowned the horizon, Great Buffalo and Red Deer helped Little Wolf face the issue head-on by selecting members for two groups: *the hunters* and *the followers*.

The hunters—mostly pre-teen boys, and girls just beginning to flesh into womanhood—from the best of those left in the village. None of these were experienced, but this would change for those who survived today.

The role of *the followers*—selected from the stronger, heartier older women, and children too young for the hunt— came afterward. In anticipation of success, the women were told to pack axes, knives, scrapping tools, buffalo hides, ropes, and poles. They would perform the immediate butchering of the animals, wrapping pieces in the hides. The packages would be tied to any of several travois[16] for transport back to the village.

---

[16] Travois - A frame structure used by indigenous peoples to drag loads over land, ice, or snow. The basic construction consists of a platform or netting mounted on two long poles, lashed in the shape of an elongated triangle. Additional poles, bound across the two main poles, were used to stabilize the frame and support the load being carried. When dragged by hand, the travois was sometimes fitted with a shoulder harness to ease the work. A travois could be loaded by piling goods atop the bare frame and tying them in place or by first stretching leather over the frame to hold the load being dragged. It is considered more primitive than wheel-based forms of transport. Wheeled vehicles excel on roadways, however, a travoise is superior when used on forest floors, soft soil, snow, etc., where wheels would have encountered difficulties. It is possible for a person to transport more weight on a travois than can be carried on the back.

For the time, *the followers* were held in reserve on a hillside. From there, empty bellies grumbling, they watched the line of young hunters—many of them their own children—march off. They hoped to hear the trumpet sounds that would signal their opportunity to swing into action as well as a chance to celebrate. They used these thoughts to shut out those of failure and continuing hunger.

By the time the sun broke the horizon the group of young hunters found a herd of buffalo. They divided into two groups—one behind Red Deer, the other behind Great Buffalo— and began shadowing them. Strung out single-file the groups walked alongside the herd to get the animals used to their presence.

Little Wolf eyed the buffalo just a few short paces away and then asked. "Which animal do we select?"

Running Elk, eager to get started, jumped into the conversation, "When do we attack?"

Wide-eyed, Great Buffalo shook his head. "This group doesn't have enough experience. They wouldn't be able to handle a whole herd, particularly not with animals this size."

"Hunting," Red Deer added, "is a game of waiting. We wait for the right time so we don't scare off our prey."

Leading the way, the pair from the caravan eased the group of youths closer to the horde. Sometimes moving quickly, other times moving slowly, they used courage, patience, and quick action to drive a wedge between the main pack and a small cluster of animals.

By late afternoon the group had managed to maneuver their prey onto the high, rolling meadows. There weren't many animals, but it would provide enough fresh meat to help Little Wolf's people… if their luck held.

Pulling back just before dusk, the group let the animals bed down for the night. The would-be hunters made camp on a hillside overlooking the meadow and set a couple of their young hunters as guards to keep watch over the herd and protect it from other predators.

Great Buffalo paired up with Little Wolf while Red Deer took Running Elk under his wing. The foursome ventured across the meadow looking for small game. Just after dark, they returned with dinner—a few rabbits, snakes, a wild chicken—in hand to everyone's satisfaction.

The girl, who had been acting as cook, eagerly received the additional game. She quickly cleaned and mounted the carcasses on spits before placing them over hot coals. When she was satisfied the meal looked ready, she began taking the spits off the fires. Getting to his feet, Little Wolf took the spits from her and handed them to the nearest youths. "Split this up among your groups and then get some rest."

Little Wolf watched for a moment to make sure his orders were being followed and then returned to his mentor's side. Great Buffalo leaned close to him and lowered his voice. "Your people were excited when they started, but they seem uneasy now."

Red Deer nodded. "I noticed it too and hoped it was just pre-hunt jitters driven by hunger and exhaustion."

Little Wolf shrugged and looked at Great Buffalo, explaining, "They are worried that the animals they chased all day long will slip away in the dark."

Relieved, Red Deer smiled. "It may comfort them to know that, unless the animals are frightened, they don't usually move too far in the dark."

Great Buffalo patted the young man on the shoulder. "Tell them that we'll take turns watching through the night so the animals won't slip away."

Red Deer nodded to Great Buffalo and Little Wolf. "Talk to the others. Tell them what we expect to happen. We'll take the first watch."

Hunched around the campfire, the young would-be hunters devoured the rabbits. Red Deer and Great Buffalo strolled away. Taking seats on a nearby knoll overlooking the meadow, they listened to the night sounds. Somewhere out in the dark a small herd of buffalo grazed. If their new hunters were successful, these buffalo grazed for the last time.

Hearing muffled footfalls, the pair turned to see Little Wolf and Running Elk, flickering torch in hand, approaching.

Little Wolf opened the conversation. "What brings you out here?"

Red Deer smiled and nodded to Great Buffalo. "We are listening."

"Listening?" Inexperienced hunters, both young men looked mystified.

"The night is filled with other hunters," Red Deer explained. "We want to make sure they aren't after what we seek. And you, what brings you two here?"

"Tell us again, how this will work." Little Wolf asked. Concern showed on their faces.

Red Deer looked beyond the pair standing before him, to take in those gathered around the fire. Bellies full, the others were seemed unconcerned about what might happen next. Stretching out around the crackling warmth, they would be asleep soon. It was best that he let them rest for now.

Satisfied the best of the group were here with Great Buffalo and himself, Red Deer pulled the torch close, picked up a stick, and began scratching in the dirt. In a low voice, he explained as he drew, "We're here, the buffalo are over here, and the ravine is here."

Great Buffalo broke into the explanation. "Before first light, we'll divide into three groups, left, right, and center. We have to crawl close and startle them into stampeding toward the cliff."

"Do you think we'll be successful?" The boys' lack of experience, the fact this was an unknown, their need for reassurance, made them ask the question.

Red Deer shrugged. "The buffalo are there. We have a plan." He reflected on their chances for a moment.

Great Buffalo shrugged. "If it works, we'll be successful."

Laughing quietly, Red Deer added, "If not, we'll be experienced and can try again."

To Running Elk and Little Wolf, neither of these leaders appeared concerned.

The rest of their group lay around the camp fire. Most snored, some loudly. "Good," Red Deer said, "they're asleep. It is best that they get some rest before we start."

Little Wolf looked over his shoulder at his sleeping comrades as if to assure himself things would work out. Turning back, he was greeted by Great Buffalo and Red Deer's confident smiles.

"Quietly now," Red Deer instructed, "put the torch out and come with us. We need to see where the herd has bedded down for the night. We must move soundlessly like the night's breeze. Walk behind me, and do as I do; step where I step; crouch when I crouch; stop when I stop. Great Buffalo will follow us to make sure no one gets lost."

Turning, Red Deer sauntered into the darkness confident the others would follow. Single file, they moved across the meadow. Pausing now and then to listen or take a bearing, Red Deer pointed out landmarks and obstacles—barely visible in the dim light—along the way.

He signaled a halt when they came to a rocky outcropping. Crouching low next to it, he motioned his followers close. Nearby, a buffalo cloaked in darkness, shuffled its feet and snorted.

Barely audible, Red Deer whispered, "The herd is bedded down over there. I want to see how far it is to the ravine so we're going to stick close to this ridge and sneak past them."

The boys nodded. Rounding the ledge, the foursome crept along the ridge, putting distance between themselves and the animals. Calling another halt, Red Deer turned to look behind them. Still whispering, Red Deer said, "We made it past the herd so we can relax a little, but we still need to remain quiet."

Running Elk and Little Wolf seemed to breathe easier at the news.

To explain the next steps, Great Buffalo added, "After we reach the ravine, we'll go back to camp along the other side of the herd so we can check that flank out."

With Red Deer in the lead, they made their way forward until he determine by the sounds of their movement that it was time to call another halt. Tilting his head, he stood silently and listened. The group bunched up in a small cluster at his shoulder. A few steps in front of them, a ragged line of bushes waved slightly in the breeze. Taking a step forward, Running Elk turned to face Red Deer.

Great Buffalo grabbed the young man's arm. "Don't take another step; the ravine is right behind you."

Looking back over his shoulder, Running Elk took a couple of quick steps away from the brink.

"Everyone," Red Deer said, "listen to how the sound changes as we move away from or close to the ravine." Satisfied his charges had learned another lesson, he motioned for them to follow him as he moved away from the edge.

The brush along the ravine helped guide them as they crossed the foot of the meadow to the ridge on the other side. One hand on the wall, they traced their way along its rocky surface until Red Deer stopped short. A gentle breeze brought buffalo scent. A snort confirmed the herd's nearness.

Crouching, they crept along the ridge once again until they reached a small hill. Great Buffalo grabbed their two escorts and said, "We're back. You can breathe easy."

Surprised, the pair looked over Red Deer's shoulder. Behind him, the once blazing campfire was now only glowing coals. The group they left behind snored peacefully. It had been a good trip.

The pair broke into smiles and was about to give noisy congratulations, but Great Buffalo raised a finger to his lips.

"Each of you'll be leading a group. I want to make sure you understand the parts you'll play before we wake the others. Tell me what you just saw and how you think it will play out this night."

The sun was yet to creep over the horizon, but it would be there all too soon. The four leaders—Red Deer, Great Buffalo, Running Elk and Little Wolf—gathered the sleepy-eyed youngsters.

Red Deer stood on top of a flat rock. The additional height added to his stature giving his words more authority. "We've toured the meadow where our prizes are bedded down. We looked at the terrain and have worked out a plan." He smiled warmly, hoping to bolster flagging confidence. "We will split into three groups. Some of you will go with Running Elk; some with Little Wolf; and the rest will remain with Great Buffalo and me. Right now, starlight and a sliver of moon will provide our only light," he told the youngsters. "We can't see the herd but they can't see us either. The cliffs lay beyond the pack. The breeze is light, but blows across us toward the animals. It is not the best arrangement, but it is all we have. They'll pick up our scent, but they are used to it since we dogged them all day long." Wanting to end on a high note, he gave them a broad smile and added, "Do your job, hold your ground and don't back down. Just remember, because of your work this night, you will give your people full bellies and much to celebrate."

The thrill of victory ringing in their ears, each youngster stood a little taller, smiled a little brighter, and let their chest swell a little more. Great Buffalo, remembering his first hunt, added his words of encouragement. "It will be dawn soon and that will be to our advantage because as the night fades, we will see better. Our prey does not see well in the dark or in low light, plus they will be in a panic and not watching closely. So, move quietly, listen to your leader's orders, and follow their directions. Do that, and you will be successful."

As they moved, Great Buffalo and Red Deer ran over the details of the plan they put together earlier in their own heads. They were sure there was only one hand's count of full-sized buffalo and even fewer calves. That was okay. Their young would stick close to the adults when the stampede occurred. It was now up to their leadership to help Little Wolf and Running Elk turn this set of youngsters into successful hunters.

Signaling a halt, Red Deer had a conference with the 'men' to whisper final instructions. "We're as close as we're going to get like this. The herd is just ahead. The breeze is blowing toward them and will carry our scent with it so move as quietly as you can. They're bedded down in the mouth of a shallow valley marked by ridges on both sides. The ravine is on the far end. Bushes and other scrub cover the lip."

Great Buffalo began issuing whispered orders like a general at the front. "Little Wolf is to take his group along the right side; Running Elk is to take his along the left; Red Deer and I will lead our group up the center. Keep low, move quietly, and don't bunch up. We'll sound the ram's horn when that star touches the tip of the moon. Be ready to run when you hear it." He paused and looked at his charges. They were all young, scared, and inexperienced, but tonight's action will change that.

Red Deer picked up where Great Buffalo had stopped. "We'll make a racket and give chase from behind. Both your groups are to run alongside and make a lot of noise. The animals will panic and run away. We need to steer them up the meadow and over the cliff."

Great Buffalo nodded his agreement and added, "If they come your way, pound your drums as hard as you can and yowl like wolves. Make all the noise you can. Use your fire baskets to light the torches and wave them around. Force them forward. Don't let them pass to the side or they will get away."

Smiling confidently at the group, Red Deer added, "Stay close to them and keep making noise. Remember to stop before you get to the ravine. We want just the herd to go over the edge. Okay? Let's go."

The group split into three parties and went their separate directions. Single file, and crouched low, Little Wolf and Running Elk led their people toward their assigned tasks.

Red Deer and Great Buffalo watched them disappear into the night and then took their own positions at the front of the last group. Side-by-side, separated only by a youth carrying a ram's horn, they spread their people out in a line on either side of them, and began moving forward. The closer they got to the herd, the lower they got to the ground. By the time Red Deer signaled a halt, they were slithering along on their bellies.

Quiet, hearts beating wildly as they waited for the star to reach the signal point, they could hear the animals stir. The herd was on alert. They may have heard the muffled sounds of their approach or detected their scent on the wind. No matter, the hunters could wait no longer.

Hoping the other groups were in position, Great Buffalo nodded to the boy carrying the ram's horn. Open-mouthed and wide-eyed, the lad's nerves were evident even in this light. Swallowing hard, he shook as he put the instrument to his lips. His cheeks puffed out, but there was no sound. Inhaling, he tried again. Nothing came out.

In front of them, feet pawing the ground, a buffalo bellowed a warning. Great Buffalo attempted to soothe the animal by putting his lips to the soft flesh of his forearm and mimicking its snort.

Red Deer realized the youngster's lips were too dry to work the horn. Leaning close he whispered an order. "Lick your lips!"

Near panic, the boy noisily spewed his portion of supper.

The herd reacted immediately. Hearing the strange noises, the animals still lying down were on their feet in an instant and joined the ones already milling around.

"Spit! Do it!" Red Deer commanded.

Suppressing the urge to retch again, the youngster managed to produce a pitiful quantity of juice. Licking his lips, he pressed the horn to his mouth and filled the air with sound. The rest of the group began filling the air with noise by banging drums, barking, and yowling like wolves.

This cacophony of sound exploded with little warning, and the startled animals ran, veering to the left as they did. Red Deer's people ran noisily after them. He hoped Running Elk's people were ready. The herd was headed their way.

Running Elk's group was ready. They waited until the animals were almost there before their torches flared into life, and they began a deafening barrage of drumming.

Turning away from this new terror, the lumbering animals picked up speed as they tried to make good their escape by slanting to the right. A noisy barrage from Little Wolf's quarter blocked their passage. Boxed in on three sides, the only escape lay ahead and the animals did their best to flee in that direction. Left, right, and center, everyone gave chase. They waved their torches, howled, and banged drums as they did their best to keep up with the terrified animals.

Running away from the clamor, the herd ran forward toward the cliff. In their panic, the animals changed from solid ground to treading air in a heartbeat, and then nothing as they hit the ground at the base of the cliff.

The youngsters, realizing their efforts were successful began to cheer and dance. Great Buffalo found the lad with the ram's horn. "Let the women know that they can get started. Blow the horn and continue to blow until you hear a response." The lad put the instrument to his lips just as the sun's rim started over the horizon. That morning, it was not the sun's rays that woke the anxious women.

###

Great Buffalo stirred. Something tickled his ear. Still asleep, he pawed at this unwelcome intrusion then pulling his sleep robe closer, he turned over hoping to be rid of the nuisance. The hunt had been a long day and night's work, but it was a success. The new young hunters rightfully celebrated their success. The women, hearing the long-awaited trumpet, reached the bottom of the cliff and began the task of tending to the night's results.

He remembered stumbling back to the village, answering a few questions, and falling onto his sleep pallet. All that he wanted now was to catch up on missed sleep. The fly continued to pester him. Death in his eyes, he sat up quickly ready to destroy this bothersome creature. A smiling Red Deer, feather in his hand, greeted him. Behind him, peering over his shoulder, crouched a giggling woman—a girl, really. He recognized her as the one he had watched turn the spit the night before the hunt. "Rise and shine my friend. We have more work to do."

Great Buffalo fought to clear the cobwebs from his brain. `"Eh? More work. The hunt was a success." *What is he talking about, more work? Haven't we done enough? Aren't we supposed to be finding out about salt?*

Red Deer jerked his thumb over his shoulder toward his companion. "Remember Appanoose[17]? She was the one that cooked the rabbits last night and then helped with the hunt. Her mother, Running Wolf's wife, had the girl wake me this morning. She is fixing our breakfast—salted fish, fresh seabirds' eggs and stoned cooked bread—doesn't that sound good?"

---

[17] Appanoose - Sauk word meaning "child"

Great Buffalo scratched his head and yawned again. "I don't understand. Why would she go through all that trouble for us?"

"Probably because I told Appanoose you are a great shipbuilder. The villager's boat has a hole in it. She and her mother think that because the hunt went well, we worked magic. They think we can use our magic to fix their boat."

Great Buffalo made a face. "We taught them how to hunt, why would we care about their boat?" Great Buffalo yawned and scratched his head. *What was behind his wanting to get involved in another job?*

"We helped them hunt, but they need more." Red Deer nodded toward the smiling girl. "If we can help with the boat, they could get more fish for them to smoke and salt ... ahhh salted fish. I'm sure the villagers, Running Wolf, and his council will smile on us and probably grant us anything."

Great Buffalo rubbed some sleep from his eyes and glanced at the girl, hopeful expectation in her eyes. Now, he understood Red Deer's message. *Salted fish. Red Deer was smart. He got his idea over without letting Running Wolf's daughter know their true motives.* Great Buffalo looked Red Deer in the eyes and nodded. "Well, I guess it wouldn't hurt to take a look."

Red Deer smiled. From the twinkle in his partner's eyes, he knew that they had reached an understanding.

Appanoose led them along the trail from the village. From a distance, seeing the vessel sitting on the beach, the boat looked sea-worthy. Up close, it was a different story.

"The accident happened one evening while we were returning to shore," Appanoose told them. "It was right after we realized that our people were not coming back and we had to learn how to take care of ourselves." Apponoose made a face. "We never handled the boat before. The men were the ones who went out and dropped the nets." She shrugged. "It didn't look that hard. I guess that shows you how little we knew. Inexperienced and working in failing light, the waves pushed us into the rocks out there and ripped a hole low in the side. Water started pouring in. We paddled like we were possessed and that barely got us close enough to wade ashore." She made a face, disgusted at their luck. "Because we lost the boat, we lost most of our catch. We were left on the beach, no catch, and no boat."

Red Deer peered into the hole. The ship, a flat-bottomed, single-masted vessel, appeared to be made of woven reed coils wrapped over a wooden frame that sat on a raft. These were held in place with twisted cords.

Besides the gash that opened the side, the rocks snapped at least three of the wooden poles that made up the floor. *They were lucky to have made it ashore,* he thought. On the plus side, behind the mast, benches for the oarsmen and their foot blocks were still in place. Beyond the benches and in front of the tiller, stood the derrick the fishermen would use to haul in their nets.

Great Buffalo looked at the water lapping along the shore at the base of the hill. It was some distance from the water to the place where they stood. "How did the boat get up here?"

"It was a lot of work," Apponoose said. "We had to cut and trim trees, then figure out how to get them under the boat. Once we solved that problem, we attached ropes and everyone pushed and pulled it forward. To keep it from sliding backwards, we placed upright timbers behind the craft as we moved it. We stopped only to move rollers from the back to the front." Her voice cracked and she stopped her narrative. A tear ran down her cheek and she swallowed a sob before continuing. "It was a lot of exhausting work to get it up here...." Her emotion-filled voice trembled as she spoke. "When we got it here, we took a closer look and figured out that we couldn't fix it."

Great Buffalo put a comforting hand on the girl's shoulder, an act that surprised Red Deer.

There was a long silent pause before she continued. "The hunt was a success," she explained, her quiet voice showing the strain of their lives, "but we can't always be that lucky. If . . . when the herds move on, we'll still need food or we'll be like we are now . . . starving. Fishing could keep that from happening or at least lessen it."

Inwardly, Great Buffalo winced. Her words struck a familiar note.

Forlorn and red-eyed, Apponoose leaned against the side of the vessel. "What do you think, can you fix it?" It was a desperate plea.

Great Buffalo, chin lifted, a determined look on his face, asked, "The people that are left, can they still weave bundles like the ones on the ship?"

Not giving the girl time to answer, Red Deer scratched his head. "Where are the timbers you used as rollers?"

Appanoose looked up, tears still running down her cheeks. This sudden barrage of question was wished for but not expected. Her heart beat faster. Afraid she misunderstood their motives; she tried not to get her hopes up lest they be smashed. "The rollers are stacked nearby and, yes, the women can still weave." Standing tall, she looked from one to the other for confirmation. "Does this mean you will help?"

"Yes," the two lads chorused.

The last of the coils of reeds fell away exposing the wooden scaffolding beneath. Inwardly, Great Buffalo made a face, but he remained stoic[18]. "The damage is greater than I figured," he whispered to Red Deer.

His partner nodded, "It's good we not let on. As long as they believe we can do this, they won't lose heart."

The pair walked around the bared wood, examining the way it was put together. Picking up a broken stave[19], Great Buffalo turned to Little Wolf. "Have your people cut some trees as long as this vessel the same thickness as this piece. To get started, we'll need about two hands worth."

Little Wolf turned to his sister, Appanoose, and passed the instruction along. The boys and Little Wolf watched her leave, shouting instructions to the villagers as she walked. Turning back, Little Wolf voiced some questions to Great Buffalo. "Some of the poles in the bottom are broken. What about them? Will the ship float with broken poles?"

"No it won't, but I plan on using some of the rollers to replace them. They're about the same size. We can cut more rollers if we need them."

"I agree they're the right size, but how will you fit them in place?"

Great Buffalo squatted and pointed at the exposed timbers. "Look at how these are put together. Set some of your people to work with their spears. I need them to drill holes through each pole, like the ones you see here. We will drive pegs from one into the next."

Satisfied by that answer, Little Wolf turned and left. He would guide the workers in this task.

By mid-day, the villagers had located and cut the required number of trees. The stacked trunks, branch-less—even the nubs carefully carved away—lay on the beach next to the naked hulk that had been the ship's frame.

---

[18] Stoic - not affected by or showing passion or feeling; *especially a* firmly restrained response to pain or distress

[19] Stave – One of the thin, narrow, shaped pieces of wood that form the sides of a cask, tub, or similar vessel. It may also be a stick, rod, pole, or the like.

Great Buffalo motioned Apppanoose to his side. He held up a broken stave, fitting the pieces together. "See how this is carved?" He held it out, giving her a chance to look it over.

"It is the same all along the length until the ends are reached," she observed. "Each end is trimmed back about two finger-widths to form a peg. It has two holes. These are about a hand's width from the top and bottom. A third hole is made about midway in the middle of this indentation made in the center. Why is it made like this?"

He knelt next to the bare frame and motioned her closer. "Look here, where the frame is still held together." He pointed to an unbroken upright, one of many around the edges of the hulk. "The pegs on the ends fit into holes drilled in the poles, top and bottom, that run along the outside length. This is so the staves can stand upright. To hold them in place, another set of shafts run on a slant left to right and right to left between uprights. An indentation is made at the spot where the two pieces cross. A cord is threaded through the hole in the center of each. It helps hold the dowels in place, but lets them flex a little."

Puzzled, Apppanoose wrinkled her forehead as she thought about that bit of news. "Why would they need to do that?"

"The willow tree sways in the smallest breeze, but survives winds that blow the sturdy oak over. The ship is like the willow tree, it needs to flex and bend, but not break."

When the broken ship had been taken out of the water, the villagers used rollers, ropes, and muscle-power to drag it up hill.

Repairs completed, the vessel was placed on rollers once again. Rows of timbers, about a forearm's length apart, were placed upright in front of the craft. These were to keep it from moving downhill too fast if any of the ropes slipped. The villagers fastened ropes to its frame at several points, wrapped them around trees behind the vessel and, letting them out slowly, they eased the craft downhill to the water. Because of these precautions getting the repaired vessel back into the water was easier than getting it out.

Eased over the last roller, the craft floated across the surface, bobbing gently with the motion of the waves. Seeing this, a cheer arose from the crowd and they began singing and dancing.

###

Red Deer made sure the craft was securely fastened to several sturdy trees on shore. After everyone's efforts, he didn't want to forget this vital task and then allow the vessel to drift away. Great Buffalo was busy inside checking for leaks.

"So far, it appears watertight," Great Buffalo yelled from the bottom of the vessel. "When you're set, join me and we can finish up."

Red Deer eagerly splashed through the water and scrambled over the side. Great Buffalo, still inspecting the vessel's nooks and crannies, lay on his belly in the bottom. Getting to his feet, he gave it one last sweeping glance. "Looks dry," he said. "I think it will stay afloat. When we raise the sail, it will be ready for us to try out."

"Good," Red Deer agreed. "Everyone will be anxious to see that happen. What do we have to do next?"

Great Buffalo looked at the gathering on shore. Locating Little Wolf's sister, he called out, "Appanoose, we are ready for you."

The girl turned and yelled excitedly to a group of women clustered around her. This was the moment they waited for and needed no further encouragement. Armed with long-handled paddles the women scrambled aboard, eagerly taking a place at each oarsman's' bench. Ready to man the tiller[20], Appanoose stood beside Great Buffalo. Next to her stood a young boy with a drum to beat cadence[21] for the oarsman—another of Great Buffalo's ideas.

Red Deer elbowed Great Buffalo, bringing him out of his reverie. "Grab a rope and we can raise the sail."

The sail, a large woven mat, had been draped over a spar[22] and fastened in place. Ropes, secured to the frame near the rudder, ran up through a tallow-filled[23] hole near the top of the mast and down to the spar that held the sail. Lubricated, the ropes would slide through the holes smoother. As an additional measure, Great Buffalo had the drummer boy run forward to the mast with a bowl of tallow, which he used to coat the ropes.

Together, Red Deer and Great Buffalo began pulling the lines to raise the upside-down, triangle-shaped sail. It soon turned into a race to see which one could raise their side first.

The breeze began filling the sail before it was completely raised. Excitement on shore grew. The vessel moved forward and the women got ready to paddle. The thrill was short lived. No one had remembered to untie the cords that had kept the vessel from drifting away. It jerked to a halt. All those on board lurched forward at the sudden halt. Some found themselves sprawled on the deck. The sail rushed

---

[20] Tiller - A tiller or till is a lever attached to a rudderpost (American terminology) or rudderstock (English terminology) of a boat that provides leverage in the form of torque for the helmsman to turn the rudder. The tiller can be used by the helmsman directly pulling or pushing it, or it may be moved remotely using tiller lines or a ship's wheel.

[21] Cadence - The beat, time, or measure of rhythmical motion or activity

[22] Spar- A stout rounded, usually wooden (as a mast, boom, gaff, or yard) pole used to support rigging.

[23] Tallow - The white nearly tasteless solid rendered fat of cattle and sheep used chiefly in soap, candles, and lubricants.

downward blanketing most of the area behind the mast and everyone there. Lost under the covering, they crawled around under looking for a way out. The women began to giggle and soon everyone on the beach roared in laughter.

###

Speaking as they walked, Little Wolf, covered from head to foot in thick layers of mud, led the way along the path to the beach. "When we discovered the value of salt, we forgot our old ways. For as long as anyone can remember, my people harvested salt. We relied on trade goods for the other things we needed. Those that hunted or fished left with the stranger. Until you arrived, we were starving because we didn't have anyone to show us how to hunt or fish. You taught us how to hunt and you showed us how to repair our boat."

"Now that your people have harvested the meat and carried everything back to the village, they can dry the buffalo skins by spreading them out in the sun, pelt side down," Red Deer explained.

Great Buffalo was not to be left out, "Stake down the edges and scrape the inside clean. Then cover it with a thin layer of salt and leave it in the sun to dry."

"Once we were great hunters like you." Little Wolf replied. "Once we knew how to do all those things. Because of you, we are learning what we once knew."

Red Deer acknowledged his remarks. "The hunt was a great success. Your people did well. You have enough to eat until the caravan arrives and then you can trade for the goods you need."

Great Buffalo nodded. "Life will be better once again," he added, "but you mustn't forget how to hunt and I think you should build more boats."

So far, Little Wolf hadn't explained where they were going, but Great Buffalo and Red Deer felt it was leading to something important.

Little Wolf scowled. "Before the stranger came, we had lots of salt. Times were good. But that's all gone. The caravan will be here before we have enough salt to trade unless…"

"Unless what?"

Behind them, a drum within the village sounded loudly. Little Wolf's pace quickened.

Red Deer stopped and looked back toward the village. "Do you have a drum for everything? What's that one for?"

Little Wolf picked up the pace. "The tide is coming. We must hurry or you will miss it."

Playing ignorant, Great Buffalo asked, "Tide? What's that?"

"The great sea is like a sleeping man." Reaching flat ground, Little Wolf broke into a run, shouting over his shoulder as he did. "The water goes in and out when it breathes. If we hurry, you can see for yourself."

Accepting this explanation, Red Deer and Great Buffalo joined in the sprint for the beach. Catching up with their guide, they ran three abreast, one on each side of Little Wolf.

Hurrying, Little Wolf continued his narrative. "Salt harvesting has been our secret. It's something few people outside the tribe have seen." He looked at his pair of new friends hopefully. "Because the hunt has been successful and the fishing boat is in the water again, the council thought— we all thought—you could look at the ways we collect salt. It's a desperate idea, but because you've traveled far and seen much, perhaps you can help us improve our methods. If we could harvest salt faster, we'd have some to trade when the caravan arrives." He looked at them optimistically.

Red Deer shrugged. "We could take a look." Smiling, he added, "I don't know if we'll come up with anything, but, if we do, will your people be ready to make changes?"

"They'll be ready."

Rounding the final bend, the trio stepped onto a rocky rise that bordered the beach. It stood at the foot of the bay and sheltered a rugged flow of black lava that sloped away from watery incursions. The sand-fringed rise appeared to cross the distance between the two bluffs—the one containing the Sea People's village, the other covered with the heavy forest where they had first camped with Aditsan.

Waves, driven by the tide, spilled over the crest of the divide and ran down the slope to form a shallow pool in the lava bed. A low wall kept the water from escaping.

Little Wolf waved an arm in the general direction of the open water as he spoke, "Climb to the top of the highest mountain and you can see the water stretching out to the far horizon. Out there, I believe it's as deep as it is wide, but over here in the pool, it's shallow."

Red Deer pointed at a pillar setting on a rocky ridge a little way offshore. Waves broke around the rocks.

Before Red Deer could ask, Little Wolf said, "My people built that pillar on the rocks to mark the water line when the tide is out. When the tide returns, the sea fills most of area between here and there with water."

Nodding, the fellows gave polite attention to the young man's explanations and followed Little Wolf into the shallow pool. Their progress was greeted by swarms of mosquitoes.

Taking time from swatting at these flying, biting pests, Red Deer looked at Little Wolf disdainfully. "What do your people do about these bugs?"

Little Wolf snickered at their dismay. "Before they come here, they do what I did and cover themselves with a thick coating of mud.

Making a face, Great Buffalo said, "I wish we had known that before."

Ignoring his remark, Little Wolf went on, "Sometime in the past, those who came before us, discovered this plain. At high tide, the sea water washes over the crest and creates this shallow pool. The lava was rough, but they carved two pools out, this one and another one beyond it."

Red Deer looked around the first pool. "What happens in these pools? What do they do? Why do you need a second one?"

Little Wolf motioned for the others to follow him as he waded through ankle deep water. The trio reached the back of the first pool and looked down at the next.

Little Wolf explained, "When the tide creates the first pool, it's just like the sea, they're equally salty. But before the tide returns, the water here has become saltier."

Little Wolf stood with his foot on a wooden mechanism. Hand-carved to fit a niche in the rim, the device blocked the flow of water. "This next pool is lower than the first and the water shallower. Before the tide returns, this gate is opened, and the water drains from the upper pool to the lower one through this channel."

Greater Buffalo took time from battling mosquitoes, to ask, "Then what happens?"

"Workers sweep the last drops from here down into the next pool and then fit the gate back in place."

Red Deer and Great Buffalo inspected the gate and the area around the each pool. A mound of broken lava fragments, decorated the fringe surrounding each pool. Scraps leftover from when the pools were originally hewed from the lava. Beyond these mounds, the terrain was rough and alternated between pockmarks and shards. Unlike the smooth bottoms of the pools, it was not something that would be easy to walk across.

Unlike the first pool, the second one sat in a bowl, wider and longer than the first. Like the first, it was carved out of the lava. Unlike the other, the bottom, here, was blanketed with sand. The exposed back wall displayed telltale rings marking past water levels. They looked from one pool to the next. "What happens here?" They chorused and looked at each other. Why would they have two pools?

"The water in the second pool is saltier than the first. Even though more water is added every day, this pool becomes saltier. After a few days, a layer of salt builds up along the bottom. We scoop it up, separate the salt from sand, and replace the sand we take out."

Red Deer stepped into the second pool and was greeted by another barrage of flying insects. The water here was so shallow it barely covered his toes. He scooped up a handful of water. It was warmer and tasted saltier than seawater.

Still in the first pool, Great Buffalo surveyed both pools. "The crust along the bottom, does it always take the same number of days to form?"

"No, it's better now in summer than during the Long Cold." Little Wolf watched him, still fighting clouds of bugs as he walked through the water. Their guide waited patiently but finally asked, "What do you think?"

Red Deer laughed. "I think the people who come here must put on a pretty heavy coat of mud." Great Buffalo stopped waving bugs away long enough to slap his knee and join in the laughter.

Little Wolf smiled. "Yes, they do." Resuming a somber stance, he asked, "Now, what do you think? Can you help?"

Exiting the pool, Red Deer found a tree limb. He positioned it upright against the back wall and placed rocks around its base to hold it there. Taking his knife, he marked the stake at the waterline. Straightening up, he rubbed dirt from his hands as he looked at Little Wolf. "I need to come back here before the water from the first pool is allowed to drain into this one. When the time comes, it will help prove me right. If it works the way I think, we'll have to go back and talk to the council because we'll need some workers to make changes."

Chapter 5: The Harvest

Standing in front of Running Wolf and the old men that made up his council, Red Deer said, "In your own words, those who came before you learned how to harvest salt and for as long as anyone can remember, your people have always done so."

Great Buffalo joined in, "When you discovered its value, you forgot how to hunt and fish."

Sitting on either side of Running Wolf, council waited with growing irritation, while they listened to this pair of lanky youths and thought rebellious thoughts: *These were not men, but smooth-cheeked boys, neither one old enough to sprout hair on their chins. How does one successful hunt, one repaired fishing vessel, give them the right to lecture Council on something already known?*

"Over time, your people also forgot something else. You harvest salt, but forgot how it came to be discovered. That is the problem you now face."

That did it! The council, usually stoic, now displayed their turmoil. How dare strangers come and talk to them like this. Running Wolf fought to bring calm to the meeting. "What is your solution?"

Red Deer continued with his explanation. "The sea fills the pools, but it's the sun's warmth that provides the salt."

"How do you know this?" White Hawk shouted angrily. "What proof do you have?"

Ready for the question, Great Buffalo replied, "You're able to harvest more salt now when it's warmer than you can during the Long Cold. Have you ever asked yourself why?"

The question created uproar among council members. The boys, arms folded defiantly across their chests, gave the council a cold stare. Running Wolf allowed the council to continue so they would exhaust themselves and be in a better mood to listen.

When the council finally grew silent, Red Deer was able to continue. "The water in the second pool is warm. A stake I placed in the pool in the morning showed less water at the end of the day. The wall at the back carries marks of past water levels."

Discussions, much quieter than the previous chaos, broke out between council members. The two boys sat quietly while council members argued back and forth.

They needed time to decide, but with the caravan drawing closer every day, time was something they didn't have. Wanting to move on, Great Buffalo nodded to Running Wolf, prompting him to bring the group to order.

When quiet resumed, Great Buffalo began again. "To improve the harvest, you need more pools. These will need to be bigger and shallow—not as deep as the old ones that feed them. You need to get started now if you want to have salt by the time the caravan arrives."

More discussion followed, but in the end, the council agreed. Everyone was put to work carving out the new pools.

The coals of Tigal's campfire glowed between them as Red Deer turned the pheasants on the spit.

Sitting across from Aditsan and the two youths, Tigal asked, "Tell me boys, did you have trouble finding us?"

"No, sir," Great Buffalo said. "You told us which villages you planned to visit and the trail you'd follow. For practice, Aditsan made us lead the way so we gave him a trip he'll remember."

Aditsan allowed his composure to slip just a little and made a face. Watching his reaction, Tigal hid a smirk.

From his duties over the campfire, Red Deer continued their narrative. "From the seacoast, we cut over the hills and through the forest until we came across your tracks. Then we followed till we found you."

"How did you know it was our tracks?"

Both boys laughed. "Dung from a wild herd is spread out, but your caravan travels in a line. Droppings from your animals, and other evidence of your passing, are pungent enough for a blind man to follow," Great Buffalo explained.

Slapping his knee, the caravan leader joined them in laughter, but soon grew sober and asked, "Do the Sea People know where you are?"

"No, sir," Red Deer explained. "They sound a drum for everything so we told them we weren't accustomed to village life and needed quiet."

Great Buffalo nodded. "We told them we'd go hunting and get some pelts to trade but would return every few days until the caravan arrived. We'll be sure to go back to them two or three days ahead of your arrival. They should suspect nothing."

Tigal smiled thoughtfully. "Good. Were you able to learn anything?"

Red Deer handed the spit of roasted bird to Great Buffalo to carve and distribute while he placed another over the coals. "Yes, sir," he said. "We learned several things. Two moons before, a stranger arrived from a tribe called Kam Na Udo. He came offering trade and disappeared after taking most of their salt and their young hunters with him. They've never returned to the Sea People and no one knows what happened to them. Those left in the village had forgotten how to hunt. When we arrived, they were starving and almost out of salt."

The Caravan Chief sat in shocked silence for a moment. "How are they now?"

Handing Tigal a piece of roasted meat, Great Buffalo explained, "We took some of them hunting, and now they have fresh meat. We even helped repair their boat, and they began fishing. They were impressed. Hoping to increase their salt production, they asked us to look at how they get it. We suggested some changes which they followed. After they carved out the first couple of new pools and saw how well they worked, the Sea People got busy making even more pools. When we left, they were starting to harvest greater amounts of salt and should have enough to trade."

At that news, Tigal brightened. "So they'll have salt to trade, and you know how it's done."

"Yes, sir," Red Deer said. "But, I believe I have another improvement, one I didn't tell them about. I need some help from a cook… and lots of firewood."

"What are your plans?"

"I want to boil the water. We can have better salt by boiling the water."

"What will this do?"

"The Sea People use the sun's warmth to get salt from the sea water. The salt forms along the bottom of the pool. To make it easier to collect, they cover the bottom of the ponds with a layer of sand. When they harvest the lumps of salt, they get the sand too. This mix has to dry and then they toss it in the air. The sand is light; most of it blows away, while the salt falls back. They get salt, but there is still some sand mixed in with it."

"Boiling the water will make better salt?"

Red Deer shrugged. "If it works, we'll be better off. If it doesn't, we're no worse off."

Thoughtfully, Tigal drew on his pipe. "How do we prove this?"

"After everyone returned to the village for the night we went back, gathered pouches of water from the pools, and brought them with us." Red Deer took the spit off the fire and examined the pheasants. "These are almost done." He licked his lips as he put the birds back over the fire. "I want to put the water in a cooking pot and set it to boil over the fire. The salt should be left when the water is gone"

Tigal nodded approvingly. "I'd like to see this. My clan chiefs will see we have all the firewood needed." He looked at the bird roasting over the fire. "I think those birds are done, and I'm hungry. All my wives cook…." Tigal tilted his head toward the two boys and added, "… but, I've daughters you should meet. They cook and would make good wives."

Red Deer laughed. "Both Running Wolf and White Hawk made us the same offer." He paused as if some idea had just occurred and finally said, "Since the hunt, there were many nights when Great Buffalo didn't share the lean-to with me. Why is that?"

Great Buffalo kept his eyes down as he carefully carved the roasted bird and made no comment.

The cunning old man joined Aditsan and Red Deer in laughter. "Men of your abilities," the caravan chief said, "will be in demand. It will be interesting to see how you deal with these new opportunities. Meanwhile, my wives… and daughters will give you whatever help you need…."

As they had done many times before, Running Wolf and his council sat across from Tigal and his clan chiefs. "Tigal, my friend, it's good to see you again. Our people want to welcome you. Everyone is eager to trade."

The caravan chief responded, "We've traded with your people since you and I were boys. It's unfortunate this may soon end."

Shocked by these words, no one said anything. Recovering first, Running Wolf, though shaken, managed to stammer out, "B . . . b . . . but why? We've always traded, always exchanged our salt for your goods. I don't understand."

"The trade has always been to your advantage. My people have had to give much to get salt. They want no more of it." Surrounded by his somber faced clan chiefs, Tigal sat quietly, his face equally emotionless.

"What will you do? It's a necessary trade item wherever you go. We're the only ones who can provide it."

Tigal shook his head. "You were the only ones, however, we now have the knowledge and can make salt—a better salt than you have—when we want. No longer will we have to pay your prices. When we travel, I can show others how to make salt like ours."

White Hawk, no longer able to restrain himself, spoke out, "My Chief, no one else can make salt. He's bluffing." Smug in his assertions, he sat back, arms folded across his chest.

Tigal nodded to one of his attendants. The man stepped forward, laid a rawhide out, and stepped back. The caravan master instructed, "At your convenience, place a small sample of your salt there, and I shall do likewise. We can compare the two."

Running Wolf sent White Hawk to fetch the sample. The two sides sat quietly waiting for his return. It was not long—although to Running Wolf, it seemed long—before he returned. Tigal knew from the haste White Hawk had shown they were afraid he was not bluffing. They were right.

With a slight tremor in his hand, White Hawk poured an off-white substance onto the rawhide and sat back. Tigal nodded to his attendant. The man stepped forward again, produced a small pouch, and poured the contents—a sparkling fine grained white crystal—on an adjacent area of the rawhide.

Running Wolf, White Hawk, the council all leaned forward to peer at the samples. Tigal gave them a moment and then said, "Go ahead, taste it and see. Check its purity. I want you to know I've spoken the truth. We have the knowledge now."

Wetting a finger, Running Wolf stuck it in the new sample and put it to his mouth. Tasting it, his eyes widened. The others, quick to follow suit, had similar reactions. Running Wolf and his people huddled together and spoke in low tones. Tigal and his men waited quietly.

"Where does this come from?" Running Wolf was shaken.

"We have the knowledge. If we choose, we can make our own or we can show others—your tribe, another tribe, maybe many tribes—how to make it."

"It's all we have." White Hawk gasped.

Hanging his head, Running Wolf acknowledged, "True. If others could do this, we're lost."

Tigal was thoughtful. "Well… maybe we could make an arrangement."

Running Wolf looked up eagerly. "An arrangement? What kind of an arrangement?"

White Hawk and the council leaned forward, a spark of hope burned in their eyes.

"We will share our method with you and only you. It will let you provide two grades of salt: the kind that you have always provided and this better grade. In return, you must give us more for each trade item."

"Even with two grades, if we do that for all the caravans, it will be our downfall."

Tigal laughed. "Treat the other caravans however you wish. They aren't my concern. I promise to keep the methods secret . . . while it is to my benefit. The fact that you can provide two grades of salt will be better for them, and they will be happy to pay whatever price you want. Now, do we have an agreement?"

Huddling together, Running Wolf and his people spoke in low tones once again. Finally, he straightened up, looked at Tigal, and said, "Yes, we should share a pipe to mark the agreement and then trading can begin."

Arranged along the beach, the clans displayed their trade goods and bartered with the Sea People. Aditsan and White

71

Hawk trailed behind their leaders as they strolled along the beach talking about times past, but keeping a careful eye on the business being transacted.

Shouts from up the beach caught everyone's attention. Hollering and pointing out to sea, a group of youngsters, bored with the business of trading, came running up the beach from where they had been playing. Shading their eyes, many of those took a break from bargaining to look for the source of the children's excitement.

Too far out to make out great detail, it appeared to be the remains of a ship that suffered through foul weather. Heading toward the rocks—the ones that Appanoose had once encountered—that protected the beach, the vessel looked as if it were unmanned, or, at least, poorly guided.

Concerned for those on the ship and for the ship, itself, everyone started waving and shouting as if those aboard were unaware of the rocks.

Suddenly, Great Buffalo yelled at Running Wolf, "Your vessel, where is it? Send men out to help them."

If it were anyone else but this one, Running Wolf would have been upset; however this boy voiced another good idea. He turned to White Hawk and ordered, "Make our vessel ready. Send men."

Having heard Great Buffalo, White Hawk had anticipated his chief's request and only needed to hear the words from the chief's mouth. The village's fishing vessel lay on its side, above the high tide line, when not in use. Because of the shortage of able-bodied men, a group of women quickly dragged the ship into the water. Great Buffalo, Red Deer, and—at the last minute—Aditsan joined them. With everyone aboard, they manned the paddles and pointed their ship toward the approaching vessel. The women broke into a chant, their paddles dug into the water with each rhythmic tone, and their efforts propelled the ship toward the approaching vessel.

Seemingly a derelict, it was larger—probably twice the size in length and width and taller—than the villager's fishing boat. It appeared to be made of coils of reeds, row upon row, stacked atop of each other, and tied, one row to the next.

As they came alongside, Great Buffalo grabbed one of the ropes dangling over the edge and trailing in the water. Testing it to make sure the other end was secure; he pulled himself up the side and disappeared over the railing. Red Deer started to follow, but Aditsan stopped him. They waited, listening for some sign—sounds of combat and conflict, a call for assistance, or a shriek of joy. There was nothing.

Chapter 6: The Ship

Typical for others his age, waiting was not Red Deer's best feature. Questions, seemingly as numerous as the grains of sand on the beach, ran through his head. He wanted to grab the rope and follow Great Buffalo, but Aditsan's heavy hand on his shoulder restrained him. Their boat bumped gently against the larger vessel, marking the passage of each swell. The women, though nervous, sat quietly, paddles raised in the air. They were ready to shove off at the first sign of trouble.

Above them, Great Buffalo stuck his head over the rail. "It's okay. There are only three on board. The man is hurt and pinned under some wreckage too heavy for the children, a boy and a girl, to move. They jabbered something at me, but I don't understand a word they've said. Come up. They're scared, so don't make any sudden moves."

That was the only invitation Red Deer needed. Slipping out from under Aditsan's grip, he grabbed the rope, scampered to the top, and disappeared over the rail. Aditsan followed immediately after him, stopping to peer over the rail before swinging himself aboard.

Seeing a grown man board alarmed the youngsters. Protectively, the boy moved in front of the girl. Each clutched something that could pass as a weapon.

"It's okay, we mean you no harm," Great Buffalo called out to them comfortingly.

At the same time, Aditsan smiled, held his open hands out in front of him, but did not move from his current position. Instead, he uttered a few words that sounded to Great Buffalo like the gibberish the boy and the girl had used.

At first the pair appeared surprised and then puzzled by Aditsan's words, but then they seemed to relax.

Great Buffalo shrugged. "They spoke, but I didn't understand them, and they don't seem to understand me.

Move slowly, we need your help over here." Both he and Red Deer were near what appeared to be the ship's stern, near a crumpled mass of tangled ropes, woven mats, and broken timbers. Nearby, on his knees, Red Deer worked at clearing away some of the debris.

Aditsan took a step toward them only to discover the deck was made of woven mats stretched over the wooden poles. The mats had lost their tension and sank under his weight. He staggered and lost his balance, ending flat on his back. Great Buffalo did a sloppy job of covering his laughter; Red Deer, also a witness to the event, tried unsuccessfully to hide his chortles by diving behind a heap of mats. Laughter from the boy and girl broke out behind him. Aditsan regained his feet, but was unsure of how to proceed.

"Look for the sticks that run across from side to side under the mats and walk on them," Great Buffalo instructed.

Gingerly, Aditsan picked his way over to them. Buried amidst the mats and tangle of ropes, a man lay pinned under some fallen timbers, the apparent remains of masts and sails. Kneeling near Red Deer, he surveyed the situation. Two large timbers, one directly on the man, the other laying across it, pinned him in place.

Aditsan waved his hands as he explained, "The bottom timber has him pinned down. The top timber is holding the bottom one in place so we need to move it first, but be careful. He may have some broken bones." He looked at Great Buffalo and then Red Deer to make sure they understood before he continued, "Get on the other end of the first timber, and we'll see if we can lift it off."

The boys scurried over and positioned themselves opposite Aditsan. From their place up front, the boy and the girl watched everything carefully. Aditsan squatted over the timber, looked over at Red Deer and Great Buffalo, and then nodded. Straining, the trio managed to lift it enough to ease it off. The man, lying on the deck, let out a long, painful moan. From behind them Aditsan heard the girl sob.

Quiet until now, the boy suddenly became noisily frantic, and gestured toward the front of the vessel. At the same time, the women in the fishing boat also began shouting warnings. Aditsan motioned to Red Deer who scrambled to his feet and sprinted over the slats to where the boy and girl stood at the rail. Looking over his shoulder, he yelled back, "We're almost to the rocks near shore." Turning back to the pair of kids, he asked, "How do you stop this?" Not understanding the words he spoke, they gave him a blank look before finally coming to life.

The boy ran forward, gesturing as he did. The girl followed. He stopped near a coil of rope and pulled out a wooden bar. It held a flap in place. Without the bar, the flap fell, providing a clear path to the water below. Red Deer did not know what to do until he saw the rope was attached to a boulder. The boy and the girl bent and began inching this heavy rock toward the edge. Red Deer called to the others and then joined the boy and the girl in their efforts. Progress was slow until Great Buffalo and Aditsan joined them. They watched the coil unwind as the rock tumbled over the side and into the water. The boy didn't lose time watching it fall, but shouted something unknown and started for the other end of the boat. Following the running figure, the others found another set up similar to the one they just left, but this time they knew what to do. The rock-anchors, front and back, hit bottom and began dragging through the sand, slowly bringing the vessel to a stop. Everyone on board raised their hands and yelled joyfully. They were joined in their cheers by the women alongside in the fishing boat as well as everyone on the beach, even though they weren't sure what was being celebrated.

Gathered around the man still pinned under the last timber, Aditsan tested the weight. It wouldn't budge. "Tell the women in the boat that we're going to need more help," he told Great Buffalo. He was sure neither the man nor the children understood his words, but judging by their actions, their intentions were clear, and this trio of strangers appeared to relax.

"Go ashore," Great Buffalo told the women, "and bring back some of Tigal's bigger men, about one hand's worth." They nodded and began rowing for shore.

Aditsan sized up the area. A timber lay across its victim. Above him, a wooden beam swiveled lazily on a pivot post. Its long arm ran overhead, but out of reach. "How much rope do we have? Get some untangled and laid out here, then one of you go stand on the far side of the beam," he said. Red Deer and Great Buffalo moved quickly to follow his orders. Aditsan knelt down and beckoned to the young boy to step forward. The youngster stepped within arm's reach and carefully watched this unknown man.

Aditsan looked up, gestured at the beam over their heads, and then he held out his forearm and pointed to it. He looked at the boy to see if the youngster had a question. The boy's face was passive, showing neither recognition nor question. Aditsan picked up a short piece of rope and pointed to the coil that Red Deer and Great Buffalo had made. The boy remained passive. Once again, Aditsan pointed to the overhead beam, then his forearm. Taking the piece of rope, he draped it over his arm so that one end dangled from each side. Dropping the cord, he stood and raised his arms overhead. It was obvious that he was too short to reach the beam without help. Hoping his message was clear, he knelt and picked the boy up under the armpits, sat him down on his own shoulders before he stood up. Surprised by this action, the boy grabbed a handful of Aditsan's hair in an effort to keep from falling off.

"Give him the rope and point to the overhead beam," Aditsan told his companions. Red Deer handed over the rope while Great Buffalo jumped up and down pointing at the beam. The girl, yelling something in their unknown tongue, joined in the pandemonium. Suddenly, everything came together and the youngster tied a knot in the rope, twirled it around, and flung it into the air. It came down in front of

Great Buffalo, on the other side of the beam. By quickly grabbing the knotted end, he kept it from slipping away. Happy with his success, Aditsan knelt and let the boy slide off.

The fishing vessel returned, and five burly men clambered aboard. Aditsan called them over, and they secured the line around the fallen timber. With half of the men on the rope and the other half on the timber, they were able to lift it enough that Aditsan and Great Buffalo could slide the injured man out of his trap. He moaned as he was moved, but two tearful children were there to comfort this now freed man.

"…once we removed the timber," narrating the day's events for Tigal, Running Wolf, and White Hawk, Aditsan sat with them around the evening campfire, "we made a pallet to help get the injured man ashore, and the rest was easy."

Tigal nodded, but didn't necessarily agree. "I recall several trips back and forth, first to inspect the vessel to see if it were still seaworthy, then to tie ropes and attempt to drag it away from the rocks and closer to shore." The caravan master shook his head in disbelief and looked at Running Wolf. "I had all my people, and you had all your people pulling their hearts out, and it barely moved. Then one of your women spoke up and asked why we didn't wait for the tide to come in. It would raise the ship up, and the waves would bring the vessel to shore." He shook his head again. "Exhausted, we decided to wait. What harm could it do? The tide came and helped us move the ship… just like she said."

Aditsan slapped his knee and laughed. "It was just like I said… easy!"

Running Wolf smiled, but it didn't last long. "Do we know anything about these people? Who they are, or where they came from... and why?"

Tigal surprised Running Wolf and White Hawk. "Yes," he said. "We can answer all those questions."

Chapter 7: A Woman

Stunned, Running Wolf and his companion looked at their guest wide eyed and finally managed to ask, "I don't understand, how...."

Tigal held up a hand, cutting him off. I know it is a surprise so let me tell you why this is so. "A few summers ago, we were traveling along the shore trail—maybe two hands' worth of moons south of here—when we came to Gray Seal's village...."

... Bathed in the afternoon sun, Gray Seal and his advisers sat outside their council hut. Tigal and Aditsan sat were also there, separated from the villagers by their small cook fire. One of Gray Seal's wives passed out bowls of thin stew while another passed around gourds of chicha.

"It looks like everyone is packing up," Tigal observed. He watched the organized chaos around him, definite signs of a village preparing to leave.

Gray Seal nodded his agreement. There was no hiding the fact, and he had little reason to do so even if he could. "If you had arrived a day or two from now," he said, "we would have been gone."

Tigal was surprised. "Gone ... but why? You have always said this place was good to you."

"We must search out another home."

"Really. Why is that?"

Sadly, Gray Seal shook his head. "The place has now become cursed," he said. "A few days before this last full moon, there was a storm. It was greater than anything we had ever experienced. A day or so afterward, we found a young woman—almost dead, clinging to wreckage—and brought her to the village to care for her. It was a mistake."

"Really." Interested in hearing more, Tigal stroked his chin, but remained quiet hoping his counterpart would continue.

Gray Seal, eyes downcast, stared into the flames of the pitiful fire for a moment before continuing. "Everything about her—clothes, looks, language—was different from anything we had ever encountered. The next day, the ground under our feet shook violently. That should have been enough of a warning, but we ignored it. The following morning, the sun came up blood red and shone through heavy gray-black clouds. Dirt and ash fell from the sky and covered everything. Believing these signs to be a test of our goodwill, we persisted in caring for the girl. A day or so later a giant wave rose up from the sea and took everyone and everything near the shore. My people said they thought the woman was cursed and her arrival put a curse on the village . . . . If we stayed . . . if we kept her . . . all would be lost."

"Amazing," Tigal said. "The girl, what happened to her?"

Gray Seal, no appetite for what he felt must be done, shifted nervously. "Well, what could we do? To remove the curse, when the tide was out we tied her to a pillar near the water's edge. If the sea would not claim her before we left, we would know that it is our job to sacrifice her and show our good faith. It will be our last act. Our hope is that it will give us the peace we seek."

"A girl that would enrage the sea in such a manner," Tigal said. "I would like to see her."

Wide-eyed by the request, Gray Seal stuttered and stalled before finally voicing his decision. "All . . . all . . . right, I'll take you to see her, but be warned that you too may become cursed."

###

The sullen girl could feel the returning tide lap at the feet. Tied to the makeshift pillar that held her in place, she knew that she would spend yet another night treading water. Four men approached, drawing her attention away from her current plight.

Some of the group's members—the one she had come to know as 'the chief ' and his adviser—were familiar to her; but, this time there was a new pair with them. The one she thought to be 'the chief ' and his aide stopped short. Shifting guiltily, he held up a cautionary hand and said something— maybe 'she is evil, go no closer' or 'look at what we caught'— in their unknown language, but the other two appeared to ignore him and continued closer.

As they approached, this pair split up, coming to a halt one on each side of her. Hands on hips, they inspected the wooden pillar—a hastily cut tree, its branches mere nubs— and the rope that bound her there. Tied to her left wrist, the cord wound around the post and then passed through a hole—drilled side-to-side—near the top. Exiting the hole, the rope wound down and was tied at her right wrist. Her bindings were loose enough to allow some freedom of movement—she could choose to sit or stand, to face the pole or turn away—but it was secure enough to keep her restrained.

The older man, himself most probably a chief, began fingering the beads of her necklace as if appraising their value. Satisfied with that, he ran his hands over the fabric of her clothes, certainly different from the heavy animal hides he wore.

Unaccustomed to this treatment, she tried to lash out at him but was stopped by the lighting-swift movements of the younger man. Having anticipated her reaction, he grabbed the cord above her head and yanked her hands up before she could strike. Rage and frustration boiled within her. She filled the air with what could only be sharp curses, gave the younger man a swift kick in the shin, and then braced herself for his rebuking blow. What she got in return was much

worse. He produced a sound universal in any language—
laughter. She was humiliated. Tears welled up. She turned her
face away, not wanting her adversaries to see her in this
moment of weakness. Gentle fingers softly touched her chin,
pulling her face back until the men could see the tears flowing
down her cheeks. Her tear-filled eyes met the young man's,
and they pleaded with him for mercy and rescue.

While the pair gazed at each other, the older man
returned to the one she thought to be 'the chief' and began
talking. While the language was unknown, the sound and
gestures were unmistakably those made when bargaining.
Each pause in the older man's speech was greeted by a violent
shaking of 'the chief's' head. Finally, after several rejections,
the older man called to the younger to join him and they
strolled away. The girl called out after them several times, but
the men ignored her petitions. As the group grew more
distant, her hope faded and her calls finally broke down into
wails of despair.

"Amazing," White Hawk said. He shifted nervously and
asked, "What happened next?"

Tigal remained silent for a moment, as if he were
recalling the events. "Well, what could I do? Gray Seal was
adamant about needing to sacrifice the woman to remove the
curse. I tried to talk him out of it, even offering considerable
goods—her weight in furs and salt—in trade for her.
Reluctantly, he would not change his mind and planned on
executing her at the next sunrise. I decided we could not stay
there and watch, so I had the caravan pack up, and we moved
on."

Running Wolf's jaw dropped. He was incredulous.
"You... you left? How could you do that? What happened to
the woman?"

Tigal smiled and turned to Aditsan. "You tell them."
His aide smiled and took up the narration . . . .

Chapter 8: Rescue

"My chief, I, Aditsan am unhappy about leaving the girl to her fate." The younger man walked next to the caravan leader while those around them scurried to break camp and move on. Even in this confusion, he hoped this private moment would give him time to change his master's mind.

The caravan master smiled slightly but directed his attention to the actions about them. After a long pause, to Aditsan it seemed like a lifetime, his leader spoke. "You looked in her eyes. Did she capture you then?"

"I bear the mark where she kicked my shin. If she has any feelings for me, I'm sure it is hate."

The caravan master placed a fatherly hand on the young man's shoulder. "My son, passion is passion. I've found that the distance between love and hate or hate and love is but two short steps."

Aditsan looked bewildered. Tigal did not wait for him to recover, but went on as if nothing had happened. "You are not happy leaving the girl to the fate Gray Seal has defined. Neither am I, my son, but what would you have me do? I saw the marks on the girl's wrist. They are raw from her efforts to free herself. I pointed this out to Gray Seal when I bargained with him, but he refused all my offers. They believe this is the only way to lift the curse. If we try to seize by force what is not ours, Gray Seal's people will fight like wildcats or slay the girl outright. I see great losses on both sides."

"Oh," Aditsan said. "Then there is nothing we can do?"

Tigal stopped in his tracks and looked at his gloomy young friend. "No, I didn't say that."

Aditsan perked up.

"When we can't fill our needs by negotiations, or by force, we must resort to using subterfuge and trickery. Are you willing to risk your life?"

Aditsan smiled. What plan did his leader have? "Tell me more."

Having Aditsan's full attention, Tigal began, "I told Gray Seal, even though it is late in the day, we will break camp and move on. I felt the sacrifice was not right. The sea could become upset and rise up again. We don't want to be here in the morning when that happens."

Mystified, Aditsan said, "Okay, but how will this help her?"

Tigal studied the sky. "Soon, there will be a storm," he said. "Do you feel the change in the air even as we speak? I think Gray Seal is too worried to have noticed the clouds gathering on the horizon. Before nightfall, I expect that we'll have to find shelter. Meantime, gather two of your trusted friends—two of my wives will go along to comfort the girl—and cover your bodies in the black from burnt firewood. It will help hide you in the dark. I saw dugouts overturned on the beach not far from where the girl is kept. I will leave it up to you to find a way to distract the guard, cut the girl loose and get away. Down the shore, about three days travel for the caravan, is the village of Spotted Deer. His village sits on top of white bluffs, but there is a beach where your boats can land. Their chief is a friend. We'll meet you there."

"It is a good plan, but what about Gray Seal? What if he comes after you?"

"If Gray Seal chases after the caravan, and I expect he will, he will find only what I want him to find—nothing."

Before nightfall, Aditsan and his small group left the caravan. Imitating a hunting party, they followed an animal trail that meandered around until it came to the shore some distance away from Gray Seal's village. Depending on the pounding waves to wash away their tracks and add to the mystery, he and the others sprinted along the beach just below the water line.

A rocky ridge cut across their path, curving away from their goal. Aditsan climbed to the top and, in the fading light, peeked over the crest to survey his surroundings.

In front of him, lay Gray Seal's village, the beached dugouts, and one, two, possible three guards patrolling the water's edge. Squinting, Aditsan could still make out a forlorn figure, bound to the post, while she struggled to keep her head above water.

Behind him, on the side protected by the ridge, the sea remained calm; but, on Gray Seal's side, the uninhibited waters pounded the shore. Clouds heavy with rain, driven by winds, rolled in. The storm Tigal promised would begin any moment.

Aditsan left Bornbazine[24], the older of the two wives Tigal sent with him and most of their supplies on the ridge. Safe from wind and rain, she squatted under an animal skin tarp, protecting the lantern that would help guide them through the darkness. She would wait there for his return . . . or until sunrise.

Rain! The storm broke just after nightfall. It came in heavy, dense clouds, pushed along by gusting winds. Visibility, at times, was cut to three or four man-lengths. Along with the rain came the pounding surf.

Crouched low to avoid detection, the remaining party left the shelter of the rocks and continued along the beach below the water line, but not so low that the surf would bowl them over. Ciqala[25], the younger and smaller of Tigal's wives with him, carried a bundle of leaf-covered vines securely held close to her body. The two men carried a simple log raft between them. It was a few poles lashed together, just enough

---

[24] Bornbazine - An Abnaki Indian name meaning "keeper of the flame," she is one of Tigal's wives.

[25] Ciqala - Dakota word for "little one," she is another one of Tigal's wives.

to carry one person. Aditsan wore a knapsack across his chest and led the way.

Reaching the dugouts, he signaled his friends to turn the vessels over and get them ready for the water. Posting the two men there to wipe out all traces of their efforts, he had Ciqala don her vine costume. Aditsan would have preferred her wardrobe be actual seaweed instead of vines, but they did not find enough for the task. He hoped that, from a distance, in the dark and storm-driven rain, the vines would suffice.

Ciqala tied a length of cord from her wrist to the raft before they picked it up and waded into the water. Circling around, they would be able to come up behind the pillar. If anyone saw them, it would appear as if they emerged from the depths of the sea.

Aditsan did not see Gray Seal's victim until, coughing and spitting, she broke the surface and fought to regain her feet. Swallowed by the surf, the girl struggled to use the ropes that bound her in an effort to climb higher on the pole that kept her in place. Wet as they were, the nubs of the branches were too slippery for her to hold. Each pounding wave washed her back and pulled her under. Aditsan knew she would not last much longer in this storm.

Shadowy movement on the beach confirmed there were at least two guards there. He smiled. In this weather, the night, and with the pounding surf, the men were close enough to witness the events about to take place, but far enough away not to be a threat.

Towing the raft behind her, Ciqala fought to stay on her feet against shoaling waves and rip currents. Nearing the backside of the pillar, Aditsan motioned her closer. In her wet disguise, she staggered through the waist-deep water and climbed up on his shoulders. From this position, her charcoal-blackened legs and her cloak of vines dangled down in front and covered both him and his knapsack.

The plan he had worked out in his head seemed so simple and straightforward he had felt sure that it would work. As he wallowed through the violent waves, weighted down with the woman on his shoulders and pulling the raft, he was not so sure.

For them to be successful, he needed to stay on his feet and get the guards to see him, that is, to see the image he and Ciqala created: a dark figure, taller than any man, and covered in seaweed. If this happened, they would report that a creature rose up out of the stormy waters to seize the girl and spirit her away. Otherwise, if they just cut the girl loose and swam away with her, it would rouse Gray Seal's suspicion.

Fighting to work her way higher on the pillar, Gray Seal's victim finally noticed this dark figure lumbering toward her and solved Aditsan's dilemma with an ear-splitting scream. The gusting winds carried the sound to the guards. The guards peered into the darkness and saw the girl striking useless blows at a large, dark figure as it engulfed her. They heard a couple additional muffled cries and then saw the figure, back to them, pause before moving toward deeper water. It disappeared, leaving no sign of the girl behind. In less than two heartbeats, the men broke and ran from the beach.

The girl's screams still ringing in their ears, Aditsan and Ciqala, fought to remain upright in the pounding surf as they struggled to reach the pillar. Finally, he felt the rough bark under his fingers. He also felt the blows the frightened girl rained down on them. Any one of which could knock him off balance and destroy their charade.

"Get a good grip on the top of pillar and then cut her ropes," he said, hoping his hoarse whisper was loud enough for the woman on his shoulders to hear, but not so loud that the guards would. "I'll grab her and try to calm her down."

Not understanding his words, they would make no difference to the girl except if she realized that it came from a human and not a beast.

One arm around the pole, he reached out for her. Still in a panic, she tried unsuccessfully to skitter away from him, but he managed to pin the terrified victim between himself and the post. Unable to calm her, he drew back a fist and sent a jab to her chin. She went limp.

"The ropes are cut, and I have the new one in place," Ciqala, still riding on Aditsan's shoulders, replied from above. "I pulled the raft closer and will hold on here while you finish. Let me know."

Aditsan located the raft and laid the unconscious girl on it. Holding that bobbing bed in place, he cut off her clothes, being sure to rip them in several places, and then opened the knapsack. Greeted by the smell of animal blood, one of the two critical elements he brought, he reached in and extracted the few small pieces of seaweed they had found. Holding them tight, he dipped the remnants of her clothes in the container before threading the seaweed through the material. He finished his subterfuge by tangling some of the garments up in the new cords before setting the rest adrift. When they were found, it would appear the creature from the sea slew the girl, perhaps ripping her to shreds, and carried her remains away.

The tattered and frayed ends of the new rope brushed his face and reminded him to coat them as well. Satisfied, he gathered the remains of her previous bindings. It was the final step in this stage of their deception.

Not finding the old cord, or finding the old cord cut at the top would make Gray Seal's people skeptical. However, blood on tattered cord, giving the appearance of a violent end, would confirm the guard's story.

"I am ready to go back," he said. Receiving Ciqala's two-handed pat on the head, he turned and pushed the raft ahead of him into the pounding surf and darkness.

###

With Ciqala still perched on his shoulders, Aditsan stumbled through the surf as he followed the same circuitous path they used on their approach. If he was observed, he wanted it to look as if the sea creature was returning to the depths.

Another attention-getting, two-handed pat on the head and then Ciqala leaned down to whisper in his ear, "Sir, I believe the guards ran from the beach. We are further away, and I cannot see them anymore. If you think it is safe, I could climb down and help you move the raft?"

No sooner had he nodded when he felt his vine covered assistant slither down his back and take a position at the front of the raft. With her help, movement became less of a challenge.

Aditsan's men had the dugouts in the water near shore when he and Ciqala returned. The rain and pounding sea had helped erase all traces of their being there. The girl, unconscious until now, stirred and suddenly sat up.

Ciqala quickly clamped a hand over the girl's mouth, muffling her outcry. Holding her face close to the frightened girl, she lay a finger over her own lips and said, "Shhh." When she felt the girl relax, Ciqala slowly removed her hand, but remained alert in the event she had to repeat her actions.

The wide-eyed girl, not sure if this was more of her captors' work, peered through the rain and darkness, in an attempt to figure out what was happening. A young woman covered in vines shared the raft with her. The cords were still around her wrists, but she was no longer tied to the pillar. Instead, she was naked and sitting astraddle a small raft. Between shoaling waves[26], her feet touched the sandy bottom

---

[26] Shoaling Waves - This describes the effect by which surface waves entering shallower water increase in wave height.

and she could hear their waters break nearby which meant she was close to shore. Around her, three men worked to set dugouts adrift. They pushed them in different directions and turned some upside down as if they had been capsized. Was this disbursement to mimic the work of the storm? Would their efforts mislead her captors so this party could escape with her in the remaining boats? Was she better off or not? She had questions, but no answers and didn't understand the language they spoke.

Their work done, the men pulled the last two vessels close to the waiting women. Ciqala motioned for the girl to climb in the closest one, then turned and started loading the bundles of vines in next to her. One of the men picked up the raft and put it in the remaining boat. Sitting in the middle, the girl appeared uneasy until Ciqala also climbed in with her. At the stern, Aditsan pushed the vessel into deeper water and then clambered aboard. The other men followed in their dugout.

After much effort, the pair of vessels reached the calmer waters on the lee side of the ridge. A small light, unseen from shore and hardly noticeable from seaside, guided them to their meeting place.

Bornbazine, holding water and pemmican, greeted her companions at water's edge. The girl ate ravenously. Their hostess left only to return with a tunic. She coaxed the girl into slipping it over her head. Fed, refreshed, and now clothed, the girl relaxed and appeared more at ease among the men.

Rested, the men brought the remaining supplies down and split them between the two vessels. To continue their success, Aditsan knew they must put distance between themselves and Gray Seal. The storm was subsiding. By morning's first light, the villagers may overcome their fears and begin to venture to the beach. Long before that would happen, his party needed to be far way. By keeping a sharp eye out, travel, even in the dark, would be easier now that the waters were calming.

Chapter 9: Abooksigun

The boat's prow ground to a stop in the sand, startling the exhausted girl awake. She bolted upright. Strands of vines, pieces of the bundle where she had cushioned her head, were still mixed in with her hair. She was near panic until she realized where she was. Pretending not to notice her reaction, the others jumped out of their vessels and began tugging them up on the beach to prevent their drifting off. The girl leaped out and joined them in their efforts.

With the dugouts safely ashore, the men busied themselves taking the raft apart. Hands on her hips, the girl looked around. Low in the sky, the morning sun shone through a thin layer of fog. She did not know how far they traveled, but there was no sign of the place where she had been held. The hills beyond this beach were covered in brush and trees. More trees, taller trees rose up behind them. Nearby, a shallow stream exited the brush. Unable to understand their language, she didn't know who her rescuers were or their intentions. She didn't know where she was, but she knew she was no longer in the place where she had been held, and her rescuers were kind to her. On the other hand, in the beginning her captors had also been kind to her.

The man, the groups' leader, motioned the women over. He could see the girl still had the remnants of the cords attached. Not wanting to leave evidence behind, the cord had been severed, freeing her from the pillar, but not removed. Taking her by the hand, he said something the girl didn't understand to one of the women. She pulled a knife and stepped forward. The girl gasped and started to back away. Still holding her hand, the man held up the loose cord and laughed. She had heard the same laugh the day before. The one who rescued her was the same man whose laughter then had caused her so much humiliation. In a flash, she brought her free hand up and laid an open palm across his cheek.

"Ow!" Surprised, Aditsan blinked at the ferocity of the attack. His face grew stern. Wagging his index finger under her nose, he shook his head and issued a sharp rebuke. "No!"

Fire in her eyes, the girl glared at him. Aditsan, seeing the look on her face, broke into laughter again. He was brought to his senses by another sharp slap across his cheek. It was his turn to glare.

Mimicking his earlier actions, the girl wagged a finger under his nose, shook her head, and said, "No!" It was her first word in this new language.

Attempting to be solemn faced, Bornbazine, knife still in hand, stepped forward and cut the cords at the girl's wrist. Turning quickly, she joined the others in finding busy work while they hid their smirks.

Having run out of other tasks, the wives gathered up all the empty water bags and handed them to the girl. Ciqala picked up the bundle of vines she had worn. Bornbazine reached into the dugout and picked up two spears. One was an ordinary implement with a smooth shaft, which ended in a pointed stone head. The other also had a pointed stone tip, but it was carved from end to end and had a collar of bird feathers. She slung the two spears over her shoulder and motioned to the girl to join them. The trio of females followed the stream into the forest. As they walked, Ciqala— still attempting to hide the evidence—cut the bundle apart and then cut the vines themselves into smaller pieces, discarding each piece in a separate spot in the brush.

The stream widened, creating a shallow pool. The girl watched as Tigal's wives looked around cautiously checking for threats. Finding no immediate danger, the women removed their tunics, waded into the chilly stream, and began bathing, using sand to remove the black charcoal from their skin. With a wave of the hand, the pair invited the girl to join them. She did not hesitate.

In the water, Ciqala motioned the girl over and curiosity drove her to join the younger one. Close together, Tigal's young wife reached out a hand and ran her fingers over a set of marks high on the girl's arm.

The girl smiled at Ciqala's puzzlement over the tattoo[27] and said, "Hono[28]." Attempting to imitate the movement of the creature, she wiggled her fingers over the water's surface and repeated the word. She watched Ciqala, who appeared fascinated by this marking; continue to run a finger over the symbol. It was something that Tigal's young wife had not noticed in the dark. Bornbazine waded over to see what had captured Ciqala's interest. A little chatter between the women followed their exam, but it was all gibberish to the girl.

Their quick bath finished, the women waded out and donned their tunics. Then, moving a few paces upstream, they paused to fill the water bags. Across the pool, the brush rustled, and a black bear pushed its way out. The women froze, hoping the animal would drink then go away without noticing them. A slight breeze blew across the pool. It carried their scent right to the bear. The animal reared up on its hind legs, sniffed the air, and then roared out a challenge.

---

[27] Tattoo - A Polynesian (Tahitian/Samoa) word meaning means 'to mark an object' such as a person. It describes the tradition of applying by hand (permanent) markings to the subject's body that defines their rank and title or that of their family, in the community. Polynesian tattooing is considered the most intricate and skillful tattooing of the ancient world. They believe that a person's mana, their spiritual power or life force, is displayed through their tattoo.

[28] Hono - Polynesian (Hawaiian/ Tahitian) word for Green Sea Turtle. Turtle can be the most important and popular element in Polynesian culture. It's connected to many meanings and the most common ones are long life (eternity), wellness, fertility, union, family and harmony. It also symbolizes the navigator. Turtle plays an essential role in Polynesian culture. The sea is regarded as the source of food and Polynesian people believe that it's also the world beyond, in which they will rest after death. Because turtles can freely move between the sea and lands, Polynesian people believe that they will bring them to their destination and final the resting place.

Bornbazine handed Ciqala the plain spear and the pair, spears at the ready, stepped in front of this unknown girl, thinking they would slowly back away from the threat and defend themselves if they were attacked.

The girl had a different idea. Pushing between her two protectors, she took a deep breath, cupped her hands around her mouth, and roared. The bear, not used to this type of reaction, seemed unsure of what to do next. After wavering back and forth a few moments, it finally decided that these opponents were not to be cowed, dropped to all fours, and disappeared into the brush. Cautiously, the women filled the water bags and headed back to the beach.

The men had been busy. Like the women, they had taken time to scrub away their burnt-black disguise. The raft, like the vines, was nowhere to be seen and each dugout was now equipped with an unusual three-legged scaffold. Suspended from the top of the device, a shaft ran side-to-side, and it supported the hides that had doubled as Bornbazine's shelter while she waited for their return.

Tigal's wives passed out pemmican and the water jugs, and conversation ensued between the younger of the two women and the three men.

The girl, left out because of the language barrier, could only guess at what was being said, but was sure she was the center of focus by the glances her way and by the body language of the storyteller.

Ciqala, her hands up and fingers curled like claws aptly described the bear. A toned-down version of the girl's roar told what happened next. Everyone looked at the girl and smiled. They did not give her a pity smile nor a sarcastic smile but one of admiration.

Bornbazine, carved spear in hand, stepped forward. Taking one of the girl's hands, the older woman placed it on her own shoulder and said, "Bornbazine." Then she placed her hand on the girl's shoulder and said, "Abooksigun[29]."

---

[29] Abooksigun - Algonquin word meaning "wildcat."

Finally, she took both the girls hands and placed them on the spear, wrapping the fingers around the shaft. Smiling, she let go and stepped back, leaving the girl standing alone holding the spear upright. Looking the girl in the eye, Bornbazine repeated, "Abooksigun." Then she turned to the others and repeated the word. Everyone smiled and shouted, "Abooksigun."

The girl did not know what the word meant, but it did not matter. What did count was that they had given her a name. She was no longer an outsider, but had been accepted and now was one of their people.

If the wind cooperated—that is, if it was directly behind them—and the sea was but a gentle roll, their voyage should have been an easy two-day trip from the beach where Abooksigun was given her name to the village of Spotted Deer. Aditsan's party would have arrived before Tigal's caravan and they would have had time to relax. Because of the wind and sea, the first leg of their travels was slow and made with great effort. It now appeared to Aditsan that they would be arriving after Tigal. Even worse, if the caravan master feared they had been lost along the way, he might move on before Aditsan's party arrived.

Not wanting this to happen, Aditsan pushed them as much as he could, but he also had to allow time for them to get out of the dugout's cramped confines. If a suitable beach presented itself, they stopped along the way to rest and came ashore to spend the night. As they traveled, Abooksigun, driven by the need to make her wants known, learned additional words. She also used the opportunity to teach her companions new skills.

By mid-day, the exhausted group spotted a good landing spot and pointed their canoes toward shore. After ensuring the area was secure, the group flopped down on the warm sand to rest and then dropped off to a light sleep.

The sleepers woke to soft pounding. To their surprise, Abooksigun had taken apart the sail rigging on one of the dugouts. The pieces were laid out nearby, and she was about to start on the second vessel.

Aditsan jumped to his feet, a multitude a thoughts racing through his head. *What is she doing? I should have posted a guard. Why didn't I post a guard?* "Stop!" He yelled, "What are you doing?"

Abooksigun looked up from her work to see the man who was their leader running toward her, a panicked look on his face. It was her turn to laugh at him. She stretched out her arm, palm toward him, and said, "Stop!" She was not sure what it meant, but it was the first word he had used when he started her way.

It was effective.

He stopped, calmed himself, and then continued, but at a slower pace. He could see that their lack of a common language was going to make understanding a challenge. *If only she knew a few words in Common Trade[30], we could talk.* Arriving at her side, he looked back and forth between the two dugouts, and then he looked at her with raised eyebrows, held his hands out, and shrugged.

Abooksigun laughing softly, took his hand, and led him over to where she had the sail and timbers laid out. Taking a stick, she began drawing two crude ship outlines in the sand. The difference between the two was the way the sails were rigged.

Using her stick, she pointed out that one had a square sail, and she pointed from the sand picture to the dugout she had not dismantled. The design of the second vessel showed

---

[30] Common Trade – A mixture of words and signs (sign language) used by various tribes who didn't share the same language. By this method, trade was able to take place.

a triangle–shaped sail. She pointed from that picture to the vessel where she had been working.

Aditsan looked back-and-forth between drawings and vessels and scratched his head. For all her work, he was still lost and, in case the look on his face wasn't enough, he shrugged.

Hampered by this language barrier, Abooksigun suppressed her frustration and patiently began drawing again. This set of diagrams also showed two vessels, but they differed from the others because the viewer would have to be looking down from above.

Abooksigun used great patience, a lot of gesturing, and several trips between the diagram and the vessel without clearly making her point. She finally plopped down next to the dugout feeling she was no further ahead than when she started. Aditsan dropped down beside her. Taking advantage of the break, Bornbazine and Ciqala passed out water and pemmican.

Like the others, Abooksigun sat quietly, munching on her midday's ration. A wind gust stirred the leaves on nearby bushes and gave her an idea. She sprang to her feet and covered the ground to the bush in a heartbeat, leaving everyone with their mouths gaping. She searched the bushes, selecting only the largest leaves to bring back. Facing her audience like a teacher, she pointed to the sail, pointed to her diagram, and then held up a leaf. Ciqala gave an excited squeal and snatched the leaf from Abooksigun's hand. Returning to the dugout, she held the leaf next to the sail and, nodding excitedly, looked to Abooksigun for confirmation saying, "Yes? Yes?"

Finally, Abooksigun thought, somebody understands. With a sigh of relief, she smiled and said, "Yes."

Ciqala hopped up-and-down, "She is telling us something about the sails."

Aditsan tried not to make a face. He knew the girl had ideas about the sail, but he didn't understand what she wanted to do. He turned to look at her and shrugged.

She looked at the group to make sure all eyes were on her, then, holding another leaf in both hands and broadside to her, Abooksigun blew. Everyone watched it puff out a little. Not waiting for questions, she turned the leaf on edge and blew again. Nothing happened. She looked at the group to see if anyone discovered what she was trying to teach them. Expressionless, they sat there waiting for her to continue. What do I do now?

She heard the leaves stir. The sound was followed by the flapping of the sail, and she knew what to do next. She grabbed one of the men and pulled him over to where she had been working. The crossbar lay there, sail still attached. She picked it up, handed it to her recruit, and faced him into the wind. The sail ballooned immediately almost bowling the holder over. While he steadied himself, Abooksigun took Aditsan by the hand, and they walked over to the diagrams. She pointed in the direction of the man struggling to hold the sail and then pointed out each of the drawings of the vessel under full sail. Leaving him standing there, she returned to her recruit. Like the leaf, she turned him edgewise to the wind. The sail, robbed of the breeze, collapsed.

Abooksigun waited a few moments for this idea to sink in then turned her recruit at an angle to the wind. The sail billowed again, almost as much as before when it was full on. She left her recruit, marched back over to Aditsan, pointed to the man holding the sail and then the other set of drawings.

Aditsan recognized the idea. "She wants to arrange the sail so that it will work even when the wind is not at our back," he told the others. Turning back to her, he nodded and said, "Yes."

Not wasting time, Abooksigun tugged people around and used hand signals to set them to work on tasks she assigned. They completed the modifications to the first vessel by mid-afternoon. It even included something new—an outrigger[31]. Aditsan didn't know what purpose it served, but she was insistent.

When he turned to begin work on the second vessel, she grabbed his arm and pulled him back, then motioned everyone to help carry the modified dugout into the water.

---

[31] Outrigger - In an outrigger canoe and in sailboats such as the proa, an outrigger is a thin, long, solid, hull used to stabilize an inherently unstable main hull. It is the part of a boat's rigging that is rigid and extends beyond the side or gunwale of a boat. The outrigger is positioned rigidly and parallel to the main hull so that the main hull is less likely to capsize. If only one outrigger is used on a vessel, its weight reduces the tendency to capsize in one direction and its buoyancy reduces the tendency in the other direction.
The outrigger float is called the *ama* in many Polynesian and Micronesian languages. The spars connecting the ama to the main hull (or the two hulls in a double-hull canoe) are called *'iako* in Hawaiian and *kiato* in Māori (with similar words in other Polynesian languages); in Micronesian languages, the term *aka* is used.
The outrigger canoe (Filipino and Indonesian: *bangka*; New Zealand Māori: *waka ama*; Cook Islands
Maori: *vaka*; Hawaiian: *wa'a*; Tahitian and Samoan: *va'a*) is a type of canoe featuring one or more lateral support floats known as outriggers, which are fastened to one or both sides of the main hull.
Smaller canoes often employ a single outrigger on the port side, while larger canoes may employ a single-outrigger, double-outrigger, or double-hull configuration (see also catamaran). The sailing canoes are an important part of the Polynesian heritage and are raced and sailed in Hawaii, Tahiti, and Samoa as well as and by the Māori of New Zealand. Unlike a single hulled canoe, an outrigger or double-hull canoe generates stability because of the distance between its hulls rather than due to the shape of each individual hull. As such, the hulls of outrigger or double-hull canoes are typically longer, narrower and
more hydrodynamically efficient than those of single-hull canoes.
Compared to other types of canoes, outrigger canoes can be quite fast, yet are also capable of being paddled and sailed in rougher water. This paddling technique, however, differs greatly from kayaking or rowing. The paddle, or blade, used by the paddler is single sided, with either a straight or a double-bend shaft. Despite the single paddle, an experienced paddler will only paddle on one side, using a technique such as a J-stroke to maintain heading and stability.

After boarding, Abooksigun indicated he should do likewise. With the two of them onboard, she unfurled the sail and shoved off.

Running with the wind, the dugout skimmed across the water. Aditsan watched as the shore, where they had left their friends standing, grow more distant. Thumping the side of the boat, he caught Abooksigun's attention, pointed toward shore, to show he wanted to go back. She nodded and began working ropes that adjusted the sail. Using a paddle, she turned the boat's nose toward shore, but not where their friends stood. Now traveling crosswind, their vessel made a smooth, quick journey toward the beach.

Aditsan watched as the distance back to land shrank. However, judging from the direction they were heading, they would reach shore a long way from where they left everyone else. Perplexed by the idea, he thumped the side of the boat again. Abooksigun looked up and smiled. He pointed forward to the shore, pointed toward the rest of their group, and then shrugged.

A twinkle in her eye, she gave him a warm smile and nodded. Adjusting the ropes once again, she used her paddle to turn the boat's nose toward the spot where the rest of their party waited. Their arrival was greeted with shouts and cheers as everyone waded into the water to congratulate them.

Aditsan hopped out of the dugout. "This worked great! It was unbelievable… except for steering, a paddle never touched water." He looked up at the sun to see how much time they had before nightfall. Pointing to the other vessel, he started to organize a work crew. "We can change the other dugout. It should go faster since we're experienced."

The group cheered and started for the other dugout but halted when Abooksigun yelled something in her own language followed by, "Stop!" Abooksigun tried to keep her face expressionless and her thoughts to herself. *What are they thinking? They'll never be able to sail a boat like this without practice, and one canoe is not big enough to carry everybody. What can I do to resolve this?*

The only solution to present itself would be to use the other dugout as the outrigger. If I put that together, I could handle the sail and the new vessel would carry everyone.

Under her direction, and with many hand motions, she had the second boat brought close to the first where she started taking all the poles from its mast system. Everyone stood around quietly watching her. Finished with that task, Abooksigun pointing to the newly stripped vessel and then the outrigger. There was no objection—maybe because they had no idea what she was going to do next, no one asked questions. To the surprise of the watchers, she bent down and removed the outrigger then began laying the extra mast poles, horizontally, between the two vessels.

Aditsan motioned to the others. "She wants to use the second canoe as the outrigger. Let's give her a hand."

Working together, they notched the poles and the dugouts where they intersected. To keep these in place, they tied ropes to the outside end, ran them under the ship's bottom to come up and get tied on the other side. They repeated the process for each cross member to make sure the pieces were secure.

Abooksigun stood back and looked at their work. Satisfied, she motioned to Aditsan. After testing the ropes and poles, he nodded to her and then the others. They shoved the vessels, now made into one, into knee-deep water, and everyone boarded. Aditsan, paddle in hand, took a spot at the end of a canoe ready to steer. To handle the rigging, Abooksigun sat opposite him, in the other vessel. A few paddle strokes and the sail caught the wind. They were on their way again, but no one had to struggle.

Seeing the village atop the white bluffs brought joy to everyone. It would be a relief to be out of the confines of the cramped dugout. Shortly afterward, their boats dug into the sandy beach near where the village's fishing boats.

Villagers taking care of the day's catch or tending the nets, gathered around Aditsan's unusual vessel. Aditsan directed his group to hold the canoes at the shore while they waited for the chief. There was no doubt in his mind that they had been seen since they had made no attempt at concealment. Word of their approach would have been sent into the village giving the chief time to prepare for the strangers' arrival. As predicted, the crowd on the beach parted allowing the Chief and his council to pass.

Aditsan stepped forward, held up a hand in greeting, and said, "Great Chief Spotted Deer, I Aditsan bring you greetings from Chief Tigal."

Spotted Deer returned Aditsan's greeting, and added, "Chief Tigal's runner brought word of his caravan's approach as well as your expected arrival. We have prepared places for you to wait for him."

Like his leader, Aditsan enjoyed the story being told and delighted in the anxiety their guests displayed. "Yes, the caravan made a big display when they left Gray Seal's village, but myself and my friends soon broke off from the main group. We found a place where we could cover our bodies with black from burnt firewood. As night fell, and just before a storm broke, we crept back along the shore to the village." He paused and looked at their guests while he let their anticipation build. "We knew where they were keeping the woman, so we distracted the guard, cut her loose, threw her on a raft we brought, and headed back up the beach."

White Hawk's puzzlement was written across his face. "Back up the beach? I don't understand. Why go back up the beach?" Did he voice the question that was running through Running Wolf's mind as well?

"We relied on the waters to hide our tracks. We would have been robbed of this assistance if we had gone up the trail," Aditsan explained. "If they would have found even the smallest sigh of our being there, they would have suspected Tigal's hand in this. As it was, they sent a small party after the caravan to make sure she was not there. Tigal counted on them doing just that. Since Gray Seal's men did not find her, they would think that since she came from the sea, the sea returned to claim her." He paused and looked at the two men across from him. Both Running Wolf and White Hawk nodded, accepting the wisdom of these decisions. "A great story, but how will this help?"

Tigal took a long draw on his pipe. "The girl, the one called Abooksigun, the one who Gray Seal had found and was ready to sacrifice, was from the village of these new people and can speak their language."

Running Wolf recovered from his shock first. "From the same village? That is good, but what happened to this girl?"

Tigal, having decided that the pipe's spark was gone, took a brand from the fire, held it near the bowl of his pipe, and nodded to Aditsan to finish the story as he worked to re-light his pipe.

"What happened to the girl?" Aditsan asked. "That's easy. She's my wife!"

Chapter 10: Who Are You?

In his nightmare, the stranger was back on his ship in the raging storm. He and the ship's captain struggled with the rudder. The cargo boom[32] tore loose. A crewman grabbed the ragged end of the rope that had secured it, but the ship's erratic movements threw him off his feet.

"Hold the ship's bow into the wind. We'll capsize if it turns sideways," the captain shouted. "I'll go help the man on that line; the rest of my crew are gone."

The wind tried to push the vessel sideways. Fire-from-the-sky[33] lit up the darkness. Through the driving rain, the stranger saw the two men at the boom. Then a wave rose up, crashed over the rail, and the men were gone—swept away in a heartbeat.

The ship felt like it was about to roll over. *If it did, would I be able to save my children? Where are they?* Another wave crashed over the bow and came rushing back to swallow him in its ebony clutches. From somewhere in that darkness, a woman, a stranger, called to him.

"Kauwa[34]! Where are my children?" he demanded. Still half-asleep, the long tendrils of the nightmare fading ever so slowly, the stranger lurched forward from his pallet. The pain of his injuries pushed away the last vestiges of his dream. Beads of sweat bathed his body. Propped up on one elbow, he tried to peer through the dim light.

---

[32] Boom - A long pole extending outward from the mast of a derrick and used to support, or guide, objects being lifted or suspended.

[33] Fire-from-the-sky - This is how they described lightning because they recognized that it sometimes started fires.

[34] Kauwa: Polynesian word for the slave class/caste. These were people taken as prisoners of war or their descendants. The kauwa are identified a tattoo mark about the eyes, or on the forehead.

A young woman and a girl knelt nearby, speaking their foreign tongue in low tones. The girl left in a hurry and the young woman turned her attention to him.

"Kauwa! Where are my children?" he repeated his demand.

"I am not a Kauwa," Abooksigun said coldly. "Lay back, or you'll strain yourself… and treat me with respect or you'll never hear me speak again," she cautioned.

The stranger from the boat recognized her voice from his dream. It was she who had called him. The man took a closer look at her. She did not have the markings of a kauwa nor did she carry herself like a menehune[35]. He reconsidered his words and finally, cautiously asked, "Wahine[36], who are you? Why are you here?"

Abooksigun softened, a slight smile painted itself across her face, and she knelt close by his pallet. "I'm here… to listen to your answers to my questions." She offered him a wooden bowl with water.

He looked at her. A cold stare had replaced her quiet smile. Gritting his teeth against the pain, his free hand snapped out toward this impertinent girl. As fast as he was, she was faster, easily catching his hand in midair and twisting it away from his intended target. With a quick snap of her wrist, she flung the bowl in his face. He felt the sharp, coldness of the water and then a quick jerk that pulled him off balance. Collapsing, he shrieked in pain.

"If you want to get back on your feet, don't try that again," she warned him. "We've gone out of our way to help you. Your children are safe. They are well fed and playing with our children. If you want that to continue, answer my questions… otherwise, I'll have to ask these people for help… and they will do whatever I ask."

---

[35]Menehune: A derisively term used to refer to the lower, worker class, just slightly above that of the slaves (kauwa).
[36] Wahine: A Polynesian word meaning woman.

The stranger lay back, knowing that for the time being there was no way he could do anything but cooperate. "What questions do you have?"

"What is your name?"

"I am Chief Aweida of the house of Nauru," he replied quietly. Because his aggressive approach had gotten him great pain and little co-operation, he had to resign himself to the role he must play, even while his mind reeled with questions he was not able to ask. *Who is this woman who felt free to order him around like a servant? Where did she learn to speak his language? I have many questions, but for the time being, they will have to wait. I must act subdued for the moment to gain time. Right now, I will listen to her questions and keep a close eye on her reaction to my answers.*

She did not blink but went on with her questions. "How many ships came with you from 'Avaiki[37]?"

He jumped as if a burning coal had dropped in his lap. *How did she know I originated from Avaiki? How did she know they sent out more than one ship?* He looked at her, surprise written all over his face. Having lost the pretense of calm, he blurted out his questions. "Wahine, who are you? How do you know these things?"

---

[37]'Avaiki: Depending on the particular Polynesian culture and language, the name '*Avaiki* has several variations (some of which are *Havaiki*, *Havai'i*, or *Hawaiki*, though *Hawaiki* or the misspelling "Hawaiiki" appear to have become the most common variants used in English). The name referred to their original home before they travelled across the sea. Linguists have reconstructed the term to Proto-Nuclear Polynesian *sawaiki*, which is the term associated with the afterlife and death. Other possible cognates of the word *Hawaiki* include *sauali'i* ("spirits" in Sāmoan) and *hou'eiki* ("chiefs" in Tongan). This has led some scholars to hypothesize that the word *Hawaiki*, and, by extension, *Savai'i* and *Hawai'i*, may not, in fact, have originally referred to a geographical place, but rather to chiefly ancestors and the chief-based social structure, that pre-colonial Polynesia typically exhibited. They feel that there is no real contradiction in Hawaiki being the ancestral homeland (that is, the dwelling place of the ancestors) and the afterlife, which is also the dwelling place of the ancestors and the spirits.

The woman smiled and gave in a little. "My name here is Abooksigun, but I am not from here. Three summers ago, my ship left 'Avaiki. It was caught in a great storm. Everyone else was lost, but I managed to cling to the wreckage. Finally, after many days, I washed up on shore. I was held prisoner by the people that found me. They were going to sacrifice me, but, then these people… the ones who found you, rescued me."

Aweida's head spun. *The time she spoke about . . . her ship lost… everything fit. It had to be her.* He bowed his head reverently and said, "Your majesty."

###

"The man's name is Aweida," Abooksigun said. "He and his children are Naacal[38]. They are from 'Avaiki—the same place that I came from." She paused and looked at her audience. Across the fading campfire, four people—Running Wolf, White Hawk, Tigal, and Aditsan—sat in silence and listened.

"Originally, there were three ships in the group. A storm came. The captain wanted to turn back, but Aweida—under orders from his superiors—wanted to, needed to continue," Abooksigun said. "They had faced bad weather before, but the captain felt this would be worse. He was not able to

---

[38]Naacal: The name of an ancient people and civilization first claimed to have existed by Augustus Le Plongeon and later by James Churchward. Though there is no scientific or archaeological evidence for the existence of the Naacals, various later fictional works have made use of them. In Andre Norton's Central Asia novels, two main characters are Nacaals. She identifies Draupadi from the Mahabharata and the Hindu deity Ganesha as Nacaal survivors who advise humanity. She describes two warring factions among the Nacaals who have different aims and pursuits. Her Nacaal civilization existed as islands in an inner Asian sea and they eventually perished.

convince Aweida. The ships became separated. The storm grew worse than any they had ever experienced. Afraid the children might be swept away, Aweida tied them to a post while the others tried to save the ship." Abooksigun grew silent, poking at the coals in the campfire, lost in thought, perhaps remembering her own experiences.

Looking up from this self-assigned task, she realized the others were watching her, waiting for her to continue. "The timber that held the sail broke and pinned him under the debris. Waves covered the ship. They swept the others away. Had he not been pinned down, the waves would have taken him as well. After the storm passed, the children managed to free themselves, but they could not free him. The vessel, too damaged to be seaworthy even if they had a crew, drifted for several days before they arrived here."

Running Wolf looked at Tigal hoping the caravan master would not object to his question. "Why are they here?"

"They were sent on a search."

Running Wolf made a face. Her answer did not help him, and he needed more. "A search? What were they searching for?"

Abooksigun looked him in the eye and replied, "Me. They were sent to search for me."

Chapter 11: Help Us

Running Wolf's jaw dropped. "Why would they risk everything to search for you?"

His surprise was not shared by Tigal or Aditsan. After her rescue and before they became husband and wife, Abooksigun sat down with Aditsan and told him her story. The tale she told, if it were from anyone else, would not have been believed. Even coming from her lips it was hard for him to swallow. When he recovered, Aditsan relayed her story, less some details, to his leader.

"Here, I am called Abooksigun, but, before I arrived here, my name was 'Aukai[39]. I, like Aweida, am Naacal. Like he, I started my journey from 'Avaiki. That was more than three summers ago." Abooksigun paused to give time for her words to register.

"The difference between us is that I was running away, and he was sent to bring me back." Abooksigun pulled the sleeve of her tunic up and revealed her tattoo. "I carry the mark of Hono, the sea turtle, and, like him, I wandered the waters. Before my grandfather's grandfather's grandfather, my people took to the sea in their canoes and traveled from island to island in order to learn new methods and trade for new items."

The group of listeners stirred and a low murmur flowed between them before quiet returned. A slight nod from Tigal indicated that she should continue.

Abooksigun put a water bag to her lips and took a few sips while she collected her thoughts. "In many ways, the Naacal in their travels are like Tigal and his caravan," she said. "We differ only slightly: he depends on his knowledge of the forest and the land he travels; the Naacal travel over water

---

[39] Aukai - Pronounced (AOO kaee) Hawaiian name meaning Seafarer

and depend on their knowledge of migrating birds, Koala[40], the great fish, and the stars to find their way.

When the distances grew longer, or when there were many people to carry, the Naacal—those that came before this time—learned how to build bigger vessels. These could carry people, animals, food, and trade goods. Because they travel far, they often set up colonies along the way. The people in the colonies would trade with the locals and then barter the goods they gathered with ships that came from afar."

Always interested in more trading partners, Tigal focused on the potential for trade. "What kinds of goods were bartered?"

"Aweida's vessel is like those that would visit the colonies. It carries cloth, beads, and several sealed jars. He said there were samples of spices and perfumes—some from the land of Punt[41] near the Great Sand Sea[42]. He planned to use these items as barter for goods and information."

---

[40] Kohala - The Hawaiian word for a humpback whale.

[41] The Land of Punt, also called Pwenet, or Pwene by the ancient Egyptians, it was one of their trading partners and was known for producing and exporting gold, aromatic resins, African Blackwood, ebony, ivory, slaves, and wild animals. The exact location of Punt is still debated by historians. While it is not know for sure, most scholars today believe Punt was located to the southeast of Egypt, most likely in the coastal region of what is today northern Somalia, Djibouti, Eritrea, Northeast Ethiopia and the Red Sea coast of Sudan. However, some scholars believe there is strong evidence that point instead to a range of ancient inscriptions, which locate Punt in the Arabian Peninsula. This leads to possibility that the territory covered both the Horn of Africa and Southern Arabia.

42 The Great Sand Sea – called "The Empty Quarter" (The Rub' al Khali) is the largest sand desert in the world, encompassing most of the southern third of the Arabian Peninsula. The desert covers some 650,000 square kilometers (250,000 sq. mi) and includes parts of Saudi Arabia, Oman, the United Arab Emirates, and Yemen. It is part of the larger Arabian Desert.

Running Wolf was perplexed. "The Great Sand Sea... what is that?"

Abooksigun waved a hand toward the sea now blanketed in the blackness of night. "You are familiar with the sea?"

Running Wolf, silent, nodded. *What kind of question is that? My village sits near the edge of the sea. I grew up here. There had to be more to her question.*

"You know the sea is very large, larger than anything any of you have ever seen, is that right?"

Again, the Chief of the Sea People nodded in silence. *Where was she leading me?*

"When you look out there, what do you see?"

Running Wolf shrugged. "Water," he said. "As far as the eye can see, there is nothing but water." Still perplexed, he looked again at the water and then squinted as he looked at her. Her questions seemed pointless.

Abooksigun smiled, almost shyly, as she triggered her trap. "Now picture a sea like the one in front of you, but made of sand. It even has waves, giant waves, some taller than three or four men, and all are made of sand. The wind blows and the bits of sand move, and in a day or two the wave has shifted. As far as the eye can see, there is nothing but these waves of sand. That is the Great Sand Sea."

Water, sand, it made no difference to White Hawk. His interests lay in the practical aspects of having more people— perhaps a warring people—at their gate, White Hawk asked, "The place where he came from, how far away is it?"

"Not that far," she answered, and pursed her lips. "Depending on the winds and weather, a good sailor could reach there in two or possibly three moons' time." To her, it was a reasonable figure, stated no differently than if she told someone that this place was right around the next bend. To Running Wolf and White Hawk, not used to travel, the idea of being on the water that long was incomprehensible.

White Hawk was the first to recover. "Who are you to them that they would come all that way?"

"My father was chief wayfinder[43] for the Naacal."
Abooksigun scanned the faces of her audience. "I learned
how to navigate from him and I honed my skills under his
direction. His sister married an evil man, one we named
Pupule Uku[44], who, I believe, killed my father and made
himself chief. Then, believing he could rule everyone, to
control everything across the sea, he wanted me to teach my
skills only to those of his choosing. When I objected, he
threatened me with a forced marriage. The person he chose
was a brute, even worse than he was. I fled." She paused and
scanned the faces of her audience again. Do they believe me,
or do they think my actions are only those of a strong-willed
girl?

White Hawk opened his mouth to speak, but Running
Wolf stopped him by asking, "So… has anything changed
that you would go back?"

"Yes. Pupule Uku is dead, killed in a war he started. So is
the one he would have had me marry, but the Naacal are left
in turmoil. It is hoped my return will bring some calm to the
Naacal."

"Bring some calm?" White Hawk struggled with the idea.
"You're a wayfinder, a navigator of waters, how would that
bring calm?"

Shoulders back, chin jutting out just a bit, Abooksigun
looked at him. "You're right, I am a wayfinder, a navigator of
waters, and I have been trained by the best." She paused a
moment, giving them time to adjust. "However, I am also
next in line for the throne," Her answer surprised everyone,
but none more than Aditsan.

---

[43] Wayfinder - Navigator

[44] Pupule Uku - Hawaiian words meaning (Pupule) Crazy (especially
referring to a mentally deranged person) and (Uku) Fleas or head lice (as
in 'undesired' little critters in your hair').

Chapter 12: The New Ship

Leading Aditsan, Great Buffalo, and Red Deer into the forest, Abooksigun described the type of tree she hoped to find. "We will be at sea a long time. For our ship, we must find trees that will stand up to the weather and the salt water."

Puzzled, Aditsan questioned her, "Are the trees the Naacal use different than the trees here?"

Abooksigun shook her head. "Not that much different." She paused to scan the stand they were passing through before continuing. "For the ship's hull, we'll need a fat tree, with a long trunk."

Aditsan looked around. "We're in the middle of the forest. How big a tree do you need?"

"If we stand on opposite sides and stretch our out arms as if to hug, our fingers should barely touch, and the length should be at least several hands' worth of men laid end-to-end, and we . . . ."

Hearing that description, Red Deer made a face. While not that familiar with ship building, the figure seemed large. He was not the only one surprised by the number. Great Buffalo interrupted her immediately, voicing the question that Red Deer was thinking. "Why do you want such a big tree?"

Abooksigun's jaw dropped, but then she realized that her audience had no experience with the task in front of them. "It seems long now, but once we set off on our trip, there could be as many as two hand's worth of people with all of our supplies. We will be living together . . . night and day . . . for three moons' time." Raising an eyebrow, she looked at the pair of young men and added, "You'll find that this space grows smaller every day we're at sea."

Red Deer ventured, "How about tying a couple of trees together? Will that work?"

"Probably not," Abooksigun said. "I don't think we could fasten the parts together well enough that they wouldn't come apart in a storm."

First to recover from the shock, Great Buffalo pointed out a timber felled by a recent storm. "How about that one? Will it fit your needs?"

Abooksigun walked the length of the tree, inspecting every inch. "It has to be long but not too long," she mumbled and finally passed judgment. "Perfect." Turning to Aditsan, she said, "We must talk about getting workers here to help turn this from a tree into a ship."

Red Deer looked around. "Here, in the middle of the forest, we're going to turn this into a vessel?"

Abooksigun laughed. "Well, we're going to get started here by removing the branches and splitting the trunk up the length. That will give us two hulls. If nothing else, each piece will weigh less, and that should make it easier to get it to the water."

Great Buffalo led Aditsan around the work site. The tree, now two overturned hulls, lay on rollers. Workers, women and children from Running Wolf's tribe alongside some of Tigal's men, scurried around it like ants on a sweet treat. "After we got the limbs trimmed off, we made a line on both sides of the trunk the entire length. Then we turned it so one line pointed up in the air. The let us drive stone wedges into the trunk along the line."

Aditsan nodded his approval. "The trunk was thick, too thick for the wedges to go through. How did you get the log to split?"

"We drove the wedges as far as we could, even used poles to push them deeper, then we rolled the trunk over and did the same to the other side."

Aditsan smiled appreciatively. "I see that worked."

"Well, not right away, but eventually."

"Okay," Aditsan said, "so what are they doing now?"

"Abooksigun said the Naacal scrapped the bark off the timbers and then coated the bare wood with a mixture of tree saps to seal the wood. That way, the hulls wouldn't soak up water . . . at least not as fast and not right away."

Aditsan clapped Great Buffalo on the shoulder. "It looks like you have everything going well. What needs to be done before we can sail?"

Great Buffalo gave a wry smile. "We have to get the hulls down to the shore; securely attach the framework that will tie the two hulls together and support the decks; set the masts and rudder. In short, it will be a while."

Red Deer and Great Buffalo moved around the finished vessel, checking each detail and pointing out changes for Little Wolf and Appanoose to have their workers fix.

Aditsan and Abooksigun watched Red Deer and Great Buffalo as they directed the work. "These two have grown into young men before my eyes," Aditsan said.

"Yes," Abooksigun agreed, "and it appears that Little Wolf's sister has noticed at least one of them. Great Buffalo better watch out."

Chapter 13: Returning

Seagull cries, the flapping of the sails, the slurp-slurp-slurp of the boat as it cut through the waves, the steady rocking of the deck, lost in thought, none of these disturbed Aditsan. The boat they traveled on was taking him away from all that was familiar. As the vessel slid across the water, he watched the land, and the security he knew, disappear over the horizon. First the shore, then the treetops, and finally the mountain peaks—it was if all the landmarks he had known were being swallowed by this unending sea. He sighed.

At the helm, Abooksigun heard him and beckoned him closer. "Are you sorry you decided to accompany me my husband?"

Caught in the act, Aditsan smiled shyly and said, "I wouldn't miss this for the world. It's just that I am not sure I'm comfortable on this much water with no land in sight." He took a seat next to her and put his hand over hers on the tiller.

His remarks earned a hearty laugh from his wife. "We won't see our goal for a while, but I promise you, my husband, that by the moon's turn, we will see land."

As if deep in thought, Aditsan stroked his chin then tried to hide the twinkle in his eye as he said, "I think Tigal will be happy if it means a new trading partner."

Raising an eyebrow, she gave him a wry smile. "A new trading partner? Is that why Tigal was so eager to help us get the vessel ready and let you come along?"

"He is always interested in new opportunities, but he also knew he wasn't going to be able to keep me there so it is a good compromise."

A squeal followed by laughter from the forward section caught their attention. Red Deer and Great Buffalo were playing a game of keep-away with Aweida's children while their father stood back and watched.

Aditsan watched them for a few moments, listening to see if he could catch any of the words. "How are the lads doing with learning the new language?"

"Aweida said they are learning fast. Arapeta and Areta keep them on their toes so that helps." Abooksigun gave him a long glance. "How about you? You'll need to learn the language if you're going to try to barter with them. They are shrewd negotiators so given the chance the Naacal will clean you out. Of course, as sharp as they are they may do that even if you speak the language as good as they do."

Aditsan glanced over his shoulder. "It looks like it's too far to swim back so we better get started with the lesson then."

Abooksigun smiled at him. "You mean lessons, don't you?"

"What? Lessons?"

"Yes, lessons. While we're here, we'll start with sailing and reading the sea and the weather. See those clouds? See how they hang low in the sky?"

"Yes," he said. "They're from yesterday's storm and mean that the weather should be good for a few days."

"Very good. How did you know that?"

"It means the same thing when we traveled over land. What else?"

Abooksigun nodded. "Okay, you can read some clouds. You'll need to be able to read the sea currents, recognize sea birds and know which ones fly far out to sea and which ones stay close to land. If that's not enough, to master your skills as a wayfinder, you'll have to recognize the stars and their paths through the sky as well as when the wind blows. Talking about wind, how are you at handling the sails?"

Caught, Aditsan smiled sheepishly, but stared straight ahead. "Not a problem."

Abooksigun knew better. She bent herself around to look at him straight-on. "Really?"

Aditsan, smile now gone, remained emotionless while he continued to be fixed on some point on the horizon. "Yes," Aditsan said. Unable to hold his expression under her gaze, he finally broke down and added, "With the wind directly behind us, it's not a problem."

Half asleep, Red Deer hung on the tiller and mentally marked the position of the Morning Star[45]. He nudged Great Buffalo into wakefulness and told him, "Better mark the star's location on the chart and then go forward to wake Abooksigun. The star will disappear below the horizon soon. She made it clear that she wants to check our work."

Both lads remembered all too well the early lessons on navigation and the need for accuracy that Abooksigun had given them.

Great Buffalo looked at the rawhide circle fastened to the top of the short pillar in front of them. Fastened to the circle's center sat a free moving shaft, equipped with two hollow bones, one on each end."

"It's a sighting device," Abooksigun told them when they first laid eyes on it. "When your caravan travels, Tigal knew that the sun rose in the east and set in the west, but how did he tell how far north or south he was?"

Great Buffalo shrugged. "We just followed the animal trails through the forest and used landmarks—mountains, rivers, lakes—to help us. I was getting to know them pretty well."

---

[45]Morning Star, a name for the planet Venus when it appears in the east before sunrise

Red Deer scratched his head. "What happens if you want to go to someplace you've never been before?"

"That's easy," chided Great Buffalo. "You just get somebody like Aditsan to take you there like he did the first time we went to the land of the Sea People."

"If you look around, you'll see there are no landmarks out here," Abooksigun said. "As a wayfinder, you must know your location. Like Tigal, we use the sun to know east and west. We also use the moon and stars to know how far north or south we have traveled. To do this, sight through the holes in the two bones to line up the right star and then carefully place a colored token at the correct point on the chart.[46]"

"Why does it matter?" Great Buffalo asked. "Wouldn't it work the same if it pointed in the general direction?"

"For a trip of one day, a small error would still guide you to the general vicinity. A small error made every day during a week's trip, would mean you would have to paddle around a lot to find the port you seek. For a trip of two moons' time, like ours, you will be completely lost before you start. From the beginning of any trip, food and fresh water are rationed. If a ship has to paddle around to find a safe port because the

---

[46] Polynesian sailors used special navigation method to make long voyages across thousands of miles of the open ocean. They were able to travel to various islands using only their own senses and knowledge passed by oral tradition from master to apprentice, often in the form of song. In order to locate directions at various times of day and year, Polynesian navigators memorized important facts. They needed knowledge of weather and the seasons of travel, when the winds blow and which direction. Other skills navigators needed include knowing the nature of wildlife species, how they travel, and where they gather. The direction, size, and speed of ocean waves, the colors of the sea and sky, especially how clouds would cluster at the locations of some islands. While these navigators depended fundamentally upon these factors, they used the heavens for navigation, since stars and planets were their most dependable "landmarks" on the open oceans. They memorize the motion of specific stars that is where they would rise and set on the horizon during different seasons of the year. To help them, the navigators used elaborate visual images—charts fashioned like darting parrotfish, triggerfish, or even the circular base of a gourd with lines burnt in to show the meridian of Hawaii.

wayfinder was careless, guess who is going to be the first one thrown
overboard so the others have a better chance of survival."

"But you're here with us so that won't happen, right?" Red Deer
interrupted in a vain attempt to save his friend. It only made things
worse.

"I am here, now . . . but what if I weren't?" She turned to him,
eyes sparking fire.

"But . . . but . . ." Red Deer started, scrambling to find the right
words to sooth her scorching glaze.

"But nothing! What if I were swept overboard? What would you
do then? Everyone on board this vessel must be prepared to do any job.
Otherwise, they put everyone else at risk"

###

Great Buffalo shook himself. Both boys understood that
a star's location was important not only as a guide, but it
would allow them to escape yet another scolding from
Abooksigun. "That's something I don't want to go through
again. I'll get Abooksigun up. If she misses this chance, she
won't get another until just before sunrise tomorrow, and that
won't make her happy . . . and she will make our lives
miserable."

Red-eyed, Red Deer peered at the sea. The morning
breezes filled the sails as they skimmed over the water.
Turning his head, he looked over his shoulder at the ship's
wake. During the night, the path they created glowed.
Abooksigun said it was from small plants in the water, but
that seemed like a story told to little children. Whatever it
was, it was no longer visible in the dawn's light. After seeing
schools of fish fly out of the water as if they were birds
stampeding across the sea in front of a wolf, small, glowing
plants were believable. Right now, there were no flying fish
and no glowing plants; there was only a slight roll for as far as
he could see.

"Good job, helmsman," Abooksigun said. She approached carrying a welcomed breakfast tray. His stomach growled in anticipation.

"You're sailing a straight line these days and not all over the ocean." Putting the tray aside, she gave him a warm smile before bending to check Great Buffalo's sightings. "Another good job," she said. "I'm glad to see . . . ."

"Look!" Red Deer shouted, cutting Abooksigun off in mid-sentence. He pointed out to sea. Before their eyes, a great whale broke the surface of the water, sucked in another breath, and dove again. No sooner had it disappeared from view, when another broke the surface, and then disappeared below the waves. The boys watched open-mouthed at the creatures' display.

Pounding feet signaled the arrival of Aditsan. "What was that? Is it going to attack?"

Abooksigun laughed good-naturedly. "No, it won't attack" she said. "Some call the great fish Paikea[47] others call him Kohala[48]. It's big, but unprovoked, it is quite harmless."

Aditsan breathed a sigh of relief. "If it attacked, our ship wouldn't have a chance against something that big."

"Big," Red Deer repeated. "I counted two hands from the time I first saw it to the time its tail disappeared under the water. That would make it more than ten man-lengths long. I have never seen anything that big."

Abooksigun nodded and began passing out the morning's rations of food and water. "Through the ages, my people have passed many stories down from one generation to the next. There is one about a young man, Kahutiaterangi[49], who lived in Hawaiki. He was one of the

---

[47] Paikea - Maori word for a humpback whale.

[48] Kohala - The Hawaiian word for a humpback whale·

[49] Ruatapu, Kahutiaterangi, and Pike - Characters in a Maori legend used to tell how they reached New Zealand·

sons of the great chief Uenuku. Kahutiaterangi's half-brother, Ruatapu, who was born of a slave wife, was jealous and wanted to become chief so he build a waka, which is a canoe. When it was finished, he lured Kahutiaterangi and his highborn brothers aboard, and took them out to sea to sink the boat and drown his rivals.

Kahutiaterangi managed to save himself by reciting a prayer calling on his ancestors to protect him from Ruatapu's wrath. His ancestors called Paikea up from the bottom of the sea. The great fish lifted him up and carried him away on its back. Together like this, they swam for many days and nights through fierce storms, thunder and lightning until the whale was able to put him ashore at Aotearoa[50].

Kahutiaterangi, now the sole survivor of Ruatapu's evil took the name Paikea in memory of the assistance his ancestors provided.

Still angry, Ruatapu called out an incantation to turn himself into a giant wave and pursue his rival. He was unable to catch the pair before the great fish deposited Paikea ashore. In his rage, doubled now because he was no longer able to turn himself back into a man, Ruatapu shouted out his threat to return to fight him as the great waves of the eighth month."

Her tray empty, Abooksigun checked to make sure everyone had something to eat and drink. "In Aotearoa, it is tradition to name the chief's first born male Paikea to remind the people that the great fish is friendly and helpful."

Aditsan shook his head. "What other surprises lay out here?"

---

[50] Aotearoa - The most widely known and accepted Māori name for New Zealand. It is used by both Māori and non-Māori, and is becoming increasingly widespread in the bilingual names of national organizations. Since the 1990s, it has been the custom to sing New Zealand's national anthem, "God Defend New Zealand," in both Māori and English.

Abooksigun shrugged. "Mako[51] is a creature you would want to watch for, especially if there is blood in the water. He's about as long as you, my husband, are tall. He has a big fin on his back and many sharp teeth in his mouth."

Having heard her description, the two boys quietly moved away from the rail. "Don't worry, my friends," she told them, "it's not likely that Mako would come up here to get you."

Great Buffalo shook his head. "I don't know, I just think it was safer back on land where I only had to worry about bears and lions."

Abooksigun put a comforting hand on his shoulder. "Kohala is big, but generally quite harmless and seeing him now means that we are getting close to Hawaiki."

"We're near Hawaiki!" Red Deer perked up at those words and clapped Great Buffalo on the back. "Did you hear that?"

"I heard," Great Buffalo said. "After this long on the water, I will be happy to be able to walk on dry land again."

Abooksigun held up her hands. "Wait! We'll be on dry land soon, but only for a short time. Hawaiki is only one stop along the way. Naacal, our goal, is at least three more stops."

Aditsan and Abooksigun strolled through the market. Vendors called out their offerings, each trying to out-shout the other.

Now and then Abooksigun would stop and haggle with a vendor. Red Deer and Great Buffalo, loaded down with goods she had acquired for the next leg of their trip, followed

---

[51] Mako - Among the Maori of the southern tribes, Mako is the word for shark, although because of pronunciation differences, Mango is more common with the rest of the Maori while Mano is the Polynesian word.

along behind. Aweida's children, happy to be unconfined, raced around the others.

Aweida, trailing behind everyone, paused and squatted down to select a piece of fruit from a vendor's basket. He glanced toward the others. Feeling they were far enough ahead that he wouldn't be heard over the bedlam of the marketplace, he caught the vendor's eye. "Send word ahead," he told the man. He quickly glanced toward Abooksigun. She was busy haggling with a vendor, not watching him. "She has been found and is returning," he said.

The vendor looked Aweida in the eye and gave him a slight nod, then sharply grabbed the fruit out of Aweida's hand as if insulted by the way the negotiations went. Aweida stood up wiping his hands, turned and walked away.

Aditsan, not involved with the vendors, had been casually looking around when he spotted Aweida squatting at the vendor's mat. It struck him as curious, maybe even out-of-place. A few small steps put a small cluster of people between he and Aweida. Now he could watch without being seen.

From his new position, he could not hear the words spoken, but Aditsan watched the exchange between Aweida and vendor. He saw Aweida glance quickly, nervously in Abooksigun's direction; turning back, there was another exchange; the vendor gave a slight nod. The move was a hidden signal obvious because it was a hidden signal. Then the meeting broke up and Aweida left to rejoin Abooksigun. Previously, Aditsan was suspicious of Aweida, but had no reason. Now that he had a reason, he would keep quiet, but keep his eye on Aweida.

Chapter 14: Arrival

Breakers. It had been a long time since Abooksigun heard the sounds waves make as they crash into foam on beaches and reefs[52]. On the tiller, she leaned back and watched a sea bird effortlessly ride the breeze. Everyone else stood at the rail, listening to the booming rhythm.

For Aweida and his two children, it was a sound they longed to hear. For Aditsan and the two boys, it was the first time they had heard anything like it. For all of them, it was an opportunity to enjoy their first sight of Naacal with its white, sandy beaches and its lush, green forests coating the cauldron's[53] ridge. The smoky cone of its fire-mountain [54]peeked over the top of the ridge.

The children and the boys raced one another to see who could be the first to point out some new feature. For her, the sound of the breakers brought back old memories—good and bad—and she wondered what she would find when they landed. She remembered the life she left behind when she ran away. Aweida had spoken of the turmoil and chaos that followed the death of her father's murderer. She did not know what the situation was now since he had been gone almost as long as she had.

The sun was setting. Their chances of reaching her homeport in daylight were growing slim. That was okay. She leaned toward the idea of having a chance to scout around before she made her entrance.

---

[52] Reef - A ridge of rocks or sand, often of coral debris, at or near the surface of the water.

[53] Cauldron - also called a caldera, is a cauldron-like volcanic feature usually formed by the collapse of land following a volcanic eruption.

[54] Fire-mountain – an active volcano.

Abooksigun glanced at the sail. Lost in her thoughts of returning, she had not given it enough attention and the inconstant wind, a warning of pending storms, left it near lifeless when she needed it most. Caught in the current, there was nothing she could do but ride a wave and aim for a good spot to cross the reef. If she failed, their boat would crash into the rocks and be pounded to pieces.

"Paddle hard. Your life depends on it," she called to the others. "We need to use the swells[55] to cross the reef, otherwise we could be crushed." At her direction, everyone grabbed their oars and began stroking the water with a cadenced beat.

"Even if the sail were filled, this would still be hard work," Great Buffalo complained.

Red Deer nodded. "At least the sail is working, though not well. Not too long ago, it stood slack without so much as a sparrow's breath to fill it." He shuddered. "I hate to think of how many days we rowed before the winds came back. In the heat, it seemed like forever."

Abooksigun selected a spot to cross the reef and turned the bow toward it. Luck was with them. The sail billowed out. "Paddle hard and don't let up," she yelled. Ahead, turbulence pointed out the obstruction below the surface and the previous wave, having struck the reef was on its return. The wave they rode rose up cresting just in front of them and then began collapsing on top of its receding counterpart. At the last moment, she yelled, "Paddles up," and watched as

---

[55] Swell - In the context of an ocean, sea or lake, a series of mechanical waves that propagate along the interface between water and air and so they are often referred to as surface gravity waves. These series of surface gravity waves are not generated by the immediate local wind, instead by distant weather systems, where wind blows for a duration of time over a fetch (the length of water over which a given wind has blown) of water.

everyone's oars rose into the air. Their vessel scooted smoothly across the reef and into the slack water[56] beyond.

Oars still up in the air everyone looked back at Abooksigun for the next order.

She laughed. "We're safe now, you can relax."

Dusk blanketed the area by the time they spotted bonfires ahead. Aditsan, his turn at the tiller, called Abooksigun and pointed. "There're fires up ahead. What does that mean?"

"Come around and head for shore," she said. "Those fires mark the mouth of the harbor. There are another set on the other side so approaching ships can find a safe way into port."

In response to her request, Aditsan adjusted the sail and worked the tiller, forcing the boat to come around. Satisfied with the results, he finally asked, "You're almost home, how come you want to head in here?"

Quietly, she mulled over the best way to answer his question. She had brought him and the lads a long way without their knowing the whole story. "When I left, everything was in upheaval because of Pupule Uku and the conditions he created. Groups of people took sides. Long hidden hatreds were exposed." Abooksigun looked into her mate's eyes so that he could read the truth of her words in hers. "I didn't just leave, I escaped. I ran away. Aweida left here after I did. He said the turmoil continued. I fear that it may be worse than he let on," she paused, and then continued. "It has taken many moons for us to get here. At

---

[56] Slack Water – Usually used when discussing tidal flow, this is a when the water is completely unstressed, and therefore there is no movement either way.

each stop along the way, I found other wayfinders and questioned them."

Aditsan shook his head. "I did not mention this before, but I have reason to suspect Aweida. I'm not sure what he's up to."

She paused and looked out across the quiet waters to the line of white that marked the place where the pounding surf met the reef. "The answers given to my questions were mixed. Even with the best of them, I didn't like what I heard. For now, this is as close as I want to get. I would like to set up camp and take time to look around... quietly. Maybe talk to some old friends before I make my presence known. Don't you think that's a good idea?"

Before he could answer, the prow[57] of the ship ground to a halt in the soft sand.

"Move quietly now, until we get our bearings," Aditsan cautioned the others. Great Buffalo, Red Deer, and Abooksigun eased over the reef side of the boat and quietly followed him through the knee-deep water to the beach. Aweida stayed with his children on the ship.

Reaching the bow, Aditsan crouched and looked around. The beach, up to the ring of forest shrubs, appeared to be empty. He leaned back and whispered to the others. "I will cross to the forest. If all is well, then each of you scurry across, otherwise retreat to the ship and leave."

Before Abooksigun or anyone else could object, he was gone. Staying low, he zigzagged into the growing darkness.

---

[57] Prow/Bow - This is the part of the bow above the waterline. Together, they are the forward-most section of a ship's structure that cuts through the water. The terms prow and bow are often used interchangeably to describe this most forward section and its surrounding parts.

Frozen in place, everyone waited for a signal to follow or retreat.

Many heartbeats passed before a whistled birdcall sounded. Great Buffalo was on his feet and racing into the darkness; Red Deer right on his heels. A few moments past and Abooksigun followed, but at a slower pace. If there was trouble, if a trap had been sprung, she believed she could stop before becoming another of its victims.

In the dark, Great Buffalo collided with Aditsan. Having heard the commotion, Red Deer managed to pull up short of knocking them over. Even in the darkness, both boys could see the scowl on their leader's face. "Secrecy," Aditsan growled his reminder.

Light from a small campfire shone through the trees. Aditsan lay one finger over his lips, pointed towards the fire, and then to a worn path through the trees. The boys lined up behind him and the trio crept up the path until they reached a clearing. It contained a few simple huts. Beyond this clearing, they saw another campfire through the trees.

The air here was heavy with the scent of animals. Aditsan began carefully picking his way along the path between the huts. Just a few steps in, he tripped a small snare. Not one made to catch an animal, but one created to raise an alarm. Freed, a clay jar swung into a rock and noisily smashed to pieces. Disturbed by their arrival, the animals, mostly geese, began to cry out. In another pen, pigs snorted and grunted. Hoping that anyone at the next campfire would pass this off as night prowlers, the trio continued forward. They stopped short of the second opening to look at what lay ahead.

Two huts stood face-to-face with a common fire between them. These shelters were slightly more elaborate than those they had just encountered. A woman bent over her cooking, while an old man, a carving in his lap, worked on finishing the details.

Without stopping his work or looking up, the man spoke, his voice low and calm. "Come sit with us by the fire and share our meal. We get so few visitors out here." He stopped, laid his carving knife aside, and looked up directly at Aditsan.

Aditsan stepped forward, one hand behind him motioning the boys to stay back.

"The others with you could join us also. There is enough for all to share." His eyes were dull, emphasizing the approach of his fading sight.

Caught off guard by this old man, Aditsan was speechless. "Others?" He questioned.

"Yes," the old man replied, "The two young men with you . . . and the woman who cautiously trails behind."

"You see much," Aditsan said.

The old man nodded an acknowledgement and gestured toward the woman with a slight jerk of his head. "A man can have many eyes."

Aditsan gave her a casual glace. Gray hair tied back in a neat bun; the woman was old but did not appear quite as old as the man did. He recalled what he had just seen. There were more animals in the pens and the two huts here were larger than two people needed. Others had to live here, but were either gone or in hiding. Had he led Abooksigun and his friends into a trap?

At the fire, the woman turned from her work and handed Aditsan a palm leaf covered with some kind of roasted meat. She indicated he sit across from the old man.

"It was not hard to know you were near," the old man said. "The animals grew noisy when you passed by. The young men try to make up for their lack of caution with their energy and enthusiasm. The woman that followed them crept quietly but could not get past the animals."

The two lads came in and took a seat on either side of Aditsan. The old woman handed each of them a palm leaf holding a meal similar to that given Aditsan.

"Forgive the intrusion . . ." Aditsan started to say, but was cut off.

"No doubt you are hungry. The three of you came from far away and are strangers to this land. The woman is no stranger, but has returned after a long absence."

Abooksigun stood at the edge of the clearing in the fringe of the circle of light the campfire cast. The old man turned to look toward her, bowed his head, and, with a sweep of his hand, he said, "Welcome to our humble home, your highness."

Chapter 15: Recognition

Everyone fell silent at the old man's words. The first to recover, Abooksigun scoffed at his actions. "What makes you so sure I'm the one?"

The old man jerked his head toward the old woman, back at the fire now fixing something for Abooksigun. "My mate was fishing when she saw your ship approach. Sure that your vessel was about to be destroyed, she waited, but you made it. You did what no one else could have and that told her that you had returned. " The old man stopped to chuckle, "She came back here, ran all the way, and then made us wait while she caught her breath." Unable to contain his mirth any longer, he slapped his leg and tilted his head back in a hearty laugh.

Aditsan joined in the laughter for a moment, but then took control of the situation. "Where are the others?" He hoped his sudden question would catch the old man off-guard.

"Others? There are no others here," The old man said.

"When I came here from the beach, I noticed that the place offers more than two people need," Aditsan said. "Then, when you told us your mate's story, you said 'us'. Where are the others?"

The old man recognized the truth in Aditsan's words. "I sent them off to carry the word of her majesty's return."

"Carry the word...? But, why?" Aditsan was confused. "How could you be sure she is the one?"

"It will encourage her people in this dire time," the old man replied. "I know she is the one because everything fits."

"Everything...fits?" Aditsan was still confused.

The old man shifted his posture, leaning in toward Aditsan. "Four summers ago, her father was killed by his own brother, a scoundrel. She escaped, running away to the east to the land of strangers." The old man paused for a moment, as if he were witnessing all he said unfold all over again. "Your ship came from the east. You are strangers. It is as my mate said, only one with your skills could come across the reef as you did. She knew you had to be the one."

A rustle of leaves, the crackle of brush announced the arrival of a young man, closely followed by two others. They scanned those in the encampment, searching for confirmation of the news they had received. Seeing Abooksigun at the edge of the campfire light, they sized her up, finally spotting the tattoo—Hono the sea turtle—and their faces lite up. They dropped to their knees, bending low enough to touch their foreheads on the ground to chorus, "Your majesty."

Aditsan turned to Great Buffalo and whispered, "Go to the boat and bring Aweida and the children here. Take Red Deer with you."

Turning back, he joined the old man—called Kumu[58]—and the others in discussing their next steps.

###

In the early morning sun, Red Deer and Great Buffalo sat side-by-side while the old woman—called Alamea[59]—shaved the boys' heads. Aditsan and Abooksigun sat nearby and nibbled at some cold meat while they discussed their plans with Kumu and the two strangers Aweida, his children still asleep in a nearby hut, sat behind Abooksigun.

Earlier that morning, the boys woke to find Aditsan, his head already shaved except for a long braid, dressed as a local. They took one look and laughed, pointing out that his

---

[58] Kumu – Polynesian word meaning teacher

[59] Alamea – Polynesian name meaning Precious, Whole.

newly shorn head didn't match the color of the rest of his body. Saying she could help him blend in better, Alamea made a tea from plant roots and began daubing it on Aditsan's head.

"When Alamea is done with me," Aditsan told the boys, "you're next." Raising his hands against their protesting howls, he added, "Since we don't know what tomorrow brings, you also need to blend in."

Not sure if it was necessary or just a means for Aditsan to get back at the pair for laughing, the two lads resigned themselves to their fate and played a round of rock-hide-knife[60] to see who went first.

Before they left, Abooksigun and Aditsan came over to see the boys. "You are to stay here and help Alamea and Kumu in any way you can," he told them. "Abooksigun and I are going to go into the settlement and look around. These men are going to be our guides." He paused and leaned in a little closer as if inspecting something on Red Deer's walking stick. "Keep an eye on things here," Aditsan, his voice low, instructed. "See what you can find out from Aweida's children. There is something about the man that bothers me. We should be back in a day or two…three at the most."

###

Inoa[61], the lad that fetched the strangers the previous night, led the way through the underbrush. Red Deer followed him, with Areta and Arapeta—Aweida's children—sandwiched between himself and Great Buffalo. To supply enough water for the expanded camp, everyone carried water bags. An added benefit to the trek was that, with all of them

---

[60]Rock-Hide-Knife – A selection game played the same way as Rock-Paper-Scissors, but with the technology of the time.

[61] Inoa – Hawaiian name meaning Namesake.

gone; it gave Alamea and Kumu some respite from the energy and noise that younger children produce.

Inoa signaled a halt and turned to the rest of the group. "The place where we get water is right over this hill."

Red Deer shrugged. "Why are we stopping here?"

"Sometimes the riverdragons[62] sun themselves on the sand by the water's edge," Inoa said. "They are dangerous and can be very fast."

"Riverdragons?" Great Buffalo seemed dubious. He had never heard of such an animal, but he had never seen Kohala, the great fish, or Mako, with the big fin and the mouth full of sharp teeth. "When they're not there sunning themselves, where are they?"

"In the water, sometimes they look like a log. If you look close, sometimes you can see their eyes. Other times, they lie in wait under the surface, near the river's edge. When some unsuspecting victim comes down for a drink, they pounce on them."

Great Buffalo grunted. "They sound dangerous."

Inoa scowled. "In or out of the water, they are very fast, and very dangerous." He glanced over at Aweida's children and saw that their attention was directed to a spider weaving its web. Satisfied, he dropped his voice and added, "Before two summers ago, there was no such animal here. The old ones had no knowledge of them. We had no fear. Then one day, my mother went to fetch water. A riverdragon rose up out of the river and snatched her." He shook his head as if he was trying to get rid of that image. "It happened so fast, she didn't even have time to cry out. Since then, I have made it my duty to learn as much as I can so I can kill them whenever I get a chance."

"You mean to say they live in the creeks and rivers?" Great Buffalo asked. Both boys, interest keyed, listened as Inoa described what he had learned.

---

[62] Riverdragons – Salt water crocodiles known to exist in both fresh water and salt water.

"Not only creeks and rivers, but also bathing areas. For protection at a bathing area, we've learned that it is wise to select a place with a white, sandy bottom. Then, we post a lookout in a tree to shout a warning if they see any dark shape moving towards the beach."

Red Deer nodded and Great Buffalo said, "That makes sense. Where else can they be found?"

"I've seen them at the mouth of the river where it joins the great sea and in swamps," Inoa said.

"They live in the sea and in swamps too! Is there any water they don't live in?" Great Buffalo asked.

Inoa answered quickly. "They make their nests in the swamp, like giant bird's nests, and they lay their eggs in them."

"They lay eggs, like a snake or a turtle?" Red Deer was fascinated.

"Yes," Inoa continued. "If you go there, watch the water lilies, especially those that reach out into the deeper water. These flowers have long stems that grow to the bottom. They also grow very close together. If you spot any unusual movement in the vegetation, especially if the flowers begin to disappear under the water, it is probably because they got caught on a passing riverdragon's scales and are being pulled down."

Inoa hefted the bag of stones he had been carrying. "The beach here is darker so we're going to stand back from the water's edge and throw a rock in every couple of feet. If a riverdragon is lying in wait and one of the rocks lands close, it will try to attack."

"Couldn't we just wait at the same spot and kill it when it attacks the rock?" Red Deer asked.

Inoa shook his head. "They have tough hides and are hard to kill. Even so, it is not wise to go to the same place more than once. Riverdragons watch and learn. The second or third time you go there, they'll be waiting for you. Unless you want to be their next meal, make sure you don't go to the same location every time."

Inoa put a finger to his lips and motioned the boys to follow him. Leaving Aweida's children still watching the spider, they crept noiselessly forward and peered over the crest.

The hill sloped downward spreading out into a sandy, flat pan fringed with brush and grass. Red Deer looked at the sandy indentation. *Back home, a wallow[63] like this would have been a place where buffalo would have come to take dirt baths.* He eyed the creek beyond. Overhung with shade trees, it appeared to be no more than three or four man-lengths wide and probably no more than waist deep. The sand carried marks of the many animals that had stopped to drink.

Except for a log lying under the edge of the bushes, there was nothing notable. "Are you going to toss a stone from here," Red Deer whispered, "or do we move clo...."

Inoa held a hand up, cutting him off in mid-sentence. A pair of birds, possibly some members of the heron family, swooped down to land in the middle of the sand. The two birds looked around before starting their erratic parade, darting back and forth on their long spindly legs. As they marched, they edged into the water.

An explosion of movement from the 'log' caught the unsuspecting lagging bird off guard. The riverdragon, motionless until now, had managed to pass itself off long enough that the bird became its meal.

In the shallows near the water's edge, the lead bird was startled into action. It sprang into the open air over the river in its attempt to flee the commotion behind. It managed to spread its wing before the water in front of it erupted. A second riverdragon reared up, jaws opened wide. It caught its victim in midair and gulped it down before splashing back into the water.

---

[63] Wallow - to roll about or lie in water, snow, mud, dust, or the like, as for refreshment. A place in which animals rolling around. The indentation produced by animals wallowing

Red Deer and Great Buffalo looked at each other in shock.

"Oh no," Inoa said. "We're in trouble. They've learned to hunt in pairs."

Chapter 16: Riverdragons

"What do we do now?" Red Deer, still in shock over the suddenness of the attack, watched every move the riverdragon made. Snapping its powerful tail, the animal lumbered across the wallow on its way to the river. It worked its teeth-filled jaws hungrily even though its fat belly barely cleared the ground.

Inoa put a hand on Red Deer's shoulder. "Come, we must take the youngsters back to Alamea and Kumu. We must tell them what we know. Perhaps they can tell us what to do next."

"We set out to bring back water," Great Buffalo pointed out. "No matter what they decide, we will still need water."

"There's another place. The creek is smaller and shallow. Probably not something that would attract the riverdragons, but we should still be careful."

The two youngsters had grown tired of watching the spider. Ready to move and not knowing their goal or where it was located, the brief stop, to them, was nothing more than a rest break.

They took a roundabout path to the new watering spot. The creek, though farther away, was as Inoa described it: skimpy, shallow, slow moving. Still, they kept the children back and used caution as they approached it.

Crouching, Inoa scanned the water. Red Deer and Great Buffalo, behind him, mimicked his movements.

"Not much here except for that small log," Great Buffalo said.

"Where?" Inoa looked around nervously.

Red Deer put a hand over his eyes shielding them from the sun.

Great Buffalo pointed toward where a log lay motionless, almost unseen as the top of it barely broke the surface. "Over there, near those reeds, it's barely sticking out of the water."

Inoa grunted. "Watch this," he said. Selecting a fist-sized rock from his bag, he flipped it up and into the water close to the front of the log. The water seemed to come to life as the log lunged forward.

Red Deer and Great Buffalo, surprised by this action, jumped as if poked while Inoa chuckled at their reaction. "It's a young one," Inoa said, "or we might not have been able to fool it so easily."

"Do you think we can kill it?" Great Buffalo hefted his spear. "There are three of us and only one of it."

Inoa shrugged. "They have tough skin and are hard to kill. Still, we need water, and we can't get any until we get him out of the way."

Red Deer looked over at the creek. Ripples from the earlier disturbance had all but disappeared. "We can move downstream and find another place to fill our containers. After that, we should take the young ones back to Master Kuma and Alamea, where they will be safe. Perhaps the old man has some suggestions on how we go about trapping one of these riverdragons."

Shocked, both of the other two looked at him. Neither of them could believe what they had heard.

"Trap one? Why would we want to do that?" Inoa put words to the question that puzzled both him and Great Buffalo.

Red Deer used his fingers to list his reasons. "From what you've told us, there were none here before two summers ago which means someone brought them. They make their nests in swamps. They lay eggs like birds and are multiplying. You know they have tough skins and are hard to kill, but we don't know their weaknesses. We should go into the swamps, destroy their nests, and break their eggs, but before we do, we need to know more about them."

###

Master Kuma listened carefully as the trio of older boys related the details of that morning's adventure and then asked, "How big were these creatures you call riverdragons?"

Inoa thought about the animals they saw, estimated the size of what he considered the biggest, and then said, "The largest one, the one that lay in wait for the birds, was close to three man-lengths from the tip of its nose to the end of its tail."

Red Deer and Great Buffalo nodded in agreement.

The old man lifted an eyebrow in disbelief, causing Inoa to add, "It is not a creature that would hold still while I paced off its length."

Kuma gave a dry chuckle. "What? You had no interest in providing the poor creature his next meal in the pursuit of the knowledge you seek. I think it would have considered it a fair exchange, don't you?" Before anyone could answer, the old man chuckled and went on, "You acted wisely. Now let us act just as wise and make a plan to get the information we need."

###

"Master Kuma asked Alamea to take the children collecting along the reef," Inoa told the other two. "They can gather shellfish and crabs and do a little spear fishing. These are necessary tasks, but it will be fun for them, and it will keep them occupied for the rest of the day." In his arms, he carried a rolled up fish net.

"Good," Red Deer said. Walking along side of Inoa, he carried two spears—one for Great Buffalo and one for himself—and an axe. A coil of rope hung from one shoulder, across his chest to his waist. "We will have a job on our hands just keeping ourselves safe."

Great Buffalo, on the other side of Inoa, grunted his agreement. "Are we going to the first place—where the birds were caught—or to the second place?" To better balance the carry pole on his shoulder, he shifted the rolled up sail taken from Abooksigun's boat. They could use it to throw over their prey to keep it from seeing them.

"We'll go to the second place. Master Kuma said we should start our lessons by capturing a small one," Inoa said. "When we know more about it, then we will be better equipped to take on his larger brothers and sisters."

Red Deer nodded. "Master Kuma did not get old by taking unnecessary chances, I ..."

Inoa held up his hand and put a finger to his lips. Everyone fell silent and froze in place. After listening for a moment, Inoa crept forward, motioning for the others to follow. The trio stopped when they reached a fallen tree, a palm pushed over in some pervious storm, and peered over its sheltering bulk.

Inoa pointed. "There," he whispered. "I think that's what we've been looking for, right there."

The area beyond the tree was rugged, unimpressive, supporting scattered clumps of brush and small trees. With more experience, Inoa easily spotted what his companions did not, would not have, had he not been there with them. A young riverdragon, no larger than the smallest one they saw that morning, lay basking in the sun. Ducking below the level of the log, the trio put their heads together.

"Unroll the net," Great Buffalo said. "We should approach from the tail, slowly and softly. Red Deer and I will be on either side of you with the rope, the carry-pole, and our spears. Spread the net over it from tail to nose. He'll be lively, but I'm hoping he'll also be tangled up in the net and can't get at us." Almost as an afterthought, he added, "If I'm wrong, be prepared to run." That brought a nervous snicker from his audience.

The trio climbed over the palm's trunk, spread out, and crept toward their target as the creature sprawled in the sun.

Without predators, it did not live in fear of attack and had
grown complacent. They reached the tip of the tail before the
animal stirred. Up close, it appeared more threatening than
when they crouched behind the fallen palm. It was at least a
man-length from nose to tail and would weigh more than the
combined weights of all three of the lads.

An experienced surf-fisherman, Inoa made a good cast.
The net settled over the surprised animal. It turned quickly.
Body, legs, and tail tangled in the net. It did little to slow the
creature. Head free of this minor encumbrance, it struck out
at this new enemy. Great Buffalo danced out of the way of its
snapping jaw and jabbed at its scaly hide, breaking his spear
tip. The animal, jaws gaping, lunged at him again. Great
Buffalo jabbed his spear into the animal's mouth. Not a good,
down-the-throat shot, but one he hoped would slow the
animal down. The creature bit down crushing the shaft
making it a useless stick. At the same time, Red Deer, hoping
to lasso this wild beast around the neck, cast his noose. It
closed over the riverdragon's muzzle, disabling its vicious
jaw[64].

The trio of boys realized that they had one victory, but
the battle was not yet over as the creature continued to
squirm and thrash about, striking out with clawed feet, and
swinging tail.

Great Buffalo discarded the remains of his broken spear.
"Get some more rope around his mouth," he yelled. "Then
we can roll him on his back and tie his legs and tail."

It was a job easier said than done. Great Buffalo lay half-
across the animal's back, one arm wrapped around its throat
and one hand holding a foreleg. On the tail, Inoa tried to stop

---

[64] Crocodile/Alligator jaws - Most of the muscles in an alligator's or in a
crocodile's jaw are arranged for clamping down. Despite the strong
muscles to close the jaw, alligators and crocodiles have extremely small
and weak muscles to open their jaws and these can be held shut with a
strong rope or several layers of duct tape.

this threshing whip but only succeeded in slowing it down. With the mouth finally tied off securely, Red Deer used the rest of the rope to tie the creature's feet and get him ready for the carry-pole.

###

Trussed up by its hind legs, the lifeless riverdragon hung by a rope between two adjacent trees allowing Master Kuma a safe opportunity to inspect the carcass up close. While he watched, Inoa and Red Deer worked with Alamea to harvest their kill, and check it for weaknesses.

With practiced hands, the old woman wheeled her knife and opened the animal from top to bottom. Between her and the two lads, they peeled the tough hide back and cut away long strips of meat.

Holding up a strip, Red Deer eyed the meat, curiosity written across his face. "For all the trouble they have caused, it would be nice if the meat were good for something."

Inoa paused in his work and looked out to sea. "We could use the meat for bait when we fish."

"Turtles and snakes are good to eat. Maybe riverdragons are good to eat, too," Red Deer suggested.

Alamea solved the problem for them. "Areta, Arapeta. Gather some wood and build a cook fire. You can roast some of this meat." Smugly, she looked at her two co-workers and added, "We should have an answer to your questions soon." Chuckling, she turned back to her work.

While his friends worked with Alamea, Great Buffalo kept himself busy making replacement spears. "These will be special ones, designed for this task, alone," he told them.

Arapeta ground a stick's point into a log. Under his practiced hands, smoke soon rose from the tinder under the point's nose, indicating that a nice cook fire would soon follow.

At the thought of food, Great Buffalo's stomach growled. The spears he had made took more work than usual because he made them with thicker shafts. He also drilled holes, diagonally, through the trunk and near the head, then pounded smaller limbs into the holes but away from the head. Finally, Great Buffalo fixed a new stone tip in place.

Alamea stopped her work to give closer supervision to the meat Arapeta and Areta were cooking. Gingerly poking a strip with the tip of her knife, she announced, "It won't be much longer."

Taking advantage of the break, Red Deer stepped over and inspected Great Buffalo's new design. "What is the purpose of these sticks near the spear's point?" He hefted the spear and twirled it around in his hand.

His cohort smiled. "If I ever get another chance to plant one down those open jaws, I want the shaft to go in deep and never come out."

Red Deer looked at the device and then the mystery cleared up. "Oh," he said. "Like the barbs on Abooksigun's fish hooks. The point will go in and the backward facing sticks will not come out without doing damage."

Great Buffalo laughed. "That's right. I am hoping the damage it does will keep him from eating me, but, if that doesn't work, I have something else." He reached behind him and picked up another shaft. Longer than the spears he had already shown, a sharpened rib-bone replaced the point. Cords ran up the shaft and formed a loop at the end. The loop was draped over the rib-bone to hold it open.

Curious, Red Deer looked over the implement.

Great Buffalo didn't wait for any questions but barged right in to providing an explanation. "You made a good shot with your lasso this time, but I don't think we have to risk being that lucky all the time. If we find another riverdragon snoozing in the sun," he began to pantomime the actions, "we can sneak up and slip the noose over his nose before he knows what hit him. That brings me to my final trick."

Red Deer pretended surprise. "You have more?"

"Well sort of…" Great Buffalo paused, almost embarrassed. "Nothing as good as the first two, but… well, you found the creature's heart behind all those heavy scales. I figured I couldn't wrestle all of them into submission. Barely held on to this one long enough for you to tie him down, and it was small." Great Buffalo picked up a pointed stake from a pile of stakes—like the spear, all wore barbs—and waved it around. "For a bigger one, once we get his mouth closed, we hop on his back and use my ax to pound one of these through his hide. That should do the trick."

Alamea handed a palm leaf loaded with cooked 'dragon meat over to Red Deer. "Eat," she commanded. She did not wait for a response but turned and began loading meat on another palm leaf.

Red Deer found a cleared spot on the ground near a fallen tree and sat down. Leaning his back against the tree, he eyed the contents of the leaf dubiously. "Well, the only way to find out if it's good is to taste it," he said and bit off a large chunk.

Everyone else stood there, a palm leaf full of cooked riverdragon in their hands, waiting on Red Deer's reaction.

"Well?" Alamea said. The two younger ones also looked on expectantly, waiting to hear if their work over the hot fire had been in vain.

Mouth full, Red Deer nodded and managed to grunt out, "Tas's like shik'n[65]," between bites. Hearing that, everyone else began their ravenous feeding.

Inoa, eagerly chewing a mouthful of food, sat down beside Red Deer. "With our new knowledge and these weapons, it looks like we should be ready to venture into the swamp tomorrow."

"The hide on the sides and back are tough," Alamea observed. "But the hide on its underside is thinner and cuts easier."

---

[65] Tas's like shik'n – "Tastes like Chicken" is the response many people make after tasting alligator or crocodile meat.

Kuma, who had been silent up until now, spoke up. "If you can get underneath the animal, or if you can get it turned over, then it will be much easier to kill, especially with your new weapons." He bit off another chunk of meat. "The meat's not bad, but I am interested in the hides. We should be able to make use of something that tough." He paused to belch loudly and scratch his chin. A morsel hung suspended from his fingers, stopped midway between the leaf and his mouth as if he forgot which direction they were traveling. The old man sat, deep in thought, until, after long moments, the interrupted morsel resumed its journey, and he said, "If these creatures are like turtles and snakes, they will be slower to act when it is cool." He paused again, letting his words sink in, and then added, "When you're ready to face them, I could use more hides...."

Great Buffalo held his spear upright. "Are we ready?" He shouted.

The other two grabbed the spear and shouted, "Ready!"

The small dugout, carrying the trio of boys, skimmed across the water's calm surface. Dawn was just breaking, and a chill still hung in the air. Spread out before them, the swamp was quiet. Night predators had retired to the safety of their lairs, while the day predators had not yet stirred.

Using hand signals, Great Buffalo directed their path from the bow. Previously, Inoa had told them he had watched a riverdragon mound up dirt and reeds to build a nest, lay her eggs in it, and then cover them before leaving. They pulled up at the closest mound, one of several that dotted this area.

Inoa, in the stern, kept watch while Red Deer secured their vessel to the putrid-smelling pile of rotting vegetation. Great Buffalo stood and tested his footing on the spongy material. Satisfied, he stepped out of the dugout and, using his spear as a probe, crept forward. He walked around the mound and returned. Handing over his spear, he picked up a parfleche[66] and then whispered one word, "Shovel," and then added, "Rake." He returned to the center and began digging until he uncovered the eggs. Squatting, Great Buffalo put some of them in his bag. The rest, he used his shovel to destroy before returning to the dugout.

Shoving off, they made their way to the next mound and found the eggs had hatched. Great Buffalo studied the scene for a moment and then motioned for Red Deer to join him. "We're too late," he whispered. "They've already hatched. How many shells do you count?"

Red Deer did a quick survey of the nest. "One hands' worth," he said.

Great Buffalo nodded and motioned for them to return to the dugout.

A flurry of activity greeted their arrival at the next mound. Brown rats exploded out of the nest before Great Buffalo hopped out of the dugout. Red Deer quickly followed him. The rats had dug into the mound and were eating the eggs.

"What happened?" Inoa asked from the dugout.

"Rats got here first and broke the eggs," Red Deer explained, "looks like we have allies."

Shoving off, they made their way to each of the other mounds opening each nest and destroying the eggs. The sun had risen and the swamp was beginning to stir. Having accomplished this task, the trio decided to return to Master Kuma.

---

[66] Parfleche - A Native American rawhide bag, it is similar in construction to an envelope, but can be as large as a suitcase. They were often painted, decorated, and used to carry personal and ceremonial objects. In everyday use, they were typically used for holding objects such as dried meats, jerky, and pemmican·

###

The area of wetlands they called the swamp was made up of lowlands kept marshy by overflow and seepage from the nearby river, particularly during the rainy season. The dugout made an easy exit to the river. Carried along by the current, the trio of boys relaxed as the dugout floated leisurely downstream.

The river emptied into the lagoon not far from where Abooksigun came across the reef on their arrival. For the ride back, Great Buffalo had stretched out in the bow and had fallen asleep. No longer propelled by a friendly current, Inoa busied himself setting up a lateen sail[67] so they could make progress without much effort. Midway through the effort, Red Deer heard Inoa say, "Uh-oh." Inoa stood frozen at the mast and stared across the sun-streaked waters.

Red Deer shaded his eyes and looked in the same direction. He spotted a single black fin break the surface and meander aimlessly around the lagoon. Excited, he shook Great Buffalo awake.

Not happy at having the delights of his sleep interrupted, Great Buffalo grumbled, "What...what is it?"

"Mako," Inoa announced, pointing across the water. "Mako."

Prodded by these words, Great Buffalo leaped to his feet, leaving those dreams a distant memory. "If Abooksigun

---

[67] Lateen sail – A triangular sail that was of decisive importance to navigation. The ancient square sail permitted sailing only before the wind; the lateen was the earliest fore-and-aft sail. The triangular sail was affixed to a long yard or crossbar, mounted at its middle to the top of the mast and angled to extend aft far above the mast and forward down nearly to the deck. The sail, its free corner secured near the stern, was capable of taking the wind on either side, and, by enabling the vessel to tack into the wind, the lateen immensely increased the potential of the sailing ship.

was able to sail over the reef, then why shouldn't fish be able to do the same?"

"You've dealt with Mako before?" Inoa questioned.

Faces paled by the memories, both boys nodded. "On the way here, we caught and cleaned our fish. Suddenly, the water around our vessel filled with their fins and they followed us for days."

"We should head for shore," Inoa said. He worked the sail and the bow turned toward the beach.

Before they could relax, the dugout shook violently and tipped as if they had struck a rock. The impact knocked all three lads over. They found themselves in a pile on the bottom of the vessel and grabbing for any handhold.

Great Buffalo was the first to see the cause of their problem. A creature from his worst nightmare, broke the surface, opened it large jaws, only to close them over the outrigger. It shook its head and then tried to roll over. "Riverdragons," he yelled.

He need not have yelled. His companions saw the attack. They saw others circling. Another attack and the dugout tipped and dipped until the outrigger broke.

These creatures had followed them from the swamp and were now attempting to destroy their small vessel. The far-away beach was their only hope, but to get there meant having to face Mako's sharp teeth or the crushing jaws of the riverdragons.

Chapter 17: Attacked

Great Buffalo clutched his spear as he lay in the bottom of the rocking dugout. The craft, no outrigger to stabilize it, tipped easily. Standing to take a shot would be a bad move that could upset the vessel. It would mean their end for sure.

From the stern, Red Deer yelled, "Use the rope next to you to make some loops. Maybe we'll get a chance to tie their jaws shut."

The dugout rocked from another blow. Great Buffalo, now on his knees, grabbed the edge of the craft to steady himself. A mighty head, jaws open wide, and front feet appeared over the side. Quickly, Great Buffalo grabbed one of his short, barbed spears and jammed it into that open maw. The surprised animal coughed and snapped its mouth shut but was too late to catch retreating fingers.

Picking up a spare paddle, Great Buffalo began beating on the animal. The paddle shattered under the impact of his assault. The beast reared its head back, exposing its underside. Using the shaft of the broken paddle like a spear, Great Buffalo rammed it into the creature's neck. It backed away, trailing a stream of blood and disappeared under the water.

Their relief was short lived. Another head, jaws open, broke the surface. Great Buffalo, lasso in one hand, threw a piece of the broken paddle to the beast. Instinctively, the animal's jaws snapped shut; and just as fast, Great Buffalo's noose slipped over the riverdragon's muzzle.

New to this experience, the animal tried to escape by rolling over in the water. It only wound more rope around its snout.

The black fin appeared in their midst and then disappeared under the surface. The trio held their breath as they watched the shadowy figure pass under the dugout and circle away. Mako, having sized up the situation, circled and returned. Unperturbed by the presence of this intruder, the riverdragons continued to churn the water.

Focused on the bloodied animal, the shark launched its attack, grabbing the wounded 'dragon. The pair, locked in combat, rolled and dove. Confused by this attacker, the others beasts scattered. The three lads saw their opportunity and paddled like possessed men toward the beach, not stopping until the prow gave that welcome grinding sound as it dug into the sand.

They vacated the dugout in a flash and ran, until they reached higher ground. There, they called a halt to catch their breath and survey the sea they just left. The waters were calm except for a lone fin meandering through the glass-like surface. There was no sign of the riverdragons. Keeping a wary eye out, the threesome made their way back to the dugout, gathered their belongings, and began their quick trek back to Master Kumu's settlement. It had been a busy morning and the sun had yet to reach its midpoint.

Master Kumu listened to their stories and then said, "You destroyed their nests. More importantly, except for the few you brought back, you also destroyed their eggs." He paused and shook his head. "I don't know if they followed you because of their anger or because they want to get the eggs back." He shrugged. "In the end, had Mako not intervened, it would not have made a difference."

A screech from Alamea grabbed everyone's attention. Squatting near the cook fire, the old woman had planned to fix riverdragon eggs for breakfast. However, on breaking the first one open, she found, not a yoke but a miniature riverdragon. Startled, she dropped it. No, flung it away. The creature landed, tumbling along the ground a short distance before it was able to stop this motion and right itself. Not a hand's length in size, it was defiant and managed to issue an angry hiss followed by a questioning squeak.

Answering squeaks came from the pouch. Nearer to it than the others, Alamea was the first to spot another miniature riverdragon stick its head over the edge and peer at the world. It was not alone. Other heads began appearing as more eggs hatched. Each new face hissed and began to scrutinize this new environment. Deciding that someone else could take care of these creatures, the old woman grabbed Kumu and the two youngsters, and they beat a quick retreat toward the animal pens.

Great Buffalo tried to smash the nearest 'dragon with a club, but it was too fast and would dart away.

Red Deer snatched up a basket. "Throw something over them. Slow them down. When we catch them, we'll put them in here," he yelled to Inoa.

Inoa pulled a surf fishing net from its drying rack and tossed it over the babies closest to the bag, snaring four. The two young men scrambled to catch them before they slipped through the holes in the net. It was not an easy task. Covered with the slime from inside the eggs made these lively, wriggling creatures slippery and hard to hold. A bigger problem was that even as babies, each of these animals had a mouthful of needle-like, razor-sharp teeth and powerful jaws.

Red Deer soon found that the critters were limber enough to twist back if picked up by the tail and could inflict wounds even though inverted. "Just out of the shell and they attack like the adults."

"Pinch their mouth closed," Great Buffalo said. "We need to take care of them now, not when they are fully grown so hold it down and I will take a swing at it."

Red Deer grabbed one, pinching its mouth, and held the animal against a tree where Great Buffalo smashed it with his club. He dropped the animal's carcass in the basket and joined Inoa in continuing this process until all hatchlings were dispatched.

Red Deer looked around then checked the bag used to carry the eggs. Amidst the broken eggs, one remained. A tiny nose peeked out of a newly created hole and there were muffled squeaks from within it. "Here's the last one," he said.

"Oh, good," Inoa said. "I will see if I can find Alamea and Master Kumu and get them to return." He turned to leave. Behind him, Great Buffalo leaned against the tree used when Alamea butchered their earlier kill.

Red Deer picked up the lone egg, and started bouncing it lightly in the palm of his hand when he heard a long, low rumble—from any other animal, it would have been a growl. *What kind of animal would make that noise?* He stopped bobbling the egg and looked around.

It was not any other animal. It was a riverdragon… a very large one… and it was watching him

Chapter 18: Eggs

"My friends," Red Deer whispered. Beads of sweat formed on his brow. The riverdragon focused on him and did not move. It appeared ready to strike. "Guys," Red Deer said. *How do I get their attention without causing the 'dragon to attack?*

The urgency in Red Deer's repeated whisper, cut through Great Buffalo's thoughts. He glanced over to where his friend was standing. The riverdragon was on the edge of the camp and ready to strike. "Inoa," he called. "We've got troubles." Turning his attention back to Red Deer he said, "Master Kumu said the others may have followed us because we took their eggs."

"I'd think he's right," Red Deer agreed. "How do we find out if it is after me or the egg? And what do we do next?"

"If it was after you, I believe it would have attacked by now. It hasn't and I don't believe it will as long as you have its young." Picking up the empty pouch, Great Buffalo grabbed an overhead tree limb and swung himself up. "Remember the game we played with Arapeta and his sister aboard ship?" he asked. "Make sure it's watching you then toss me the egg and run."

Once again, Red Deer began bobbling the egg back and forth. "Be ready," he said. "Here it comes."

The egg, propelled by a gentle, well-aimed toss, seemed to float through the air. Red Deer didn't wait to watch the results but turned quickly, ran through a copse[68] of trees, then headed into heavy brush. The riverdragon bellowed. Its' angry roar seemed to shake the ground.

Red Deer could hear the clatter and crunch of destruction behind him. The sound drove him forward. He

---

[68] Copse - A thicket of small trees or shrubs; a coppice

ran a circuitous route over the rough ground, tripping and stumbling through thorn bushes, cacti patches, broken volcanic-rock, and coral ridges in hopes that the terrain he followed would slow the creature down. It was his only hope.

Exploding from the brush, he tripped over Inoa, crouching in the tall grass. The force of their impact sent both boys sprawling. Red Deer scrambled to regain his feet in an effort to continue his flight, but Inoa tackled him then fought to keep him down and—a hand over his mouth—quiet.

"Shhh," Inoa told the squirming body under him. "The riverdragon is after the egg, not you. It forced Great Buffalo higher in the tree." Waiting for his words to cut through his friend's panic, he held Red Deer down until calm returned.

When released, Red Deer followed Inoa's example and crouched low in the grass. Shading his eyes, he looked over the tassels in the direction Inoa pointed to find the tree where Great Buffalo was perched.

Balancing on its tail, the riverdragon hugged the trunk and stretched itself upwards, close to where Great Buffalo had originally taken refuge. Forced by the proximity of these snapping jaws, the lad left the luxury of thick branches and moved higher. Certain death waiting below him, he clung to his new location, populated by shaky thinner branches. It was anybody's guess how long he could hold on.

"What do we do now?" Red Deer asked. "Do you think Great Buffalo can out-wait the beast?"

Inoa shook his head. "I've seen them lay motionless for long periods while they waited for some prey to come along. Right now, it is intent on getting its egg back. That appears to be its only thought." Inoa stopped speaking. A surprised look came over his face. "The other eggs were hatching. What was the condition of the egg when you had it?"

Red Deer thought about it. "There was a tiny hole in the shell, and I could hear squeaks."

"That means that the baby is trying to break out," Inoa said. "When that happens, Great Buffalo will have a bigger problem."

Red Deer looked at Inoa. "We could give the creature what it wants. Maybe it would go away."

Inoa shook his head. "Maybe it would go away, but it will remember where we live and what we've done. They are a threat to us and they will always be a threat to us. Since we've worked to get rid of them, they will look at us as threats."

Red Deer could see that Inoa was right. Letting the creature go would not solve the problem only prolong it. They needed a way to capture the riverdragon without being trapped by it. "If we had time we could dig a pit, but we don't have time."

Inoa made a face. "If we are going to act, we should do so now while the animal is focused." He rose up a little and craned his neck to look around. "On our right, there's a rugged area. Let's look there and find a place to trap it. Once it's trapped, we can make sure that it won't be a problem anymore."

"Fine, but, how do we get it there?" Red Deer questioned.

"That's a good question," Inoa said. "I had hoped you would have the answer."

###

Red Deer surveyed the camp he had vacated in such a rush. With benches knocked over and worktables crushed, it was evident the riverdragon had passed by there. At the edge of the clearing, Great Buffalo still clung to the thin upper branches of a tree, while the creature stood on its tail at its base.

Red Deer called out to Great Buffalo, "How's the egg doing?"

Great Buffalo freed one hand long enough to open the mouth of the pouch and look inside. After a quick exam of the contents, he went back to holding on with both hands. "The baby has quit trying to break out and only squeaks now and then," he said. Smirking, he added, "It looks like you've been in a fight." Even from that distance, he could see the marks the thorns left when Red Deer had made his panicked escape through the underbrush.

Red Deer ignored his remark. "We've got some rope...."

"Are you going to try to lasso its mouth shut?"

"No. Listen. It wouldn't do any good because the tail is problem too," Red Deer said. "Inoa and I have a plan and think we can trap this creature. We've tied ropes between trees—yours is the last one to hook up—and we want to slide the pouch from tree-to-tree till it reaches the trap."

Great Buffalo looked doubtful. "A rope between the trees, how will that work? Why not just take the pouch and run?"

"Because it's not a race I want to lose, okay?" Red Deer waited a moment, giving his friend a chance to consider his words, and then continued, "If the plan doesn't work, the 'dragon will get the egg, and we hope it will go back to its nest; if it does work then the 'dragon will fall into our trap. Then we'll be able to destroy both of them."

The plan sounded okay and, one way or another, it would get him down out of the tree. Great Buffalo nodded. "What's next? What do I need to do?" he said.

"When Inoa gets the rope to you, run the end through the handles on the pouch and then tie the rope up as high as you can reach. We are making a rope-slide[69]. The other end is low, so it will be like going downhill. Before you let it go, stir up the baby so the mother will follow its calls. When she's gone, climb down and follow the rise toward the noise."

---

[69] Rope-slide – A zip line.

Behind him, Inoa appeared at the crest, rope in hand. "All set?" he asked. Red Deer nodded. Inoa threw the rope to Great Buffalo and then left.

The riverdragon was uncertain why the others had shown up; why they had thrown the rope or its purpose. It was certain it would protect its young and the ground it now held. It was not willing to give up its position and loudly bellowed its displeasure.

Keeping one eye on the riverdragon, Red Deer started to back away, moving toward the place where Inoa had stood a few moments ago. "The bag on the end of the rope contains animal fat," he continued. "Put some on the straps to make them slick, and tuck the bag in the pouch with the egg before you send it on its way. I'll yell when I get to my post. Stir up the baby to make sure the mother is watching then send the pouch on its way. If she follows, you can get down. If not, we'll have to come up with something else."

Before Great Buffalo could reply, Red Deer was out of sight. He busied himself stringing the rope through the straps and tying it as high as he could get it. Time passed. It seemed like forever. He was anxious to get down.

From somewhere on the other side of the brush, both Red Deer and Inoa yelled, "Okay."

Great Buffalo rubbed the animal fat on the straps and put the bag in the pouch. With his hands covered in grease, it was hard for him to hang on and he nearly fell. Finally ready, he broke off a bough and dropped it on his waiting warden. The 'dragon snapped at the nuisance and growled at him. Knowing he had its attention, Great Buffalo gave the side of the pouch a sound whack. The baby let out a series of squeaks. Satisfied, he gave the packet a shove, launching it on its way. "I hope this works," he said under his breath.

Chapter 19: Trapped

The pouch, squeaking passenger within, slid along the rope toward Inoa in the next tree along the route. The riverdragon, hearing her helpless young, leaned back and watched the pouch for just a moment. That was all it took for her to decide to abandon her post. She backed off quickly and began racing after the baby in distress.

While Great Buffalo watched, the riverdragon began crashing through the brush. Moving with unbelievable speed, afraid that it would lose sight of the bag with its precious cargo, it soon disappeared from sight. Breathing a sigh of relief, Great Buffalo climbed down and made his way along the ridge in the general direction of the noise.

The pouch slid to a stop at the next tree. Red Deer scrambled down and grabbed it, untying the rope. The sound of chaos and destruction grew louder. The riverdragon was getting closer. He hoped the animal, even driven as it was, would soon tire. His survival depended on speed—how fast he moved and how fast the animal moved. A mistake, a miscalculation could mean his end.

Packet clamped between his teeth, he clambered hand-over-hand back up the tree and not a moment too soon. The 'dragon slammed into the trunk so hard the tree shook. It filled the air with a hiss and bellowed its rage. He felt its hot breath on his bare feet.

Near the treetop, safely out of range, Red Deer wrapped himself around a limb and followed the same routine that he had given Great Buffalo. Below him, the riverdragon continued to thunder and claw at the tree. Red Deer shook the bag. Squeaks began pouring out of it. Hearing this, the riverdragon stopped and watched as Red Deer gave the package a shove. The 'dragon quickly abandoned the tree and charged into the brush after its offspring.

Inoa waited at the last tree. Behind him sat the depression he hoped would trap the mother. Except for the area that he and Red Deer had trampled, tall grass shrouded its edge. Over this area and down the steep sloop, they sprinkled eggshells, the remnants from Alamea's attempted breakfast and the discovery that followed. He was leaving an open invitation for the beast to follow. If he were successful, it would sniff around, slip over the rim to begin a downhill run, not stopping until it was too late. Mud, topped with a scant amount of algae covered the surface of this pit.

Not evident from the rim, the edge of the slope did not blend in with the edge of the depression. A drop off, nearly waist high, collared the hollow and presented an obstacle to anything that entered and then tried to climb back out. If the riverdragon stopped at this point, it would be up to Inoa to coax it into taking the plunge.

In the distance, he could hear the 'dragon crashing through the brush. The package slipped along the rope toward him. Since it was set at a steeper angle, the pouch traveled quickly. After what everyone had been through, he did not want to lose this race so close to the goal.

When the bag arrived, Inoa peeked in and checked the egg. The hole in the shell was a little larger and a few cracks fanned out around it. More significantly, a tiny nose protruded, sniffing the air. He put a couple of fist-sized rocks in the bag with the egg then removed the pouch from the rope. Taking his cargo, Inoa scurried around the rim to the far side where he had a knotted rope—a loop in the end for his feet—secured to a tree. Sitting on the edge of the rim, feet in the loop, bag clenched securely in his teeth, he lowered himself down the two man-lengths to the bottom. Reaching the end, he hung the bag over a small bush and wrapped his arms around the rope. There—hanging about two fingers' width above the surface of the mud—he waited for the beast to come to him.

The noise grew louder and then stopped. The riverdragon had reached the tree on the far side of the rim. She nosed around. Inoa could imagine her thinking, *yes, this was the place where my baby had been, but where is it now?*

Then, from his position below the rim, Inoa could see the bulk of her huge body. He reached in the bag and pulled out a rock. Tossing it up and down in his hand, he got the feel for its weight. Satisfied he drew back and slung the projectile forward. It hit the 'dragon squarely on the head. The beast shook off the blow and continued nosing around. He had failed to get the animals' attention. This concerned Inoa. One rock left, he would have to try again.

Reaching for the bag, he slipped, nearly spilling the contents. Startled by this sudden movement, the baby began a panicky bawl. Above the pit, the riverdragon's head snapped up as she listened to these cries. He threw the second rock, hitting her again. It got her attention and she started forward toward the rim.

Inoa watched as the creature paused at the rim's edge. It swung its head back and forth as if checking its surroundings. Did it suspect a trap? He had no answer for that question; he only knew that he wanted it to follow the path they had laid out. *How do I get it to do that?*

A noise from inside the pouch provided his solution. He carefully, lifted the bag and shook it gently. The baby emitted a couple of squeaks. The beast glared at Inoa and started forward crossing the edge of the rim where she found that the tall grass hid the steepness of the slope. To slow its forward motion, it began to back-peddle in the loose sand

and managed to stop short of the drop off. Behind her, Great Buffalo and Red Deer had crept up to lay at the rim's edge. They waited to see if their plan worked.

Inoa carefully extracted the egg from the pouch, and then leaned over, low to the muddy surface. Taking great care, he gently rolled the egg into the middle of the pit. The upset baby, squeaking from this topsy-turvy ride, tried to break out of the shell.

Coming to its aid, the beast crossed the collar and found itself sinking into the soft, bottomless mud. The more it thrashed and churned, the deeper it sank. Even if it were not completely sucked under, with the walls as steep as they were, it would never get out. The pit had trapped the riverdragon and would become its final resting place.

The riverdragon had left Master Kumu's encampment a mess. The work of putting things right kept the trio busy the rest of the day. They wanted to go back to the swamp and the creeks to search out any remaining riverdragons—what had happened to the other beasts that attacked their dugout? Mako couldn't have killed them all.

Regardless of their arguments, Alamea had other ideas and made sure they stayed with the task. Late in the day, three men stumbled into the camp and interrupted everyone's plans. Two of the men were strangers. The third man was Aweida. Beaten, he was unconscious.

"We were fishing when we found him," one of the men explained. "Couldn't understand most of what he said except for Master Kumu's name, so we brought him here."

"Were others with him?" Red Deer asked anxiously. "Where are they?"

"He was alone," the fisherman said, "we saw no others."

The lads looked at one another with the same though in mind. *What happened? Where are our friends?*

Chapter 20: Lost Friends

The strangers placed Aweida on a sleeping mat in Alamea's hut. With his children at her side, she began dressing his wounds. Master Kumu questioned the two men while the trio of boys looked on and listened, but stood in respectful silence. Eventually, Areta and Arapeta returned carrying dishes of food the old woman had prepared. The men ate and left. Night was falling.

No one slept well that night. By daybreak, the trio of boys had become extremely agitated. Wishing action, they faced Master Kumu and laid out their arguments.

"Aditsan said they expected to be back by now," Great Buffalo said.

Red Deer chimed in, "They are not, and they haven't sent word. The strangers said they only found Aweida."

Master Kumu held up a hand bringing silence to the group. "Everything you said is true, but to go now would be wrong. You have no plan and don't even know if they made it to the settlement." The old man paused for a second and then waved a dismissive hand. "You haven't had anything to eat yet. If you want to do something, why don't you start there? You'll think better on a full stomach."

"I am familiar with the settlement and the places that come between here and there," Inoa said. "I could go and look around. Perhaps I could find out where they are and what happened."

"Better yet," Red Deer said, "I think Aweida has the answers to our questions. From the start, Aditsan was suspicious of him. If anything happened to them, Aweida may have had a hand in it, so he is the one we need to hear out."

"I don't disagree," said a weak, scratchy voice from behind. Everyone's head turned to the source. Feebly,

Aweida leaned against a tree outside Alamea's hut. No one had heard him. They didn't know how much he had heard. "I think it important that you know my story and what happened to your friends," he said, and took a step away from the tree, collapsing immediately. Great Buffalo rushed to his side and grabbed him before he was completely on the ground. Inoa joined him. Between them, Aweida was able to reach a position near Master Kumu and took a seat.

Alamea woke from her sleep to find her patient had wandered away. She came in search of him. "If you're going to insist on being up, you might as well have something to eat," she said. "I suppose the rest of you would like something too. You three, come lend a hand. This food won't fix itself." The three lads held their disappointment inside while they reluctantly rose to follow her. Perhaps, Aweida would speak more freely to Master Kumu than if they were present.

Grouped around the campfire, everyone ate quietly. While they ate, no one brought up the subject that was on their minds.

Finished with his meal, Aweida put his plate aside and turned to the others. "As you have already said, Aditsan had his suspicions, and he had a right to them" Some murmurs rose from those who surrounded him. Great Buffalo gave Red Deer a knowing poke. Both boys shot Aweida dark looks.

Aweida held his hands up in front of him and quickly explained, "After you found me, I told Abooksigun that her uncle, Pupule Uku, had died. This is true. I told her that the man she would have been forced to marry was dead. This is true. I told her that because of all this, the Naacal are in turmoil. This is also true." He looked around at his audience.

"What I didn't tell her is that there are two groups, one that would support her and one that wouldn't."

Red Deer shrugged. "I think, when you said things were in chaos, they knew there would be people that supported them and those that didn't." So far, Aweida had talked a lot, but hadn't explained anything.

Aweida held his hands up again. "The groups of people against her have a strong leader. Her supporters hoped that her return would help defeat him. They sent me to find her. On our return, at each stop we made, I did my best to send word ahead of her return."

Great Buffalo was tired of listening to this story. "That's all well and good, but where are Aditsan and Abooksigun?"

"We were attacked," Aweida said. "We went into the settlement and met with some friends. While we were there, a mob surrounded us. We could not fight them off. They put us aboard their great ship. Along the way, they decided I was of no value to them so they beat me and threw me overboard."

"But, where are Aditsan and Abooksigun?" Red Deer asked.

Chapter 21: Plan, Then Act

Great Buffalo grabbed his spear. "We must go to find our friends. They need our help." Red Deer and Inoa jumped to their feet and began gathering items they thought they would need.

"STOP!" Master Kumu roared—the loudest the trio had ever heard him speak. It brought their actions to an immediate halt.

"We spoke about this before," he said, now more calmly. "You are ready to run off, but you don't know where you're going and you don't know what to do when you get there."

"But our friends need us," Red Deer asserted. The other two lads nodded their heads in agreement.

"To run off without knowledge and a plan of action is the best way that I can think of for you to fall into the same trap as your friends." Master Kumu gave the group a cold stare, "What help would you be then?"

Reluctantly, Great Buffalo cast aside his spear. His two companions followed his lead. "What would you have us do?" Great Buffalo asked.

"First, start by helping Aweida back to Alamea's hut where he can recover from his injuries. He has been about as useful as he can be in his current condition."

Hearing these words Aweida began to protest and tried to rise but nearly toppled over. Master Kumu motioned to Great Buffalo and Red Deer, "Take him to Alamea. She will know how to care for him."

With someone on each arm, Aweida shuffled off still muttering protests, toward Alamea's hut where the old woman stood waiting.

When the others were out of earshot, the old man motioned for Inoa to come closer. Lowering his voice he said, "Take the skiff[70] and go quickly. Confer with the families to find out what happened and where our friends are being held. Then return here and tell us what you've found."

###

Great Buffalo and Red Deer helped Aweida onto the sleeping mat in Alamea's hut. They were about to leave when she said, "Wait, I need your help. He needs to take this potion, and he may not like it."

Hearing these words, Aweida started to protest and tried to sit up. The lads pinned him down. Though weakened by his injuries, Aweida hoped to throw them off and continued to squirm. Through flailing arms and legs, he saw Alamea, a large bowl and ladle in hand, approach and he closed his mouth tightly. His eyes spewed the venom he could not speak.

Unperturbed, the old woman spooned a ladle full of the bowl's contents into a small cup. Standing over Aweida's head she said, "Now, Chief Aweida of the house of Nauru, we can do this the easy way or we can do this the hard way, but either way, we will do this."

With her free hand, she pinched his nose and closed off his air supply. He was able to hold out for a few moments, but succumbed to the need for air. Aweida parted his lips just slightly hoping to catch a quick breath and close up again. As quick as he was, Alamea was quicker. She poured the contents of the cup through his parted lips, dropped the cup, and used her newly freed hand to cover his mouth. Unable to

---

[70] Skiff - this is a small boat, which may be paddled or sailed. Today, there are a number of different types of small crafts referred to as skiffs. Traditionally these are coastal or river craft used for leisure or fishing and can carry one-person or small crew.

spit out the liquid, Aweida sputtered and choked, but swallowed it despite his best efforts not too.

Alamea took her hands away and looked at him. His eyes burned with hatred and he continued to fight. She dipped the ladle into the bowl, filled another cup, and repeated the process. He fought less this time. Turning to the bowl again, she filled the cup and turned back. Aweida's eyes were glazing over and his struggles reduced to twitches. She lifted Aweida's head, put the cup to his lips, and coaxed him to sip the cup's contents. He did not resist.

Finished, she turned to the two young men. "You may go back to see Master Kumu. Please tell him that Chief Aweida is ready to talk now."

Great Buffalo was surprised to find Master Kumu sitting alone at the campfire. Red Deer seemed to expect nothing less. "Where's Inoa?" Great Buffalo asked.

"He had to run an errand." Kumu replied. "He will be back later and help us plan our next move."

Great Buffalo was puzzled. *In the face of everything, what kind of errand was so important that it delayed helping our friends?*

"Sir," Red Deer said, "Alamea asked that we tell you that Chief Aweida is ready to talk now."

"Ah, good, I always enjoy good conversation, and his should be a very good conversation," Kumu said and struggled to get up. "My friends, if you could help me up, I would appreciate it. These old bones don't move as well as they once did."

On his feet, with the help of the two lads, they started for Alamea's hut. Great Buffalo was as puzzled as Red Deer. "How are you going to talk with him?" he said. "The man sleeps."

"Ahhh, sometimes," the old man said, "that is the best time to talk. Men can deceive when awake. They can pretend they are what they are not. Alamea said our guest acted more seriously injured than her exam showed. This morning, with the additional help of her skills, the truth will become known, and secrets will be told. I think it will be an interesting and helpful talk."

"The children are asleep," Alamea explained. "I thought it best they sleep while we work."

"But how…," Great Buffalo started, but was cut off when the old women handed him a cup.

"You look tired," she said. "Perhaps you should drink this and you can sleep, too."

Great Buffalo took one look into the dark fluid in the cup and hurriedly handed it back to her. "I'm awake. I'll be okay," he said, a wry grin playing across his face. *I think I can get along quite well without your magic.*

"It is time we get started," Kumu said and took a seat next to the man on the sleep mat. He motioned to the others to be seated. The pair of lads took a place on either side of him. Alamea sat on the opposite side near Aweida's head, fingers wrapped around his wrist. She softly counted his slowing heartbeat, tracking the unheard rhythm. Satisfied all was okay, she nodded to Kumu.

"What is your name?" he asked the sleeping man.

"I am Chief Aweida of the house of Nauru," was his reply.

"Do you have children?"

"Yes, I have two, a boy, and a girl."

"What are your children's names?" Kumu continued with these non-threatening questions as if in polite conversation with someone he just met.

"The boy is called Arapeta, and the girl is called Areta."

"Do you like to go to sea?"

"Yes," he replied, smiling.

"Why did you last go to sea?"

"Mine was one of several ships sent out on a search."

"A search? How interesting. What were you sent to search for?"

"I was sent to search for the woman called 'Aukai."

Master Kumu nodded. One-by-one, Aditsan's suspicious were being confirmed.

The wise old man, wishing confirmation of this woman's identity, asked, "This woman you call 'Aukai is she the one who is also called Abooksigun?"

"Yes, some call her that."

Kumu was sure that Aweida had lead Abooksigun into a trap, but he wanted confirmation. "What were you supposed to do when you found her?"

"I was to get her to return to the Naacal."

"How would you do that?"

"I was instructed to tell her that both her uncle, Pupule Uku, and her betrothed are dead. Her people are in turmoil. Her return could bring peace to the Naacal." Aweida took a deep breath and stirred a little.

"How could she do that?" Kumu pressed for more information.

Agitated, Aweida groaned as if he faced his own internal turmoil. Beads of sweat broke out on his forehead. Alamea held up a warning hand then mopped his brow with a cool cloth. Taking his wrist, she began counting. After a few moments, she nodded to Kumu.

Master Kumu leaned in closer and began again. "Who asked you to bring her back?"

"Pupule Uku."

"Her uncle? Pupule Uku, the man who is her father's brother by marriage." Master Kumu provided the detail to confirm they were speaking of the same person.

"Yes, he sent me to find her and bring her back."

"He is alive, but you were to tell her he was dead?" Master Kumu asked.

"Yes, he was sure she would not return if she knew he was alive, but would return if she believed that story."

"Where is 'Aukai now?" Aweida stirred, but he did not seem to be in distress.

"Pupule Uku has her at his compound."

"And the man with her, where is he?"

"He is being held aboard Pupule Uku's great ship."

Kumu thoughtfully stroked his chin. "Why were you beaten and thrown into the water?"

"Pupule Uku wanted to make it look like I suffered and then escaped so my story would be believable."

"Believable? Believable to whom?" Kumu asked

"By 'Aukai's friends," Aweida replied dreamily.

"Why would it be necessary for her friends to believe you?"

"So they would be willing and eager to follow me back to where they could be captured."

"How would you do that?" Even Kumu seemed puzzled.

"After I told them I was attacked. They would want to rescue their friends. I would lead them to the place where 'Aukai was taken."

"Interesting, and why would he want to capture her friends?"

"He wanted 'Aukai's friends close in order to insure her cooperation and keep her from running away again." Aweida said and then he let out a long sigh.

Still holding his wrist and counting, Alamea shook her head. "We should not go further right now, or he will be completely gone."

Master Kumu nodded knowingly. "We have enough information for now and can come back for more, later."

Great Buffalo spit. "He'll remember this and won't be as cooperative next time, but we can help change his mind." Red Deer, next to him, put a hand on Great Buffalo's shoulder.

Master Kumu chuckled and waved a dismissive hand. "When he wakes, any memories he has will seem like a fading dream."

The two lads seemed to relax, but only after Red Deer added, "Still, if there's a problem, we're here to help."

Master Kumu nodded knowingly. "It is harder to wait than to act, but waiting and knowledge often saves us from rushing into a trap, don't you agree?" Without delaying to hear their response, he added, "Your friend Aditsan suspected Aweida, and the words we heard from this man's lips confirmed what we all wished were not true. I hope that Inoa's errand produces something that helps us plan our next move. Until then, we have to wait for his return."

Chapter 22: Reporting Back

Great Buffalo, spear propped against his shoulder, sat wrapped in his sleep robe with his back against a palm tree. He watched Red Deer idly stir the fire again. "How many more times are you going to play with the coals?"

"Go to sleep, my friend," Red Deer replied. "We were up most of the night and then all day, netting fish and cutting them up. I don't know what Master Kumu wants with the fish, but I'm sure we'll find out. Anyway, you've got to be as tired as I am, so I'll take the first watch and then you can play with the fire while I sleep."

Great Buffalo stretched and yawned. "Maybe you're right," he said. "Time seems to go quicker when you're asleep. When word comes, we can plan what to do next, and we will be rested and ready for action."

Red Deer watched his friend curl up under the tree and pull the sleep robe around him, a hand still clutching his spear. He seemed to fall asleep the instant he laid his head on his arm. Leaning back against a rock, Red Deer watched the flames dance and traced the embers as they floated up into the dark sky. When he looked at the fire again, it was a mere mass of ash-covered coals, their feeble light peering through their gray topcoat. On the eastern horizon, a slight glow signaled the pending sunrise. A small bouquet of flowers replaced Great Buffalo's spear. His bouquet matched the one Red Deer held. He did not know how either one got there.

Knowing that Alamea would need a fire to make breakfast, he tossed the flowers aside, stirred the coals, and then slowly added tinder and kindling. By the time Great Buffalo woke, Red Deer had created a respectable fire.

Great Buffalo sat up, looked at the flowers in his hand, and looked around. Scratching his head, he tossed the flowers away. "I guess I slept all night," he said. "You should have called me."

"I would have," Red Deer confessed, "had I been awake. I think that we had some help sleeping from Alamea."

"I thought I heard voices," Alamea said. Neither of the lads had heard her soft padding step as she came up the path.

Great Buffalo stretched. "I don't think I moved all night. Alamea, what did you give us?"

"You both worked hard yesterday. I thought you needed something so I gave you a weaker form of the potion I gave Aweida."

Red Deer elbowed Great Buffalo. "Maybe we should get some of Alamea's potion to take back with us."

"I can think of a couple of people to use it on," agreed Great Buffalo.

The old woman wagged a finger under their noses. "Great magic means great responsibility," she warned.

"When do we eat, Alamea," Red Deer asked, quickly changing the subject.

Reaching in the basket over her arm, she pulled out two small chunks of bread, tossing one to each of them. "This should be good for a start," she said, "now bring a torch and follow me."

Without another word, she started down the path for the beach. Knowing she was a woman of few words and even fewer explanations, Red Deer looked at Great Buffalo and then fell in step behind the old woman before quickly being swallowed by the dark. Great Buffalo picked a brand from the fire and followed his friend. They both knew she would tell them more when the time was right. This was not the time.

When the lads caught up with the old woman, she was walking along the beach just above the high-water mark as if she was taking an afternoon stroll. Reaching a sandy strip, she stopped and turned to Great Buffalo. "Hold the torch high and wave it back-and-forth," she instructed.

Great Buffalo held the flame up and made several quarter-circle motions, forward to his waist and then back up to where he started.

"Enough with the fire," Alamea said, "they've seen us." Before either lad could ask questions, a small dugout cut through the still waters until it came to a stop in the soft sand; two more followed the first. Each craft held four men. The occupants of each vessel hopped out and pulled their craft up on the beach.

Inoa came running up to his two friends. "I'm back and I have news of...."

Alamea cut him off by thrusting the basket at him and saying, "Pass this out to your men, and then have them hide their canoes away from prying eyes. When that's done, bring them back to our camp where we can have a good breakfast, then we can talk." She looked at him to see if he had any questions, but the look she gave stifled any response.

Turning to Red Deer and Great Buffalo she said, "You two follow me. Breakfast won't fix itself."

Master Kumu joined them after breakfast, taking time to greet each of the new arrivals individually. Finally, he took a seat and began, "It is time for us to tell what we know. Then we will be able to consider our next steps and plan accordingly."

"But sir," Red Deer interrupted, "what about Chief Aweida? Won't he hear our plans?" Not having thought about this, Great Buffalo stiffened at the prospect of having to sit on the man.

Master Kumu laughed quietly. "As you know, Chief Aweida was injured. With Alamea's help, he is resting quietly... as are his children. You need not worry my son."

Red Deer breathed a sigh of relief, and Great Buffalo relaxed. Kumu pointed to Red Deer and said, "To the best of your recollection, tell our friends what Aweida told us."

Red Deer stood before the group. All eyes were on him. He swallowed hard, and began, "The woman you know as 'Aukai, we called Abooksigun. She is our friend, and we would risk our life for her. With Alamea's help, Chief Aweida told us that her uncle, Pupule Uku, sent him to locate her and bring her back. The man whom she feared and despised, instructed Aweida to tell her that he was dead and her people were in turmoil. Her return would bring peace to the Naacal." Red Deer paused to look at his audience. They were listening, but showed no emotion and had no questions. He continued, "Aweida led our friends into a trap. He returned here, after pretending to have escaped, hoping to lure us into following him. If he had been successful, we would have been used to obtain Abooksigun-'Aukai's cooperation. It was Master Kumu's wisdom that kept us from being captured." Red Deer, having completed his story, looked at Master Kumu to see if there was anything more to add. The old man nodded and Red Deer sat down.

Kumu turned to Inoa. "What have you found out?"

Inoa rose and addressed everyone. "These men, trusted friends of 'Aukai and Master Kumu, have reached out to others to find out what they know. They confirm that Aweida led 'Aukai and her mate into a trap. She is held prisoner in his compound. Her mate—the one you call Aditsan—is held aboard Pupule Uku's great ship. Her uncle sent Aweida back to capture her friends who came across the great waters with her. He could use all of their lives in barter for her cooperation." Inoa, having told what he knew, looked to Master Kumu.

Thoughtfully, Kumu scratched his chin and then asked, "Where is this great ship where our friend Aditsan is held?"

"I am told that it is anchored off the seaside of the reef," Inoa answered.

"And 'Aukai," Kumu asked, "is held where?"

"In Pupule Uku's compound on top of the bluff overlooking the sea so she can see the great ship where her mate is held," Inoa said. "Every evening she is brought out to the overlook. From there she can see her mate marched out, tied up, and flogged."

"Our friends do not deserve this punishment," Kumu said. "We must create a plan to rescue them."

Inoa made a face. "Her uncle is wily. He separated them so they cannot plot together. As it stands, if he escapes, it puts her life in danger; and if she escapes, his life is forfeited."

"Then," Master Kumu said, "we must make a plan to rescue both of them at the same time."

Chapter 23: Action

Dusk. The time when failing light makes it hard to see detail. Just offshore, almost hidden in the shadow cast by the bluff, two dugouts skim across the calm water. Beyond the reef, Inoa could see two more dugouts. These belonged to Great Buffalo and Red Deer.

Pretending to be fishermen, his friends spread and gathered their nets. They rode the gentle swell that let them edge ever closer to the great ship and Aditsan. Inoa knew his friends would reach the ship soon. When that happened, the next part of the plan Master Kumu had laid out would be in place.

Knowing this, Inoa turned the bow of his canoe toward his own goal— the rocks near the base of the bluff.

###

For most of the afternoon, the two fishing vessels had crisscrossed the calm water outside the reef. Pupule Uku's great ship lay at anchor close by. The men aboard this larger vessel went about their tasks. Now and then, a few would pause to watch the fishermen cast their nets, spread them out, and then gather them back in once again. With two hands' worth of men aboard their vessel, no one was concerned about two small dugouts and a few men. After all, what harm could they do?

However, with every move, the dugout crews—Red Deer, Great Buffalo, and two of Inoa's friends—played their roles carefully and counted the faces at the rail as they worked their nets. Few fish were caught, certainly nothing of any size, so those aboard the larger vessel lost interest and went on with their work.

Patiently, the fishermen guided their vessels closer to the great ship where they knew Aditsan was held. By dusk, they were at the point where it was time to put the final phase of their plan into action and free their friend … or die trying.

The incoming tide eased their dugout nearer to the larger vessel. Any closer and Red Deer could reach out and touch it. He scanned the rail above him to make sure there were no onlookers and then nodded to Great Buffalo's shipmate. The man picked up a cord, slipped over the edge, and disappeared under the water. As he swam, he towed a large fish behind him on the tether. The swimmer and the fish disappeared under the ship's closest pontoon and reappeared on its other side, out of sight from those on deck. The swimmer quietly pulled himself up on the pontoon and waited for his next signal.

Continuing to act like a fisherman, Great Buffalo began the chatter that would attract the guards' attention. Whispering loudly he said, "My friend, a big one…a really big one, it's coming our way." He struck a pose, fishing spear in hand, as if he was watching a fish just out of range. Overhead, he heard footsteps and then voices. A man leaned over the rail and watched. "How's fishing?" he asked.

"Not bad here in deep water." Great Buffalo replied, unemotional, as if preoccupied with the task in front of him.

"That's a surprise," the guard said. "Usually the better fishing is on the other side of the reef.

While his friend kept the guard's attention, Red Deer picked up a rock hidden in the fishing gear at his feet and flipped it at the pontoon, signaling the man hiding there.

"We tried that. Didn't catch anything there," Great Buffalo said. "Something must have gotten them."

Sounding bored, the guard said, "We're anchored out here to be away from the fishing boats. You're not supposed to be here."

Great Buffalo's shipmate joined in conversation. "I thought you were here to guard the opening to the harbor."

Bored with the whole conversation, the guard at the rail grunted, but sudden splashing between the dugout and the ship caught his attention and raised his interest.

Grabbing his spear, Red Deer jumped to his feet and matched Great Buffalo's pose. Another splash and he thrust his spear into the water. "I got it," he yelled to Great Buffalo.

"Careful now, don't lose it," Great Buffalo chided.

Red Deer stepped back, moving the spear back and forth as if he was struggling with a large fish. After letting just a few moments pass, he surfaced a large red snapper. The fish was nearly half his own length.

"Not bad," the deck guard said and called another man over as witness.

The second man looked at the fish, appreciatively. "Nice," he said. "That will make a great meal, better than what we've been eating."

"Would you like some fish?" Red Deer's shipmate asked. "Since we caught this, we have extra."

"Sure," the pair at the rail chorused.

Red Deer waved over Great Buffalo's craft. It pulled alongside the larger vessel, and, seated, they held up a string of fat, large fish. The guards on the ship licked their lips at the prospect of the meals they would have and leaned over the rail.

The men in the dugout stood up, the string of fish stretched between them. The pair pretended to lift their offering high, tantalizing close, but just short of the guards' reach, and made a show of rocking the dugout.

"We can't reach the fish," the guards said. "Hold them higher."

In the dugout, Great Buffalo and his teammate inched up a little, but rocked their vessel even harder as they did.

Showing his disgust, Great Buffalo said, "The dugout is too tippy. You'll have to lean closer or we could end up in the water and lose everything." He gestured, encouraging the guards to lean over a little more, to stretch a little further.

He and Red Deer raised the fish once again and the guards, determined to succeed, leaned closer. It was their undoing. As the guards' fingers closed around the string of fish, Great Buffalo and Red Deer grabbed them by the wrists and yanked. Surprised, the guards were in the water before they could cry out. Dropping the fish, Great Buffalo picked up a club, ready to silence the guards if they surfaced. The lone man in the second dugout helped the swimmer—the one who had been hiding behind the pontoon—out of the water. Great Buffalo threw him his club and that man took over the watch.

From the bottom of the dugout, Red Deer snatched a coiled rope with hooks on the end. A quick throw secured the rope around the rail. Great Buffalo picked up two cudgels[71], one end of each ending in a large, heavy knot, the other end imbedded with a sharp bone blade. He tossed one to Red Deer then turned and started up the rope. Great Buffalo scurried up the rope and over the rail. Red Deer wasted no time following him.

Moving quietly, the pair fanned out and moved forward, their way lit by a hand's worth of torches placed along the length of the ship. A woven-mat awning, tied down around the edges but propped up along the front edge, sheltered the rest of the guards. They slept confident that they were safe because the night guards would raise the alarm if needed.

With steps as soft as a cat's, they crept below. In the light of a small oil lamp, the found Aditsan tied to a post. The daily floggings had taken a toll on their friend. Great Buffalo supported Aditsan's limp figure while Red Deer used his knife to cut their leader free. He was too weak to walk. Great Buffalo threw the man over his shoulder and Red Deer, weapons in hand, led the way back up the ramp to the open

---

[71] Cudgel - A short heavy club: a heavy stick used as a weapon.

deck. Reaching the place where they climbed aboard, they set the nearly unconscious man down.

"What now?" Great Buffalo whispered.

"We'll have to drop him overboard...," Red Deer started.

"We can't just drop him overboard." Forgetting to whisper, Great Buffalo's reply was clearly audible. "He'd sink. How are we going to get him into the dugout?"

Red Deer made a face. "No, I mean tie a rope around him and ...."

"What . . . what's going on?" A sleepy voice from under the awning interrupted Red Deer. Another man stirred and then sat up, scratching his head.

Great Buffalo nudged Red Deer and picked up his club. Crouching low, the pair headed toward the awning, weapons in hand. Under the canopy, others were starting to stir, thanks in no small part to the efforts of the first man. There would soon be too many for the two lads to handle.

"Remember when we started out on Appanoose's ship? Remember the problem we had with the sail?" Red Deer asked. Pointing, almost shoving Great Buffalo toward an awning pole, he darted for the other.

Great Buffalo shot his comrade a look. *This is no time to be thinking about problems when we learned to sail. Certainly not the time to think about having to dig our way out from under the heavy sail . . . . Wait! That's what he wanted to tell me.*

Red Deer swung his club as he reached his goal. The poles began collapsing under the force. Right behind him, Great Buffalo wiped out the other. The men tried to escape, but became moving lumps under the collapsing canopy.

Jumping on the awning, Red Deer and Great Buffalo began swinging their clubs at anything that moved. They continued to do so until—out of breath and sweating—the pair stood in the middle of the collapsed canopy and nothing moved.

Safe from attack, the two lads went back to where Aditsan lay. Tying a rope around him, they managed to get him over the rail and lowered into the dugout. Before they climbed down, the pair cut the anchor ropes, setting the ship adrift, then dropped all the torches over the side. With the tide coming in, it would push the vessel onto the reef.

The dugout pushed off from the great ship and the men began paddling toward the bluff.

Aditsan stirred and moaned. Red Deer pulled a goatskin drink bag from a basket at his feet and put the spout to the man's lips. "Drink! It contains some medicines. Almena said you would need help and sent it along"

"Did you rescue Abooksigun?" Aditsan asked weakly.

"Inoa is leading a group to free her," Red Deer said. "We are heading there now to give him help."

Whatever medicines Almena sent worked quickly. Aditsan appeared stronger and sat up. "What happened?" he asked.

Red Deer handed him a bowl of food. "Eat up. You'll need this to regain your strength. Great Buffalo will smear some of Almena's ointments on your back while we talk. Almena said the balm contains something to kill the pain."

Great Buffalo, rough in nature and rough in action, began applying the salve with heavy-handed motions. Aditsan did not cry out or even wince, but asked, "How did you manage to rescue me?"

Red Deer saw that the man clenched his teeth as he finished speaking. To help preserve his leader's dignity, he did nothing to show he saw this, but started his narration. "To get close," Red Deer said, "we pretended to be fishermen. At dusk, when light was bad, one of our men slipped over the side of our canoe. Earlier we caught a large fish. After we got the attention of one of the deck guards, I signaled the man in the water. He swam underwater and pulled the fish we caught earlier up to our dugout. I speared the fish and tricked the deck guards into thinking we just caught it. We found the rest of the men asleep and freed you."

Aditsan pursed his lips. "The sleepers did not wake and give you trouble?"

"Oh, they woke up," Great Buffalo snickered, "but we managed to put them back to sleep."

Aditsan snorted. He didn't know the details of the action that occurred, but he understood the message in Great Buffalo's reply. Returning to reality, he said, "When they wake, they'll be after us in their great ship."

Great Buffalo jumped in before Red Deer could explain. "The tide was coming in so before we left, we cut the anchor ropes. When they wake, they'll be surprised to find themselves aground on the reef, maybe with a hole in their vessel. Our last boat to leave spread chum[72] on the water to attract Mako and delay the guards from swimming ashore for help."

###

The rocks under the bluff pointed at the ceiling of the sky like spears. Inoa's canoe, as well as the one that accompanied it, skirted these pinnacles to reach the black-sand beach. With their boats out of the water and hidden under brush and seaweed, they located the footpath up from the beach and began their ascent. Near the top, they found a small opening—the cave's mouth. When they were on the beach, torches had lined the length of the ship. During the climb, he had not allowed himself to look at it. Now, before ducking through the opening, he would take one final glance in hopes that it would tell him whether his friends were successful. Inoa turned to look out over the sea. White froth from breaking waves outlined the reef, but there were no

---

[72] Chum/Chumming - (American English from Powhatan) Chum consists of cut up fish parts, blood, and similar bait items. Chumming is the practice of scattering "chum" across the water to attract larger fish, particularly sharks.

lights showing. Inoa smiled. It was what he hoped to see. The first part of Master Kumu's plan was successful.

Chapter 24: Closing In

In the lead, the man with the torch held up a hand as he stopped short of the exit. "We are here," he said, his voice a low whisper. "Any farther and we'll be outside the cave, and our torch will be seen."

Inoa lay his kit aside and gathered his group around to review the plan Master Kumu laid out. "My friends, our other companions signaled they freed Aditsan," he said. "Now it is up to us to free 'Aukai." The men with him, committed to the task even to the death, remained stone-faced. "I will go out first," Inoa continued. "While I get the guards to open the gates and convince them to go help those on the great ship, you two sneak behind the stockade and find a way inside." Turning to the last man, he said, "Take the torch back down and wait. When our friends arrive, bring them here."

"How will you get inside?" the torchbearer asked.

"Hit me," Inoa said. No one moved. "I need to look like I escaped when the ship was attacked, so each of you must hit me, and hit me hard." Surprised, the three men stared at him. Nobody moved. "To make this work, I have to look like I was beaten before I escaped."

The oldest man recognized the wisdom in the ruse and made the first move. Even though he probably pulled his punch, Inoa felt the impact of the blow. It sent him back a step or two. With the ice broken, the other men also began throwing punches. Inoa collapsed under the blows. The older man called a halt.

Struggling, Inoa got to his knees, pulled a goatskin container from his kit, and began dousing the contents over him. Casting the empty flask aside, Inoa explained, "I thought a little extra goat's blood might add something to my story." He made a full-circle turn and then asked, "What do you think?"

The older man took the torch and held it close while he inspected Inoa, pausing at one point to smear some dirt in with the blood. Standing back, he continued his inspection. Finally, he pronounced his verdict, "Good."

Inoa crept along the timbers that outlined the stockade, pausing now and then to peer through the slits between the uprights. Torches topped every other post, pushing back the night. Along the far end sat a long hut with many doorways, probably for the guards and their women. Another hut, clearly more elaborate than that of the guards, stood in the center of the encampment. It was quiet enough that he could hear the sound of footsteps coming close, stopping, and then retreating—the night watchman pacing in an effort to keep awake, alert. What could he be thinking? *Another long night walking back and forth from the well to the gate, or maybe he thought, how did I draw the short lot again?* No matter what was going through the guard's mind, Inoa knew getting the man's attention was critical.

With cat-like movements, the lad moved around the enclosure until he reached the front gate. Peering through the chinks, Inoa waited for the guard to reach the well and then the lad stepped back a few paces, laid on the ground, and rolled in the sand. Satisfied that he looked as if he had crawled up here from the shore, he stopped and listened. The sound of the guard's footsteps, louder now, indicated that he was nearing the gate. Inoa moaned and then called out. The footsteps paused. The guard had heard him, but needed time to decide on his next step. *Open the gate and find a trap or wake the chief of the guards and face his wrath if it is nothing.*

Steps again, quick this time, but fading. The guard finally decided to wake someone else, probably his superior. More footsteps, accompanied with voices—irate at first, dying down to anger—broke the quiet. Inoa lay his head down on the dirt and faked being unconscious. Light from a torch pushed back the darkness. He could feel its heat as they held it close and examined him. Inoa moaned and stirred.

"Water," he croaked.

Heavy hands rolled him over, pushed him into a sitting position, and forced a drinking pouch to his lips.

Coughing and sputtering, Inoa groaned and complained about the handling. Opening his eyes and found four men surrounding him. All had some kind of weapon. Two men were poised to beat off an attack, should one occur; the other two crouched nearby, carefully looking him over.

"What brings you here, boy?" a guard, probably their leader, demanded.

"The ship...the rebels ...are going to attack...I was sent to get help." Inoa motioned for the pouch. "Water," he said.

The leader held up a hand, stopping the man with the pouch. "Where did they attack?" the leader continued.

Inoa reached for the pouch, but the guard pulled it away, just out of reach.

"Where? Answer me," demanded the leader.

"On the beach," Inoa said. "We—my father, uncle, grandfather, and I—were fishing all day. We just came ashore. The men wanted our boats. They beat us. I managed to crawl away and hide."

"They were just thieves or pirates, nothing more," the leader said. Awakened at this hour, his disdain for such a trivial matter plainly showed in his demeanor. "If those on the ship suspect an attack, they'll just sail away."

"No," Inoa jerked forward, winced at his imaginary pain, and slumped back. "No, he continued softer," knowing that he had everyone's attention, "I heard them talking about the best way to attack the boat."

"Yes, and what did they say?" Begrudgingly, the leader listened, waiting for the lad to make a slip, mix up his story, or sound too rehearsed.

"After their friends came with more boats and warriors, they would paddle outside the reef in the dark. Then some would slip over the side, swim to the ship, and cut the anchor ropes. With the tide coming in, the great ship would be on the reef in no time and helpless."

The leader, wide-eyed and nervous now, fired off more questions, attempting to trip the youth up. He was unable to shake the lad, whose story was plausible. Looking out over the lagoon, the leader could see the white outline of sea foam from waves breaking on the reef. They could not see the lights from the great ship. Were they already too late?

The two men that had accompanied Inoa crouched near the stockade and watched him, one hand on the uprights, feel his way along the side as he headed for the gate. The darkness swallowed him, and he moved so quietly that it was as if he had never been there. The two men he left behind knelt in silence and peeked through gaps between the fence. They watched for a sign that would tell them to begin their task. Torches and a night-fire worked at pushing away the darkness but left deep pockets of blackness in every nook and corner. Looking between the huts, the pair could see the night watchman walk to the gate turn and stroll slowly back to a spot beyond their view. A few seconds later, he would reappear on his return trip to the gate.

In the distance, a low cry from someone in pain. It caught the guard's attention, and he stopped to listen. Another moan was followed by a muffled voice. The watchman stubbed his toe in the dirt while he pondered his next move. Finally, having weighed the alternatives, he hurriedly walked away from the gate and disappeared from view. After a few moments, the night watchman reappeared followed by three others, all armed. No one looked happy.

Expecting an attack, two of the men took defensive positions. One man, probably the guards' chief, stood back ready to sound the alarm or issue orders, while the night watchman swung the gate open. The pair watched the men venture through the gate and disappeared from view. Soon, low voices followed. It was the sign the two watchers needed.

The first man threw a lasso over the top of the palisade and quickly climbed up. Throwing a leg over the edge, he paused and caught the rope tossed his way by his companion. He looped the second rope over another pole, dropped it inside, and used it to lower himself to the ground. Crouching silently in place, he looked around. Assured he was undiscovered, he warbled a quiet birdcall. Shortly, the second man appeared at the top then slipped down the rope to land next to him. Remaining in the shadows, the pair moved along inside the stockade to the overlook. If it had been day, they would have been able to see the lagoon, the reef, and the great ship, just as 'Aukai saw it each evening. However, it was not day it was night and their only view was out the open gate to where the young lad was telling his tale to a group of guards.

Sand and gravel groaned their objections as the prow of Red Deer's canoe gouged out a landing spot. Above them, at the top of the bluff, lay the compound that held Abooksigun. Red Deer could see Aditsan clench and unclench his fingers, working his anger off. The men set to work carrying the craft higher on the beach. They left the second canoe near the water.

"'Aukai lives," A man called to them from out of the darkness. The group on the beach moved in the direction of his voice until they found him at the mouth of a cave. Silhouetted against the light of a torch planted farther back, the man who would be their guide remained invisible to everyone else. "Hurry," the figure said, "we don't have much time."

Ducking down, he disappeared into the cave. The others quickly followed the only light in that dark cavern. The pathway twisted and turned in its upward climb. Whenever the tunnel split, the torchbearer checked for the seaweed that someone had thoughtfully used to mark the route. Finally, he called a halt. "We are here," he said and put aside the torch. Everyone crouched low and followed him out into the darkness.

Chapter 25: Trickery

The chief guard's anxiety grew. He had been unable to shake the lad, whose story was plausible. It was not a stormy night, yet he could not see the lights from the great ship. Something was wrong. Definitely wrong! "Wake the rest of the men," the guard chief ordered. "If we're not too late, we can keep our captive and catch the rebels too."

From the shadows, Inoa's two men watched the quiet night turn into chaos. Guards, still half asleep crowded around their leader and tried to act eager. "You four, stay here and guard against attack," he ordered. "The rest of you, follow me."

No one saw the young man limp though the gate and slide into the shadows inside the stockade.

The leader organized the men into two columns and then, weapons in hand, the chief, two torchbearers, and the remainder of the guards trotted out the gate, down the path, and into the darkness. The men left behind watched the others depart and then closed and barred the gate. With the sound of the bar still fading into the night, the four looked at one another and shrugged. Their unspoken assessment: *There would be no attack here tonight.*

Unaware that they were not alone, the quartet drew straws to see who would remain on watch while the others slept. With that determination completed, one man began the endless walk between gate and well while the others went back to their sleeping robes. Soon, snores all but drowned out the crunch of the watchman's boots.

###

Inoa took advantage of every patch of shadows to edge his way into a hiding place inside the stockade. There he waited and listened. Soon sounds of the sleeping men punctuated the calm that had settled on the compound.

Just outside the walls a night bird's call sounded. It was followed by another. Inoa smiled. His friends had freed Aditsan and were waiting outside for him. Nearby, from within the shadows behind the larger hut came a matching call. The men inside were ready.

Inoa looked for the guard. He spotted the man peering through the chinks in the gate. Apparently satisfied that there was nothing to see, the guard turned and sauntered toward the well.

A splash of light fell between Inoa and the safety of his next set of shadows. It blocked the lad's immediate path back to the gate. To continue to be undiscovered, Inoa would have to wait for the watchman to reach the well and start back along that well-worn path. As the guard distanced himself, Inoa would be able to move freely knowing the noise the three sleepers radiated blanketed the sound of his light steps.

A pebble flew through the air and landed at Inoa's feet. He froze and carefully looked around. One of his men stood in the shadows, near the corner of the larger hut, but out of the guard's sight. The guard reached the well, stopped for a drink, and then started back for the gate. Inoa motioned for his men to follow and fell in line behind the guard.

As they reached the gate, Inoa stumbled forward passing the guard and clutched at the bar as if he wanted to raise it but didn't have the strength. Finding the young lad here surprised the guard who leaped forward to grab this stranger.

Inoa, feinting delirium, weakly mumbled, "Must go . . . help . . . grandfather . . . ." He let his voice trail off into a whisper and his body go limp.

The guard, burdened with this dead weight, let his weapon fall. It hit the sand with a soft plop as the guard lowered the body of this unknown intruder to the ground. Inoa continued to whisper and move his arms weakly, hoping to keep the guard's attention fixed on him while his friends crept nearer.

Still trying to figure out what had happened, the guard questioned the near comatose young man. "Who are you?"

Inoa continued his pretense and gave a whispered, incoherent reply. Unable to understand the lad's words, the guard leaned in closer. It would be the last thing that he remembered.

His friends lifted the bar and Inoa swung the gate open enough to let the others enter then closed and barred it again to avoid suspicion. One of Inoa's men took up the unconscious guard's duties, walking back and forth between gate and well. Before moving on, they bound, gagged, and hid the unconscious guard's body.

The group, now eight strong, slinked to where the sleeping guards lay. Surrounding the bunch, Great Buffalo took the initiative of waking the sleepers by kicking the closest in the shin. Startled, the guard sat straight as he issued a string of loud, angry oaths. Awaken by this sudden explosive noise, the others sat up quickly, but froze when they found themselves staring at the tips of spears.

One by one, the guards were pulled out of their beds, bound, gagged, tied to separate posts. Inoa's men armed themselves with the guards' weapons. Not knowing what lay ahead, Red Deer picked up a coil of rope, draped it over his shoulder, and handed another to Great Buffalo.

The group moved ahead, but still stuck to the shadows. Inoa and Great Buffalo took the lead, peering around corners before motioning the others to follow. While cautious, they felt a need to hurry because they didn't know when the chief guard and his troupe of men would return. As suspected, there was no one left in the smaller hut. The larger structure was more ornate. Great Buffalo brought a torch over, and they looked for a way to enter.

This building was made from large stones, cut to size, and fitted in place. High window-like openings allowed breezes in and smoke out. Thinking that it would be a good idea to get a look inside, Red Deer hunted for a way to climb up to that level, or perhaps to get on the roof, lean over, and peer inside.

In single file, Aditsan, Inoa, and Great Buffalo moved forward while the rest of the men remained there on guard. "I found a door," Aditsan whispered. There was excitement in his usually calm voice.

Getting a boost from Inoa's men, Red Deer pulled himself up and lay flat on the top ledge. Notched uprights, arranged around the inner edges, supported the thatched roof. The windows were right below him. He leaned over and looked, but because the walls were thick and the windows tiny, he could see little more than the opposite wall. Deciding he needed to consider another approach, Red Deer got to his knees. Muffled voices drifted up from below catching his attention. Parting the thatch, he peered through the opening.

Just inside the entrance, in the light of Great Buffalo's torch, Red Deer could see his friend next to Aditsan and Inoa on one side of the room. Across from them, on a raised dais, stood Abooksigun, her hands bound in front of her. A cord led from her to a man—probably Pupule Uku, his black hair streaked with gray—at her side. Another man stood next to him: Aweida. A smirk on his face, this culprit, having slipped away from Alamea and Master Kumu, now spoke, "See my chief, I told you I could deliver her friends."

A hard, cold rock formed in Red Deer's stomach. In spite of their efforts, his friends had walked into a trap

Chapter 26: Surprised

Red Deer knew he had to act fast before Pupule Uku could make a move and before the chief guard and his men returned and beat their way through the gate.

He leaned over to whisper to the men on the ground. "Aweida arranged a trap for our people," he explained. "We must hurry to free them and escape before her uncle's men return. Join me up here."

The first man, boosted up by his comrades, was by Red Deer's side almost before the lad stopped speaking. Turning back, the man was able to help the others.

Red Deer tied his rope high on the closest upright and turned to the men with him. "I'm going to swing down and try to hit them," he said. "Follow closely and we can take advantage of their surprise." Before he could move, the largest of the men with him grabbed the rope, leaned back and the swung forward, crashing through the thatch. The big man collided with Pupule Uku, knocking him into Aweida, who stumbled backwards until he fell off the dais where they had stood and smacked into the wall.

Recovering from the shock, everyone sprang into action. Red Deer waved the others to follow and jumped, landing on the sleeping mats below. Abooksigun tried to run, but Pupule Uku yanked on the rope, pulling her back. Aditsan and Great Buffalo started forward.

"Stop where you are," Pupule Uku shouted. Outnumbered, he looked around for support. His only associate, Aweida lay sprawled awkwardly across the dais steps, a dark pool spreading across the floor. Seeing this increased his anxiety, and he pulled a knife, holding it to Abooksigun's throat. "Stop," he repeated. "I can cut her before you can get to me."

Stopping, Aditsan held up a hand. "Release her and we'll let you leave," he said.

Pupule Uku backed toward the farthest, darkest corner pulling his hostage along with him. "Lay your weapons down and surrender. My men are waiting for my signal."

"Your men," Aditsan corrected him, "are on their way to your ship to prevent an attack that would liberate me. They'll find your ship on the reef."

Pupule Uku edged backwards toward a curtain knowing that every step he took, the angry mob facing him took a step forward. Even in this low light, everyone could see the beads of sweat that covered this wild man's brow.

"Don't do it. Don't surrender," Abooksigun pleaded. "I would rather die than for either of us to live as his prisoners."

"You have no choice," her assailant screamed. "You are mine and your friends are mine."

Focused on those in front of him, Pupule Uku failed to notice Inoa. The lad, spear in hand, slipped along the wall.

Pupule Uku held his hostage close and in front of him. When he reached the curtain, he pushed over a stand holding an oil lamp. The gourd that held the oil shattered when it hit the floor, splashing flaming oil over the stones and then down the steps. The blazing oil cut Aditsan off from his goal. Pupule Uku smiled as this wall of flame spread out between them.

Inoa threw his spear catching Pupule Uku's shoulder. The man screamed, pulled out the spear, and shoved over a second oil lamp. The flames shot even higher and smoke began filling the room. Pupule Uku pushed Abooksigun ahead of him, and the pair disappeared behind the curtain.

Shouts at the gate, followed by pounding, gave evidence of the return of the chief guard and his men. Unable to raise the men left behind, the guards would soon be scaling the walls. Aditsan and his men were trapped between the fire and the men at the gate.

"Quickly," Red Deer shouted to the men behind him, "grab the sleeping robes. Throw them over the fire."

Two men, holding the heavy robes in front of them, ran forward and flipped the blankets onto the flaming dais. Moving quickly along this path, the group ran between the flames to the curtain. Pulling it aside, Aditsan found an opening. "It leads to a cave," he shouted. "We'll need a torch."

"I still have the one I carried in here," Great Buffalo said. Waving the torch around, he led the way into the darkness. Aditsan and the rest of the group followed, but not before the men piled everything burnable in the entrance and pushed the last lamp stand over on it. The blaze it started would not last, but it would slow the guards and provide the time for Aditsan to give chase.

The smoke grew thicker, filling the room, and making it impossible to see. Coughing, Red Deer remained near the opening and called to the men still in the room. Crouching low, they followed that beacon to reach the mouth of the cave safely.

The opening led to a cave, much like the one they had used to climb up from the beach. Abooksigun and her captor were out there somewhere in the dark. As he and his men scrambled through the twists and turns, Aditsan could hear noises—her cries, his curses—ahead of them. He knew that Abooksigun was doing her best to slow her captor down, but even wounded, Pupule Uku, desperate to maintain his lead, managed to force her along.

The path split, one tunnel going left, one right. Aditsan called a halt. "Bring the light close," he said. Taking the torch from Great Buffalo, he held it low to the cave's floor and checked the pool of light for any sign that would show the route taken.

Suddenly, he straightened up, "Blood," he said, pointing the direction with his torch. His group started moving again as they tried to catch up with the fading sounds of those they pursued.

They had not gone far when they ran into another split. Ahead of them, the sounds from those they raced to catch had faded to a muffled whisper. Frantic, Aditsan waved the torch around looking, hoping to find more blood from the wounded man.

Suddenly, Inoa pointed. "There," he said, his voice, though a whisper, overflowed with excitement.

Ahead, something glistened in the twilight just beyond the boundaries of the torch. Aditsan moved closer and picked up Abooksigun's seashell necklace.

He had made it for her after her rescue from Gray Seal's people. When he started, it was something to pass the time while his group of rescuers waited for Tigal's caravan. By the time he gave it to her, it had become something more. Until now, she had never taken it off.

Like a finger, it stretched out in the dark tunnel pointing the way. Had she managed to rip it from her neck and lay it out while she and her captor stumbled along? Or, had he done this to mislead them?

Behind them came the sound of others making the descent. Pupule Uku's chief and his men had fought their way through the flames to the opening and were following. The sound of their approach grew louder while he could no longer hear anything from Abooksigun. Aditsan knew he was running out of time and needed to make a decision.

Chapter 27: Confrontation

Great Buffalo surprised everyone. He broke the shaft of his spear and held the shattered end in the torch's flame until it caught. Smiling he said, "Follow the way the necklace pointed and we'll go this way." With a tilt of his head, he motioned to Red Deer, and the pair ducked down the opposite tunnel.

Aditsan didn't waste any time arguing. The pair had barely disappeared around the bend when Aditsan said, "Let's go." The group followed him into the tunnel that had held Abooksigun's necklace.

The tunnel, which had been steep, soon flattened out. Aditsan could smell the sea air and expected to be in the open soon. Rounding a bend, he found himself splashing in water, and then they were out.

The group stood on the edge of a small cove. Across the water, two torches burned. It lit a scene Aditsan didn't want to see: Abooksigun, tied between two pillars. Pupule Uku had used her necklace to trick him into making the wrong turn, and he fell into the trap.

###

Great Buffalo's makeshift torch, the broken end of his spear, flickered weakly.

By necessity, Red Deer followed closely behind the feeble light. Surprised when Great Buffalo drew up short, Red Deer smacked into him, almost bowling both of them over.

Collecting himself, Red Deer found Great Buffalo in a crouch near the mouth of the tunnel. He had put the torch out. Beyond them, Abooksigun stood on a raised platform tied between two large pillars. She was not alone on the terrace. Waiting, Pupule Uku leaned against one of the columns and stared out across the water. A hollow tree trunk hung from an adjacent post while, nearby, another one of Pupule Uku's men leaned on a large mallet.

On the other side of the cove, light from a torch blinked into view. Aditsan and his men had exited the cave and were looking around.

Red Deer hardly had to think about it. *There isn't much time left to act. The guards had entered the cave and were rushing down the tunnels. Each time they encountered a split, the chief guard would probably divide his men, sending some down each path. It could mean that only a small handful might reach each of their locations. It could also mean that he was wrong. In either case, if we act now, we can free our friend and get away.*

Red Deer took out his knife and motioned to Great Buffalo. Pointing to where Abooksigun was held, the pair moved quietly forward.

Pupule Uku stepped away from the pillars, stopping at the edge of the stairs that led downward toward the water. "Aditsan, Aditsan, do I have your attention now?" he called. "Give up. My men are behind you. You cannot win."

"I cannot allow you to win," Aditsan yelled back.

Reaching the pillar, Great Buffalo dropped the coil of rope he carried, and joined Red Deer. The pair began trying to cut through Abooksigun's bindings. If Aditsan could keep her kidnapper's attention long enough they would have her free. A canoe, tied near the edge of the stone patio, rocked gently in the waves. *When we get Abooksigun loose*, Red Deer thought, *we could use the dugout to escape.*

The quiet ended all at once. Across the cove, three guards exited the tunnel behind Aditsan. The guards and Aditsan's men began fighting. The battle favored Aditsan's men.

Witnessing this, Pupule Uku feared his plan was falling apart. He signaled his man with the mallet who began a rhythmic beating of the hollow tree. Great booming noises, their purpose not known, filled the air and floated out over the water.

Behind Great Buffalo, someone yelled. He turned to see two guards at the mouth of the tunnel he and Red Deer had used.

"Free Abooksigun," Great Buffalo shouted to Red Deer, "I'll slow these two down." Knife in hand, Great Buffalo headed toward the pair of approaching guards.

Hearing the commotion, Pupule Uku turned to see Red Deer trying to cut the bounds that held Abooksigun. He drew his knife and, waving both hands in the air, he stumbled toward them yelling, "Stop, you're too late. You cannot free her. It is too late."

Red Deer continued sawing on the ropes, even stepping up his efforts with every stroke. If he could not free her, he was going to have to stop and face their enemy.

When Aditsan saw his mate tied between the pillars, he thought all was lost. Pupule Uku thought he had the upper hand, but the tyrant had not seen Great Buffalo and Red Deer when they emerged from the tunnel. Aditsan saw them and watched as they crept to where Abooksigun was tied.

Her captor shouted for his surrender, but Aditsan rejected the idea and kept Pupule Uku's attention focused on him. Behind him, three guards exited the tunnel. Aditsan's men turned, and a fight broke out. The guards, outnumbered, soon gave up and threw their weapons down. Aditsan decided he needed to take more action. "Our friends may need help … and soon! Tie the guards, then go back and find your way down to the other side."

Across the water, he saw men emerge from the tunnel and Great Buffalo advance to meet them. Left alone, Red Deer continued to try to free Abooksigun.

Pupule Uku, alerted by the scuffle behind him, turned and discovered to see Red Deer attempting to free Abooksigun. He waved to the man with the mallet who began hitting the timber-drum. A sonorous[73] tone filled the air and rolled out across the water. Definitely, a signal, Aditsan thought, but what was its purpose?

Never taking his eyes off the scene across the way, Aditsan watched Pupule Uku's actions. Knife in hand, the tyrant shouted and waved his arms overhead as he shuffled toward Abooksigun.

Aditsan had to move fast. He turned to give instructions to Inoa, but he was too late. The lad had quietly waded into the water and begun swimming. By the time Aditsan looked for him, the lad had nearly reached the other side. There was not enough time for him to follow Inoa through the waters and certainly not enough time to follow his men through the tunnels. Aditsan looked around and saw his only quick option.

###

With each of his shuffling, stumbling steps, Pupule Uku drew closer to Red Deer.

Knowing he would not have enough time to free Abooksigun before her captor arrived, the lad turned and started for the despot. From the corner of his eye, he saw

---

[73] Sonorous - Having or producing a full, deep, rich sound.

movement and glanced that way to see if it was a new threat. He watched as Inoa climbed out of the water onto the stone platform and started for Pupule Uku, knife in hand.

If Pupule Uku's blood-soaked tunic was any indication, both he and his plans were crumbling. The wounded man now faced two young men, both armed. A wild look in his eyes, he came to a halt. "You're too late," he said. "It has been summoned, and there's no way to stop it."

Perplexed, the two young men stopped in their tracks. "It?" they chorused.

Before he could say anything, a spear fell out of the night sky. It caught Pupule Uku high in the thigh. Shocked, the two lads watched the man in front of them sink to his knees.

His disdain evident, he jerked the spear out and used the shaft for support as he knelt there, his will to fight draining out of him. Witnessing these events, the man with the mallet quit drumming. Across the cove, Aditsan leaned on another spear and breathed a sigh of relief.

Sounds of a scuffle replaced the fading drumming noises. Great Buffalo faced his opponents. They made the mistake of attacking him one at a time. The first one lunged forward, ready to impale the young man. Great Buffalo sidestepped the move and grabbed the shaft of the spear. Pushing forward, he hit the man with a body block that knocked him off his feet. Now, armed with his opponent's spear, Great Buffalo made a threatening move toward the second guard. Seeing the look on Great Buffalo's face, he dropped his spear and quickly headed to the tunnel.

The guard on the ground looked up at Great Buffalo who glared at him and pointed to the tunnel. The man didn't wait for a second invitation. He scrambled to his feet and quickly followed his partner.

The trio of young men headed over to free Abooksigun when the water at the edge of the patio erupted. Abooksigun, the first to see the cause of the disturbance, screamed.

Before their eyes, a riverdragon stuck its head out of the water then began trying to claw its way onto the stone platform. It was the biggest they'd seen and now they knew what Pupule Uku meant when he said *it had been summoned*.

"Quickly," Red Deer shouted, "we need to free Abooksigun."

Inoa grabbed the guard's discarded spear. "No, we'd better stop this monster while it's still in the water."

Before Inoa finished speaking, Great Buffalo had a lasso ready. He tossed his spear to Red Deer, motioned him to go left, and Inoa to go right, but they were too late to keep the monster contained. It had already clawed its way up and onto the stone surface. Pausing a moment, the beast swung its head left and right as if checking its surroundings. Satisfied it found no threats, it lurched forward.

Abooksigun watched as the riverdragon crawled onto the patio and started toward the stone steps . . . and her. The only obstacles between the two of them were three young men armed only with simple weapons and, in front of them, one lone figure who knelt quietly and hoped to go unnoticed.

With a quick flick of the wrist, Great Buffalo flung the lasso. The beast jerked its head, and the lasso missed its target. It continued to move forward until, open-mouthed, it reached Pupule Uku. The tyrant stared into the open maw and then lunged forward with the spear that had supported him. It was a desperate attempt to ram it down the beast's throat and turn the brute away. He failed. The jaws slammed shut, closing over the shaft and its holder. Whatever life was left in the oppressor was now gone.

Behind the trio, shouts filled the air. The men Aditsan sent emerged from the tunnel to witness this action. "Quickly," Red Deer shouted, "cut Abooksigun down." The men fell rapidly to work.

Great Buffalo flung the lasso again and it snapped over the 'dragon's snout. The animal reared its head pulling the lad forward. Inoa ran in and jabbed his spear in the soft tissue under its chin. The animal lowered its head darted forward making everyone backup quickly.

"I am free," Abooksigun shouted. With that announcement, more men joined the skirmish line in front of the animal.

The beast now faced a ring of spear tips. If it lunged either way, those on the opposite side poked at it.

"Move it forward," Red Deer yelled, "toward the pillars."

"Why there?" Great Buffalo asked.

"So we can wrap the rope around the pillars and hold him down," Red Deer said.

The men prodded, coaxed, and teased the animal forward and up the steps. It didn't always go smoothly. Moving backwards up the stairs, it was easy for a man to trip and fall. Looking at the downed man as a tormentor, or at least a meal, the animal would try to move in that direction, but it would meet with a series of spears. While this did little real damage, the aggravations distracted the creature's attention long enough for the downed man to regain his feet.

Reaching the pillars, Great Buffalo ran between the two uprights, and the beast followed . . . as much as it could. The head and shoulders squeezed through, but the pillars were too close to allow the wider body passage.

"You two men," Red Deer instructed, "get beside Great Buffalo and lure the animal deeper to keep it from backing out."

Standing beside Great Buffalo, the men waved their spears under the animal's nose, poking and jabbing at it, to keep its attention focused on them.

"Pass the rope around the back of the pillar and throw it to me then get on the other side, and I'll throw you the rope."

Great Buffalo looked puzzled, but knew his friend had to be up to something. "What are you planning?"

"The pillars are too close to let the animal through," Red Deer said. "If we run the rope around each pole, we'll have a better chance of holding the beast there."

Great Buffalo nodded. Red Deer's plan was not only sound, it was the only idea that they had to destroy the beast.

He followed Red Deer's instructions while the others kept the animal occupied.

With the rope wrapped around the pillars, Great Buffalo waved two men over to join him. "Hold this tightly," he said. "We have to come up with a way to finish this."

Red Deer, Inoa, and Great Buffalo stood in a circle watching the beast's tail whip back and forth. The trio knew the rope wouldn't hold the beast forever. They had to come up with a plan for its demise. The beast was planning its escape . . . and when it did, it would be harder, much harder, to fight.

"It's trussed up right now, but we can't expect that to last long," Red Deer said. Great Buffalo wiped his brow. "What are your plans? What should we do now?" he asked.

Inoa glanced over at the riverdragon, stuck between the pillars and held by ropes. The thought in his mind, most likely the same thought in the minds of his friends was, *if it reared back, how long would the ropes hold?* "You're right, the beast won't be happy to just sit there," he said. "We have to act quickly."

Suddenly, torches lit the mouth of the cave. The trio braced themselves for the arrival of men loyal to Pupule Uku.

"How goes it?" called Aditsan as he stepped out of the cave. Abooksigun gave a cry of joy and rushed into his embrace. The lads relaxed, relieved that he and his men had arrived.

"Great Buffalo lassoed the riverdragon's snout," Red Deer explained. "We managed to lure it between the pillars and it got stuck, but I don't think the beast will remain captive much longer."

Aditsan, one arm around Abooksigun's waist, looked the situation over. "How come it doesn't just snap the ropes and tear into us?"

"If it gets its mouth open, its powerful jaws could crush a man," Inoa said, "but it seems that if it gets caught with its jaws closed, it is almost powerless."

Aditsan raised an eyebrow. "Almost powerless, what do you mean?"

Inoa pointed toward the beast's back end. "Well, you probably don't want to get hit by the tail or run into the claws."

"We've got to come up with a plan pretty soon," Red Deer worried, "before the creature decides to get active."

Great Buffalo nodded thoughtfully and said, "We'll need more rope . . . and that big mallet Pupule Uku's man used."

Aditsan looked at the young man. "What are you thinking?"

"Ropes on the beast's tail and men on the ropes should take its sting away long enough that I can hop up with a couple of spears and the mallet . . . ."

Inoa interrupted, "You hold the spears, and I'll handle the mallet."

Great Buffalo gave him a sharp look.

"I've lived with these monsters longer and they have taken more from me than any of you. It is only right that the last one dies at my hands."

Seeing the wisdom in his friend's words, Great Buffalo relaxed and nodded his agreement. Before he could say anything, men exploded from the cave. The two guards that Great Buffalo had chased away returned, but with more men, men who were loyal to Pupule Uku. They began to form a line, spears pointed outward. Aditsan's men, except for those holding the riverdragon at bay, turned to face them.

Abooksigun jumped between the two sides and faced Pupule Uku's men. "It's over!" She shouted. "Pupule Uku and Aweida are both dead! Put your weapons down!"

Looking at one another, the men hesitated.

Abooksigun glared at the men. "Aweida fell! Your leader left him to die in the fire you witnessed." She looked over the line of men, right to left and then left to right. They wavered under her intense glare. "Your leader brought the riverdragons here to bring terror to everyone. He tied me here as a sacrifice to his great beast, but it attacked him, and he is no more." She took a step forward, stretched out an arm, and pointed a finger toward the ground in front of them. "It's over!" she hissed. "Now put your weapons down!"

The men looked at one another and then began dropping their weapons. Indeed, it was over.

The sleek looking ship, gently rising and falling with the light waves, rode at anchor just up the beach from Red Deer, Great Buffalo, and Abooksigun. Two moons had passed since they had rescued her and Aditsan.

During that time, Abooksigun and Aditsan worked together to bring their calm leadership to the Naacal. Inoa returned to his apprenticeship with Master Kumu and Alamea.

The memory of what brought the three of them to this beach played over in Red Deer's head: *At loose ends, Red Deer and Great Buffalo had finally managed to corner Aditsan. "We have been gone many summers," Red Deer said. "We long for the lands of our people. It is our wish to return there."*

Aditsan nodded. *"Abooksigun and I owe you much. She will not be happy at this news, but she will grant you anything you ask."*

Abooksigun interrupted Red Deer's musings. "I tried to talk you out of it, but it seems your minds are made up, is that right?"

The pair nodded. "Yes," Red Deer said, "we learned many things and have many stories . . . some are stories that people will never believe."

"You could stay here with Aditsan and I," Abooksigun said. "We could use your help."

Great Buffalo leaned on the shaft of his spear. "Inoa has made sure that the last of the riverdragons are gone and he has promised to remain here with you. Master Kumu and Alamea are here to offer their guidance. Red Deer and I have been away a long time, and we are anxious to get back."

"What will you do then?" Abooksigun asked. She had been lost in her own problems, but did not fail to notice that these two had grown from boys to men before her eyes.

"Well," Red Deer said, "I will join Tigal's caravan when he returns to Running Wolf's village. With his help, I will be rejoining my tribe. I have been gone a long time . . . longer than most."

Great Buffalo shrugged, "Since Aditsan is staying here, Tigal may be looking for someone to replace him."

Red Deer snickered. "If that doesn't work, I think Little Wolf's sister, Appanoose, may have her own plans. She may have plans even if it does work."

Great Buffalo gave his friend a playful punch on the shoulder and made a weak attempt of denying that an opportunity might exist. "It has been three summers since we left Running Wolf's village," he said, "she probably found a mate, and they have little ones crawling around."

Red Deer stroked his chin as if deep in thought. "As I remember, there weren't many men her age when we sailed away. Certainly none that could qualify, in her eyes, as a great hunter, a leader, and a master shipbuilder." He shrugged and added, "Who knows? She might like the idea of becoming a caravan wife. Either way, you win."

Abooksigun nodded. "I understand," she said. "When Aditsan told me of your request, I hoped that I might be able to change your minds. Aditsan said he had heard all your arguments and tried to talk you out of leaving, but . . . from the beginning of our adventure, I knew it would end like this."

Great Buffalo nodded. "You know, we'll always remember you."

Abooksigun, a tear in her eye, said, "I know you have made your good-byes with the others. Everyone will miss both of you." She nodded to the ship riding at anchor. "I made arrangements for a fast ship to take you back. The captain is anxious to set sail."

Wading into the surf, Red Deer and Great Buffalo climbed aboard the waiting craft. They took one final look at the lone woman on the beach before the nose of the vessel swung toward the open sea.

ABOUT THE AUTHOR

The author's career spans 40 years in Information Technologies where providing documentation and training was a major part of developing applications. During this time, whether working on large-scale computers, PC's, or networked systems, the author found the success of any applications was highest when the materials were tailored to the audience to keep their attention.

The Ice Age Saga trilogy (The Shaman's Song, The Sojourner's Tale, and [yet to be released] Crooked Foot) are all written as action-adventure stories meant to entertain readers of all ages. Footnotes are included to explain unfamiliar terms or expand on descriptions. These are not stories of what was, but more stories of possibilities, of what could have been.

The author and his wife, both retired, have been married 44 years, have three adult children, and live in a suburb of Detroit.

The author maintains a website, where he writes about his books and ideas on the background he created. He may be contacted via www.evansandrew50.weebly.com.

Glossary and References

Name	Description
'Aukai	Pronounced (AOO kaee) Hawaiian name meaning Seafarer. This is Abooksigun's Polynesian name.
Abooksigun	Algonquin word meaning "wildcat." It is the name given to the girl ('Aukai) from the shipwreck at the village of the Sea People.
Abyss	In geology, a relatively narrow, often deep, fissure.
Aditsan	Navajo: "Listener". A member if Tigal's caravan, he is Tigal's second-in-command.
Adobe	A natural building material made from sand, clay, water, and some kind of fibrous or organic material (sticks, straw, and/or manure), which the builders shape into bricks (using frames) and dry in the sun. Adobe buildings are similar to cob and mud brick buildings.
Adsila	Cherokee name meaning blossom. Lady Adsila is the wife

	of Wikvaya.
Adze or Adz	A tool used for smoothing rough-cut wood in hand woodworking. Generally, the user stands astride a board or log and swings the adze downwards towards his feet, chipping off pieces of wood, moving backwards as he goes and leaving a relatively smooth surface behind.
Aggregate	A collection of items that are gathered together to form a total quantity. In construction, an aggregate may include sand, gravel, crushed stone, or slag
Alamea	Polynesian name meaning Precious, Whole.
Algard	The younger of the two guards wounded by Little Fawn (associated with safety)
Antinanco	Native American Mapuche name meaning "eagle of the sun."
Aotearoa	The most widely known and accepted Māori name for New Zealand. It is used by both Māori and non-Māori, and is becoming increasingly widespread in the bilingual names of national organizations.

	Since the 1990s, it has been the custom to sing New Zealand's national anthem, "God Defend New Zealand," in both Māori and English.
Appanoose	Sauk word meaning "child"
Arapeta	Maori boy's name meaning 'Nobel and famous."
Areta	Maori girl's name meaning 'of noble kind'.
Arroyo	A Spanish word translated as "brook", it can also be called a "wash" or "dry wash" as it is usually a dry river, creek or stream bed—a gulch that temporarily or seasonally fills and flows after sufficient rain. "Wadi" is a similar term in Africa. In Spain, a "Ramblahas" has a similar meaning.
Askook	Native American Algonquin name meaning "snake." Long Tusk's friend and Chief of Mattocks. Older now, but in his younger day, led his tribe to conquer surrounding areas. After years of soft living, he is very interested in Bright Moon's magical powers as a means of retaining his power.

Aweida	The name of the stranger from the shipwreck at the Sea People's tribe.
Attikamekey	The Attikamekey (Whitefish People) are Little Fawn's original tribe, it had been attacked and finds refuge with the Narwikin.
Bandy Legged	Also called bow-leggedness or bandiness, is a deformity marked by medial angulations of the leg in relation to the thigh, an outward bowing of the legs, giving the appearance of a bow.
Bending Willow	A Sabala woman that Little Fawn meet while being held captive
Bog	Wet spongy ground; especially a poorly drained usually acid area rich in accumulated plant material. Also known as a mire or "muskeg", bogs consist of a thick ground cover layer of sphagnum moss or similar growth. Acidic in nature and very low in nutrients they may support thin amounts of black spruce, Pin Oak, or Tamarack Larch forest. Open water is rare, but the water table is very close

	to the surface and the ground soft with many hidden sinkholes that act similar to quicksand.
Bola	Weighted cord for entangling an animal's legs: a strong cord with weights attached to the ends, used for catching animals, large or small, by throwing it to entangle the animal's legs.
Bolt	To run off quickly; to depart in haste.
Boom	A long pole extending outward from the mast of a derrick and used to support, or guide, objects being lifted or suspended.
Bore/Drill	To make a hole in or through something in the form of a hollow cylindrical chamber (a tunnel, for example) or, to form by drilling, digging, or burrowing as if with a chisel.

Bornbazine	An Abnaki Indian name meaning "keeper of the flame". She is one of Tigal's wives and is the other of the two women who are part of Aditsan's rescue party.
Brand	A piece of burning wood.
Breechcloth	A form of loincloth consisting of a strip of material (usually a narrow rectangle) passed between the thighs and secured, in front and behind, under a belt or string. (See loincloth).
Bright Moon	Daughter of Silver Waters, as a young girl she traveled with a trade caravan and later became a tribe's medicine shaman, responsible for treating the sick and wounded. The main purpose of shamanism is to understand nature and heal the sick.
Bright Star	The name Bright Moon used when she was undercover in Kam Udo's city with Crooked Foot ("Crow")
Buttes	From a French word meaning "small hill", this .is a conspicuous isolated hill with steep, often vertical sides and a

	small, relatively flat top; it is smaller than mesas, plateaus, and tables.
Cadence	The beat, time, or measure of rhythmical motion or activity
Cairn	A pile of stones used to mark a path for walkers and climbers.
Calico	Any small repeated print design. This snake was probably a Water Moccasin, also called a Cottonmouth, and is poisonous.
Canyon	A canyon or gorge is a deep ravine between cliffs often carved from the landscape by a river. It may have steep walls formed by running water. A canyon may also refer to a rift between two mountain peaks.
Capstan	In its earliest form, the capstan consisted of a timber mounted vertically through a vessel's structure which was free to rotate. Levers, known as bars, were inserted through holes at the top of the timber and used to turn the capstan.
Carrion	(From the Latin caro, meaning meat) refers to the carcass of a dead animal. Carrion is an important food source for large carnivores and omnivores in

	most ecosystems.
Carry Pole	A pole used to carry items of equal weight. For balance, the items are fastened to each end of the pole and balanced across the individual's shoulders.
Chicha	A term used for several varieties of fermented beverages, most commonly made from maize, grapes or apples, but which also describes similar non-alcoholic beverages. Chicha may also be made from manioc root (also called yucca or cassava), or fruits, and other ingredients. The drink is often consumed during festivals or provided to visiting guests.
Chochmo	Native American Hopi name meaning "mud mound." This is the chief Long Tusk meets with after Askook sends Long Tusk into exile.
Chum/Chumming	Chum/Chumming - (American English from Powhatan) Chum consists of cut up fish parts, blood, and similar bait items. Chumming is the practice of scattering "chum" across the water to attract larger fish, particularly sharks.

Ciqala	Dakota word for "little one." One of Tigal's wives and is the smaller (and younger) of the two women who are part of Aditsan's rescue party.
Clam Shell People	This is White Badger's tribe. Crooked Foot meets them and invites them to join the Narwikin.
Cleft	Geologically, a crack or a long narrow opening in a rock face; an opening, fissure, or V-shaped indentation. A hollow between ridges or protuberances.
Cob	Cob, cobb or clom (in Wales) is a building material consisting of clay, sand, straw, water, and earth, similar to adobe.
Copse	A thicket of small trees or shrubs; a coppice
Coulee	A term applied rather loosely to different landforms, all of which refer to a kind of valley or drainage zone.
Counting	In this culture, the people count on their fingers and it is done in sets of five. One hand is a count of five; two hands are a count of ten. Individual numbers are: Da (1); Jar (2); Cha (3); Tug (4); and Mux (5). For numbers six

	through ten, Pra plus the count, as Pra-Da (6), Pra-Jar (7), etc.
Creeper	A clinging plant especially one that grows by means of tendrils, suckers, or roots that anchor it to a surface
Crocodile and Alligator jaws	Most of the muscles in a crocodile's jaw are arranged for clamping down. Despite the strong muscles to close the jaw, crocodiles have extremely small and weak muscles to open the jaw. The jaws of a crocodile can be securely shut with several layers of duct tape. (Source: Wikipedia)
Crooked Foot	A boy from a prehistoric, ice age tribe called The Narwikin ("The People")
Crow	The name Crooked Foot used when he was undercover in Kam Udo's city with Bright Moon ("Bright Star")
Cudgel	A short heavy club: a heavy stick used as a weapon.
Da	See Counting.
Derrick	A derrick is a lifting device with three major parts: a stationary vertical base topped with a moveable tower equipped with a boom arm which runs

	perpendicular to the derrick tower. The base is used to keep the tower from falling over. The tower sits on the base and can be rotated freely. The tower's movement may be controlled by arms or by lines powered by some means such as man-hauling, so that the tower can move in all directions. A line, with a hook or a loop on the end, runs up the tower out the boom arm. Like a crane, it is commonly used to lift, suspend, or lower heavy objects.
Drill/Bore	To make a hole in or through something in the form of a hollow cylindrical chamber (a tunnel, for example) or, to form by drilling, digging, or burrowing as if with a chisel.
Drinking gourd	A container made from the dried shell of a bottle gourd or any of numerous inedible fruits with hard rinds.
Dugout	A dugout or dugout canoe is a boat which is basically a hollowed tree trunk
Dust devil	A miniature whirlwind strong enough to whip dust, leaves and litter into the air.

Emissary	Someone sent on a mission to represent the interests of another person.
False Dawn	Also referred to as the Zodiacal Light, is a faint, roughly triangular diffused white glow seen in the night sky that appears to extend up from the vicinity of the Sun along an imaginary line called the ecliptic or zodiac. It is best seen just after sunset and before sunrise in spring and autumn when the zodiac is at a steep angle to the horizon. It is caused by sunlight scattered by space dust in the zodiacal cloud.
Fen	An area of low, flat marshy land where decomposing plants accumulate, forming peat
Fire-dragon-from-the-sky	A fictional beast Bright Moon used to panic Chochmo's people. In truth she used Wikvaya's hot air balloon, Travels-the-air-with-the-birds
Fire-from-the-sky	This is how they described lightning because they recognized that it sometimes started fires.
Fissure	In geology, a crack or crevasse in a surface, ice or land.

Fly-Whisk	A flexible bunch of twigs, feathers, or straw, attached to a handle for use as a tool to swat or disturb flies or other insects.
Gachi	The chief of the guards in Kam Na Udo; one of Romnog's Lieutenants.
Gorge	A deep, narrow, passage with steep rocky sides. They are usually formed by running water.
Gray Seal	He is the Chief of the Sea People. These are the people who first rescued Abooksigun when she drifted ashore and then held her captive.
Gray Wolf	In Book One, this is Howling Wolf's father. In Book Three, this is the name of a different person. He is a member of rescue party.
Great Buffalo	A young orphan lad from another village, he is a porter in Tigal's caravan. He is a couple of summers older than Red Deer. The two start off as foes but end up as friends.
Great Elk	Two different individuals. In Book One, he is the mate of Silver Moon and the father of

	Bright Moon. In the Book Three, it is the name of the master brick maker of the Sabala. He befriends Little Fawn during her captivity.
Great Ice	The glacial ice-sheet, in their view, an area that the people saw as seemingly going on forever.
Great Otter	Tribal chief of the Sabala, the White Clay People
The Great Sand Sea	Also called "The Empty Quarter" (The Rub' al Khali) is the largest sand desert in the world, encompassing most of the southern third of the Arabian Peninsula. The desert covers some 650,000 square kilometers (250,000 sq. mi) and includes parts of Saudi Arabia, Oman, the United Arab Emirates, and Yemen. It is part of the larger Arabian Desert.
Gruel	Depending on availability, they boiled cereal meal (oats, rice, semolina, etc.) in water, milk, or both. May also be referred to as porridge.
Gulch	This is a deep V-shaped valley formed by erosion. It may

	contain a small stream or dry creek bed and is usually larger in size than a gully. Occasionally, sudden intense rainfall may produce flash floods in the area of the gulch.
Gully	A landform created by running water, sharply eroding the soil, typically on a hillside. Gullies resemble large ditches or small valleys, but are meters to tens of meters in depth and width.
Gut String	A tough thin cord made from the treated and stretched intestines of certain animals, especially sheep, and used for stringing musical instruments and tennis rackets and for surgical ligatures
Hands old	The people counted on their fingers. See Counting.
Hantaywee	Sioux name meaning "faithful." He is a clan-leader for Chief Honovi.
Hardpack	Soil that has been packed down either by feet or nature, into a firm layer of dirt that is structurally developed enough to prevent much penetration or deformation. It is the most

	common soil condition if the weather has been dry, and the trail is in good condition without much loose dirt on top.
Hevataneo	Native American Cheyenne name meaning "hairy rope."
Hobble	This is a device, such as a rope or strap (around the legs of a horse, for example) used to impede action and restrict, but not prevent, movement.
Hogback	A ridge formed by tilted strata; hence, any ridge with a sharp summit, and steeply sloping sides.
Hono	Polynesian (Hawaiian/ Tahitian) word for Green sea turtle.
Honored Mother	A term of respect and endearment often used by Bright Moon when she addresses her Mother.
Honovi	Hopi Indian name meaning "strong deer."
Horse	History of Modern horses (Wikipedia): Equus: The oldest species of "true" horse, Equus stenonis, was discovered in Italy, and is believed to have evolved from Plesippus-like animals at the end of the Tertiary or beginning of the Quaternary

periods. Equus stenonis proliferated into two branches, one lighter in body mass and one heavier.

Equus stenonis crossed into North America, where similar forms known as Equus scotti are common; some types (Equus scotti var. giganteus) exceeded the modern horse in size. However, all the horses in North America ultimately became extinct approximately 11,000 years ago. The causes of this extinction (simultaneous with a variety of other American megafauna) are still a matter of debate, particularly given the suddenness of the event and the fact that these mammals had clearly been surviving for millions of years previous. Often-mentioned possibilities include climate change, pandemic, or hunting by the possibly simultaneous arrival of humans. Recent studies by a team of geneticists headed by C. Vila indicate that the horse line split from the zebra/donkey line between 4 and 2 million years

	ago. Equus ferus, ancestor species to Equus caballus, appeared 630,000 to 320,000 years ago. Equus caballus was formed from several subspecies of Equus ferus by selective breeding widely over Eurasia for an extended time. The details of this process are currently a target of research by archaeologists and geneticists.
Howahkan	Sioux name meaning "of the mysterious voice".
Howling Wolf	Crooked-foot's grandfather; an elder of the tribe and leader of the tribal council
Inoa	Hawaiian name meaning Namesake
Jaleti	Salmon, the giant fish
Jerky	A meat that has been cut into strips, trimmed of fat, marinated in a spicy, salty, or sweet rub or liquid, and dried or smoked with low heat (usually under 70°C/160°F) or is occasionally just salted and sun-dried. The result is a salty, savory, or semisweet snack that can be stored for a long time without refrigeration. The word "jerky" comes from the Quechua term

	charqui, which means to burn (meat). Jerked meat was one of the first human-made products and is derived from this crucially important food preservation technique. It was essential for survival.
Kaliska	Miwok name meaning "coyote chasing deer." He is a scout for Long Tusk, and is befriended by Wikvaya and Bright Moon.
Kam Na Udo	The tribal name of the raiders – the 'People of Kam Udo'
Kam Udo	The tyrant leader who wants the city built for him to rule.
Kamaja	The great wandering herds; Mastodons, buffalo, antelope, deer, reindeer, horses
Kauwa	Polynesian word for the slave class/caste. These were people taken as prisoners of war or their descendants. The kauwa were identified by bearing a tattoo mark about the eyes, or on the forehead.
Kohala	Kohala is the Hawaiian word for a humpback whale.
Kolata	The moon in the sky
Kolenya	Miwok name meaning "coughing fish."
Kumu (also	Polynesian word meaning

called Master Kumu).	teacher. He meets with Abooksigun and Aditsan when they return to the Naacal.
Liminaka	The one that travels on its belly; a snake.
Little Fawn	A young woman. Her father is White Owl, the Shaman of the Attikamekey
Little Wolf	Son of Running Wolf, Chief of the Sea People
Logjam	An immovable pileup or tangle of logs and like debris, as in a river, causing a blockage
Loincloth	A one-piece male garment similar to a breechcloth, sometimes kept in place by a
Long Tusk	The caravan master and bandit leader who leads his people on raids of settlements and other
Magram	Local overseer in village (renamed from Newcomer then named Ramga).He accompanied
Makaio	Polynesian/Hawaiian form of Matthew
Makata	The Mastodon that Ti-gal uses in his caravan
Mamuta	The sun in the sky

Mangy	A class of persistent contagious skin diseases caused by parasitic mites. These mites embed themselves either in hair follicles or skin.
Mako, "Mango"/ Mano	Among the Maori of the southern tribes, Mako is the word for shark, although because of pronunciation differences, Mango is more common with the rest of the Maori while Mano is the Polynesian word.
Mattocks	A tribe that is led by Long Tusk's friend, Askook. The Mattocks trade with Long Tusk's caravan and he hopes to use barter Bright Moon's freedom away in exchange for trade goods. The tribe gets its name because they use a digging and grubbing tool with features

Melanesia	This is a sub region of Oceania extending from the western end of the Pacific Ocean to the Arafura Sea, and eastward to Fiji. The region comprises the counties of Vanuatu, Solomon Islands, Fiji and Papua New Guinea. The term, Melanesia, was first used by Jules Dumont d'Urville in 1832 to denote an ethnic and geographical
Makana	Polynesian/Hawaiian name meaning gift.
Meltwater	The water released by the melting of snow or ice, including glacial ice. When meltwater pools on the surface rather than flowing, it forms melt ponds. As the weather gets colder meltwater will often re-freeze. It can also can collect or melt under the ice's surface. These pools of water, known as sub glacial lakes can form due to geothermal heat and friction.
Menehune	A derisively term used to refer to a lower class—workers or slaves (kauwa).

Mesa	Spanish and Portuguese for "table", the term is used to describe an elevated area of land with a flat top and sides that are usually steep cliffs. It takes its name from its characteristic table-top shape.
Micronesia	This sub region of Oceania is comprised of thousands of small islands in the western Pacific Ocean. It has a shared cultural history with two other island regions, Polynesia to the east and Melanesia to the south. (Source: Wikipedia)

Missoula Floods	The Missoula Floods (also known as the Spokane Floods or the Bretz Floods) refer to the cataclysmic floods that swept periodically across eastern Washington and down the Columbia River Gorge at the end of the last ice age. These glacial lake outburst floods were the result of periodic sudden ruptures of the ice dam on the Clark Fork River that created Glacial Lake Missoula. After each ice dam rupture, the waters of the lake would rush down the Clark Fork and the Columbia River,
Missoula Floods: Scablands (Internet)	http://www.pbs.org/wgbh/nova/earth/explore-the-scablands.html
Missoula Floods: Slideshow (Internet)	http://www.angelfire.com/hugefloods/Video.html
Missoula Floods: Channeled Scablands (Internet)	http://hugefloods.com/Scablands.html

Mochni	This pudgy out-walker is a laky/minion of Long Tusk. She is a constant nemesis of Bright Moon. The name is a Hopi name meaning "talking bird."
Mud brick	A brick made of a mixture of loam, mud, sand and water mixed with a binding material such as rice husks or straw. Brick makers use a stiff mixture and let them dry in the sun for 25 days. In warm regions, with very little timber available to fuel a kiln, bricks were generally sun dried. In some cases brick makers extended the life of mud bricks by putting fired bricks on top or covering them with stucco
Naacal	The name of an ancient people and civilization first claimed to have existed by Augustus Le Plongeon and later by James Churchward. Though there is no scientific or archaeological evidence for the existence of the Naacals, various later fictional works have made use of them. In Andre Norton's Central Asia

	novels, two main characters are Nacaals. She identifies Draupadi from the Mahabharata and the Hindu deity Ganesha as Nacaal survivors who advise humanity. She describes two warring factions among the Nacaals who have different aims and pursuits. Her Nacaal civilization existed on islands in an inner Asian sea and eventually perished.
Narwikin	'The People'. The manner in which many primitive tribes
Night Fires	Campfires set at night to ward off wild animals or keep raiders from attacking.
Nukimba	Rats
Nunashki	When the flowers come, spring
Nunavik	Musk Ox, long haired, heavy tusk, 8 foot long, 4-5 foot tall, can weight anywhere from 450–800 pounds. Wool is soft and a good insulator.
Oceania	This (geographical) area was originally conceived as the lands of the Pacific Ocean, stretching from the Straits of Malacca to the coast of the Americas. It comprised four regions: *Polynesia, Micronesia, Malaysia*

(now called the Malay Archipelago), and *Melanesia* (now called Australasia). Included are parts of three geological continents, Eurasia, Australia, and Zealandia, as well the non-continental volcanic islands of the Philippines, Wallacea, and the open Pacific. It extends to Sumatra in the west, the Bonin Islands in the northwest, the Hawaiian Islands in the northeast, Rapa Nui (Easter Island) and Sala y Gómez Island in the east, and Macquarie Island in the south, but excludes Taiwan, the Japanese Archipelago (including the Ryukyu Islands), and Aleutian Islands of the margins of Asia. As an Eco zone, Oceania includes all of Micronesia, Fiji, and all of Polynesia except New Zealand. New Zealand, along with New Guinea and nearby islands, part of Philippines islands, Australia, the Solomon

	Islands, Vanuatu, and New Caledonia, constitute the separate Australasian Eco zone. (Source: Wikipedia).
Ogdun	The architect and construction project manager for Kam Udo
Outrigger/ Outrigger Canoe	In an outrigger canoe and in sailboats such as the proa, an outrigger is a thin, long, solid, hull used to stabilize an inherently unstable main hull. It is the part of a boat's rigging that is rigid and extends beyond the side or gunwale of a boat The outrigger is positioned rigidly and parallel to the main hull so that the main hull is less likely to capsize. If only one outrigger is used on a vessel, its weight reduces the tendency to capsize in one direction and its buoyancy reduces the tendency in the other direction. The outrigger float is called the ama in many Polynesian and Micronesia n languages. The spars connecting the ama to the main hull (or the two hulls in a

double-hull canoe) are
called 'iako in Hawaiian
and kiato in Māori (with similar
words in other Polynesian
languages); in Micronesian
languages, the term aka is used.
The outrigger
canoe (Filipino and Indonesian:
bangka; New Zealand
Māori: waka ama; Cook Islands
Maori: vaka; Hawaiian: wa'a; Ta
hitian and Samoan: va'a) is a
type of canoe featuring one or
more lateral support floats
known as outriggers, which are
fastened to one or both sides of
the main hull.
Smaller canoes often employ a
single outrigger on the port side,
while larger canoes may employ
a single-outrigger, double-
outrigger, or double-hull
configuration (see
also catamaran). The sailing
canoes are an important part of
the Polynesian heritage and are
raced and sailed
in Hawaii, Tahiti, and Samoa as
well as and by the Māori of New
Zealand.
Unlike a single hulled canoe, an

	outrigger or double-hull canoe generates stability because of the distance between its hulls rather than due to the shape of each individual hull. As such, the hulls of outrigger or double-hull canoes are typically longer, narrower and more hydrodynamically efficient than those of single-hull canoes. Compared to other types of canoes, outrigger canoes can be quite fast, yet are also capable of being paddled and sailed in rougher water. This paddling technique, however, differs greatly from kayaking or rowing. The paddle, or blade, used by the paddler is single sided, with either a straight or a double-bend shaft. Despite the single paddle, an experienced paddler will only paddle on one side, using a technique such as a J-stroke to maintain heading and stability.
Out-walker	A person who walks next to, in front of, or behind a procession and acts as a guide or escort. They may also be employed to keep porters from acting up,

	getting out of control, or running away. On occasion, they may be sent to catch runaways.
Palisades	A line of cliffs and example of such exists in NE New Jersey and SE New York extending along the W bank of the lower Hudson River. It is about 15 miles (24 km) long and, in places, reaches some 300–500 feet (91–152 meters) high. Alternately, a fence of pales or stakes set firmly in the ground, as for enclosure or defense. Any of a number of pales or stakes pointed at the top and set firmly in the ground in a close row with others to form a defense. Finally, to furnish or fortify with a palisade.
Parfleche	A Native American rawhide bag. It is similar in construction to an envelope, but can be as large as a suitcase. They were often painted, decorated and used to carry personal and ceremonial objects. In everyday use, they were typically used for holding objects such as dried meats, jerky and pemmican.
Paxotori	A sub-chief in Kam Na Udo

	army; one of Romnog's Lieutenants.
Pemmican	A concentrated mixture of fat and protein (usually meat) used as a nutritious food as a mainstay while on the trail or as a supplement when other food was available. Traditionally pemmican was prepared from the lean meat of large game such as buffalo, elk, or deer. The meat was cut in thin slices and dried over a slow fire or in the hot sun until it was hard and brittle. Then, using stones, it was pounded into very small pieces, almost powder-like in consistency. This was mixed with an equal amount of fat. When available, nuts and dried fruits were pounded into powder and then added to the meat/fat mixture. The resulting mixture could be packed into rawhide pouches for storage until needed.
Pinnacle	Any pointed, towering part or formation.
Pitch	A resin derived from the sap of

	various coniferous trees such as the pines.
Plateaus	Also called a high plain or tableland, is an area of highland, usually consisting of relatively flat terrain. Plateaus can be formed in many ways. One is due to the erosional processes of glaciers on mountain ranges; in this case the plateaus are left sitting between the mountain ranges. Water can also erode mountains and other landforms down into plateaus.
Polynesia	(From Greek: "poly" *many* + "nēsos" *island*). This is a sub region of Oceania and is made up of over 1,000 islands diffused throughout a triangular (with sides of four thousand miles) area scattered over the central and southern Pacific Ocean. The area from the Hawaiian Islands in the north, to Easter Island in the east and to New Zealand in the south was all settled by Polynesians. The indigenous people who inhabit the islands of Polynesia are termed

	Polynesians and they share many similar traits including language, culture and beliefs. Historically, they were experienced sailors and used the stars to navigate during the night.
Porridge	Depending on availability, they boiled cereal meal (oats, rice, semolina, etc.) in water, milk, or both. May also be referred to as gruel.
Porter	A person, or people, whose job is to carry burdens or baggage
Poultice	Medicine that might be converted to a paste and applied as a salve or, used dry, worn in a small bag. Its purpose is to heal bruises, break up congestion, reduce inflammation, withdraw pus, toxins and embedded particles in the skin, and to soothe irritation.
Prow	This is the part of the bow above the waterline. Together, they are the forward-most section of a ship's structure that cuts through the water. The terms prow and bow are often used interchangeably to describe this most forward section and its

	surrounding parts.
The Land of Punt	The Land of Punt, also called Pwenet, or Pwene by the ancient Egyptians, it was one of their trading partners and was known for producing and exporting gold, aromatic resins, African blackwood, ebony, ivory, slaves and wild animals. The exact location of Punt is still debated by historians. Most scholars today believe Punt was located to the southeast of Egypt, most likely in the coastal region of what is today northern Somalia, Djibouti, Eritrea, Northeast Ethiopia and the Red Sea coast of Sudan. However, some scholars point instead to a range of ancient inscriptions which locate Punt in the Arabian Peninsula. It is also possible that the territory covered both the Horn of Africa and Southern Arabia.
Pupule Uku	Hawaiian words (Pupule) meaning Crazy (especially referring to a mentally deranged person) and (Uku) Fleas or head

	lice (as in 'undesired' little critters in your hair').
Quirt	A weighted, short-handled, whip usually made of braided rawhide or leather
Ravine	A deep narrow steep-sided valley or gorge in the earth's surface worn by running water
Red Bird	After the Narwikins are attacked, she speaks out at the tribal meeting. Her family elects not to move to the island retreat and end up captured (slaves)
Red Deer	A young Narwikin man, whose mother had died, he is the son of Howling-Wolf.
Reef	A ridge of rocks or sand, often of coral debris, at or near the surface of the water.
Rift	An opening made by splitting, cl eaving, etc.; fissure; cleft; chink.
Riverdragon s (also called 'dragons).	Salt water crocodiles. They are known to exist in both fresh water and salt water.
Rock-Hide-Knife	A selection game played the same way as the modern version called Rock-Paper-Scissors, but with the technology of the time.
Romnog	The chief of the army in Kam Na Udo

Running Buffalo	The chief of the Attikamekey and Waving Grass' father.
Running Buffalo	Chief of the Attikamekey (Whitefish People), father of Waving Grass and leader of Little Fawn's people.
Running Elk	Hunting companion of Little Wolf of the Sea People
Running Wolf	Chief of the Sea People. For generations, his tribe have gathered and traded salt.
Running Wolf	Chief of the Sea People
Sabala	The village and tribe that Kam Na Udo invaded and now occupies.
Saboniti	A large wild feline with curved tusks; a Saber-Tooth tiger
Sand	Before soap was invented and before hot waters became available, sand was used to remove dirt and exfoliate the skin.
Sanity	The older of the two guard wounded by Little Fawn (associated with Algard)
Satchel	This is a bag with a cover, similar to a saddlebag but often with a strap. The strap is usually worn so that it crosses the body diagonally, with the bag hanging

	on the opposite hip, rather than hanging directly down from the shoulder. Satchels are most commonly made of leather or cloth.
Scablands	(See Missoula Floods) Also called "The Channeled Scablands" are a unique geo-logical erosion feature in the state of Washington. They were created by the cataclysmic Missoula Floods that periodically swept across eastern Washington and down the Columbia River Plateau during the Pleistocene epoch— approximately 2.588 million to 12,000 years before present (BP). River valleys, when formed by erosion normally have a 'V' cross section, while glaciers leave a 'U' cross section. The Channeled Scablands have a rectangular cross section and are spread over immense areas of eastern Washington.
Score	A set of twenty members
Scorpion	These are predatory arthropod animals of the order Scorpiones

	within the class Arachnida. They have eight legs and are easily recognized by the pair of grasping claws and the narrow, segmented tail (called a telson) carried in a characteristic forward curve over the back with the tip ending in a venomous stinger.
Scrub	A stunted tree, shrub, or bush.
Shaman	A "medicine elder" (not always a male) that uses naturally occurring products, such as herbs, to treat ailments/illness. In order to attend to the tribes' physical, spiritual, and mental needs, they had to be adept at reading body language and using primitive phycology. They were often required by situations to think and act quickly. To become a Shaman, a person would apprentice themselves to a teacher for 20-30 years
Shining Waters	From the legends of 'the people', in an earlier time, she was the medicine shaman who brought fire.
Shoaling Waves	This describes the effect by which surface waves entering shallower water increase in wave

	height.
Silver Fox	Crooked-Foot's peer and (sometimes) tormentor.
Silver Leaf	The second child of White Bird and Little Rabbit, she tells Howling Wolf that she heard a baby's cry on the Attikamekey's rafts. This was when Small Turtle was captured.
Silver Waters	The mate of Great Elk and mother of Bright Moon. She was a great shaman whom many thought of as magical. She trained Bright Moon to follow in her footsteps
Skewer	A wooden shaft used to secure or suspend meat and/or vegetables during cooking.
Skid	A plank, log, etc., often one of a pair or set, used as a support or as a track upon which to slide or roll a heavy object. A low pallet on which goods are loaded for handling or transport.
Skiff	This is a small boat which may be paddled or sailed. Today, there are a number of different craft which are called skiffs. Traditionally these are coastal or river craft used for leisure or fishing and have a one-person or

	small crew.
Slack Water	Slack Water is a term usually used when discussing tidal flow. The condition occurs when the water is completely unstressed and therefore there is no movement either way.
Small Turtle	Captured by Waving Grass and her people he acts as a diplomat to bring the two tribes together.
Sojourn, Ssojourner	A period of time when a person may stay in a place as a traveler or guest. A temporary inhabitant, a newcomer lacking inherited rights. To reside or stay temporarily.
Sonorous	Having or producing a full, deep, or rich sound
Sounding weight	A heavy weight used to determine water depth
Spar	A stout rounded, usually wooden (as a mast, boom, gaff, or yard) pole used to support rigging.
Spire	The slender, tapering part of a structure or formation, such as a steeple or a newly sprouting blade of grass that tapers to a point at the top.

Spit of land	A peninsula, possible an island, that appears to protrude from the main land mass.
Stalactites	This is a type of formation that hangs from the ceiling of caves, hot springs, or man-made structures such as bridges and mines.
Stave	One of the thin, narrow, shaped pieces of wood that form thesid es of a cask, tub, or similar vesse l. 2) A stick, rod, pole, or the like.
Stocky	Compact, having a short and solid form or stature
Stoic	Not affected by or showing passion or feeling; *especially*: firmly restraining response to pain or distress.
Strokes	Typically imposed on an unwilling subject, this is a form of corporal punishment which involves methodically beating a person or animal. It has also been called flogging, whipping, birching, and caning. Some specialized implements for it include rods, switches, and the cat o' nine tails.
Surefooted	Not likely to stumble, slip, or

	fall. Proceeding surely; unerring.
Swell	In the context of an ocean, sea or lake, a series of mechanical waves that propagate along the interface between water and air and so they are often referred to as surface gravity waves. These series of surface gravity waves are not generated by the immediate local wind, instead by distant weather systems, where wind blows for a duration of time over a fetch (the length of water over which a given wind has blown) of water.
Switchback	A path, as in a mountainous area, having a series of tight zigzag curves arranged for climbing a steep grade.
Table	When used with landforms, this is a hill, flank of a mountain, or a mountain, that has a flat top. This landform has numerous names in addition to "table." The term "flat" is relative when speaking of tables and often the name or identification of a table (or table mountain) is based on the appearance of the terrain feature from a distance or from below

	it. An example is Mesa Verde, Colorado, where the "flat top" of the mountain is both rolling terrain and cut by numerous deep canyons and arroyos, but whose rims appear quite flat from almost all directions, terminating in cliffs.
Tallow	The white nearly tasteless solid rendered fat of cattle and sheep used chiefly in soap, candles, and lubricants.
Tattoo, or 'Tatau'	A Polynesian (Tahitian/Samoa) word meaning means 'to mark an object' such a person. It describes the tradition of applying by hand (permanent) markings to the subject's body that defines their rank and title or that of their family, in the community. Polynesian tattooing is considered the most intricate and skillful tattooing of the ancient world. They believe that a person's mana, their spiritual power or life force, is displayed through their tattoo.
Tawasiki	The one who roams along the Great Ice; a large bear
Telson	The rearmost segment of the body of certain arthropods, or

	an extension of this segment, such as the middle lobe of the tail fan of a lobster or the stinger of a scorpion
The Great Ice	The glacial ice-sheet. An area that the people saw as seemingly going on forever.
The Long Cold	Winter. Seasons occurred even in the Ice Age
The Sea People	For generations, these people have harvested salt. Tigal's caravan has stopped here often to get salt to trade for other goods. This is Running Wolf and White Hawk's tribe.
The-long-sleep	Death was associated with sleep, and is referred to as "the-sleep-from-which-no-one-wakes" as well as "the-long-sleep".
The-sleep-from-which-no-one-wakes	Death was associated with sleep, and is referred to as "the-sleep-from-which-no-one-wakes" as well as "the-long-sleep".
They-That-Make-Honey	Bees. From ancient times, Bees were known for their ability to produce honey and through the ages, many cultures used honey as a sweetener but in many other home remedies.
Tigal	A merchant who leads a traveling caravan from village to

	village. They gather goods in one area and sell them in another. He is a friend of Howling Wolf and the Narwikin people.
Till	Sediments composed of a mixture of grain sizes which were deposited directly onto the sub glacial landscape during basal melting.
Till Plain	A gently irregular plain of till, which are mixed grain-sized sediments deposited by an actively retreating glacier
Tiller	A tiller or till is a lever attached to a rudderpost (American terminology) or rudderstock (English terminology) of a boat that provides leverage in the form of torque for the helmsman to turn the rudder. The tiller can be used by the helmsman directly pulling or pushing it, or it may be moved remotely using tiller lines or a ship's wheel.
Tinder	Fine, dry grasses and other materials for starting a fire.
Todie	A person who flatters and

	ingratiates himself in a servile way; sycophant: to fawn on and flatter (someone). A servile self-seeker who attempts to win favor by flattering influential people.
Tolinka	Miwok name meaning "flapping ear of a coyote." He is the advisor to Chief Honovi.
Totem	A being, object, or symbol representing an animal or plant that serves as an emblem of a group of people, such as a family, clan, group, lineage, or tribe, reminding them of their ancestry (or mythic past).
Travels-the-air-with-the-birds	The name given to Wikvaya's hot air balloon because it flew through the air with the birds. Later, Bright Moon called it the Fire-dragon-from-the-sky in order to panic Chochmo's people.
Travois	A frame structure that was used by indigenous peoples to drag loads over land, ice, or snow. The basic construction consists of a platform or netting mounted on two long poles, lashed in the shape of an

	elongated triangle. Sometimes additional poles, bound across the two main poles, were used to stabilize the frame and support the load being carried. When dragged by hand, the travois was sometimes fitted with a shoulder harness to ease the work. A travois could either be loaded by piling goods atop the bare frame and tying them in place or by first stretching leather over the frame to hold the load being dragged. It is considered more primitive than wheel-based forms of transport. Wheeled vehicles excel on roadways, however, a travoise is superior when used on forest floors, soft soil, snow, etc., where wheels would have encountered difficulties. It is possible for a person to transport more weight on a travois than can be carried on the back.
Tree hollow or tree hole	A semi-enclosed cavity which has naturally formed in the trunk or branch of a tree. These are predominantly found in old trees, whether living or not. Hollows form in many species

	of trees, and are a prominent feature of natural forests and woodlands, and act as a resource or habitat for a number of vertebrate and invertebrate animals
Tunic	A short, usually to hip line or slightly longer, sleeveless, straight, tubular garment, gathered at the waist, sometimes belted.
Valley	A valley is a depression with a predominant extent in one direction. In its broadest geographic sense, it is also known as a dale. A valley through which a river runs may also be referred to as a vale. A small, secluded, and often wooded valley is known as a dell, or in Scotland as a glen. A wide, flat valley through which a river runs is known in Scotland as a strath. A small valley surrounded by mountains is known as a hollow. A deep, narrow valley is known as a coon. Similar geological structures, such as canyons, ravines, gorges, gullies, and kloofs, are

	not usually referred to as valleys.
Vest	A sleeveless garment, worn usually over a shirt or blouse and, in modern day, sometimes as part of a three-piece suit. A waist-length, sleeveless garment worn for protection
Wahine	A Polynesian word meaning woman.
Walking Stick	A device used by many people to facilitate balancing while walking. It may be used as a defensive or offensive weapon, and may conceal a knife or sword. Walking sticks can come in many shapes and sizes.
Walled Village	A walled village is a type of large traditional multi-family communal living structure that is designed to be easily defensible. It is completely surrounded by protecting the residents from the attack of wild animals and enemies
Water under Glaciers	Glaciers form because snow collects faster than it melts. Time, cold, pressure from the weight of the snow, and additional water, turn some of the snow into ice. The surface may appear as one continuous

	expanse, but seasonal changes cause the ice to push forward or draw back, creating fissures. These may be partially or fully buried under a shroud of snow. The glacier's immense weight, combined with the friction of its movement, produces heat which creates small amounts of water. Fast flowing rivers may have been swallowed but not frozen. Beneath the surface, protected from the intense cold, the water collects, drips down, trickles and forms rivulets. The rivulets combine to form creeks, streams, and rivers. They burrow ravine-like tunnels and eat away at the snow and ice overhead.
Waving Grass	Daughter of Running Buffalo; she is the one that Little Fawn rescues from the intruders and then she later comes searching for Little Fawn
Wawakin	Their name for cold wind which blows off of the Great Ice.
Wayfinder	This is another title for a Navigator
Welt	A raised mark on the skin (as produced by the blow of a

	whip), may also be called a wale
White Badger	Red Deer comes across remnants of this tribe on his way back to the Narwikins. They later join the Narwikins.
White Eagle	One of the youngsters that went berry picking with Little Fawn, Silver Fox, and Crooked Foot.
White Hawk	Also a member of the Sea People, he is Chief Running Wolf's advisor.
White Hawk	Running Wolf's advisor (Sea People)
White Owl	Father of Little Fawn, also shaman of the Attikamekey, an elder of the tribe and a council member
White Rain	Snow was called 'white rain' to distinguish it from regular rain.

Why is Glacier Ice Blue?	In simplest of terms, think of the ice or snow layer as a filter. From the surface, snow and ice present a uniformly white face because almost of the visible light striking its surface is reflected back. Light that is not reflected is scattered by the icy grains filtering out most of the light spectrum. If the ice is thick enough, mostly blue light makes it through.
Wikvaya	Native American Hopi name meaning "one who brings."
Wye	The name of the letter Y; A wye-shaped object: a wye-level, wye-connected.
Yellow Flower	Howling Wolf's first wife (deceased)
Zagged/Zig zagged	To move in one of the two directions followed in a zigzag course : First we zigged, and then we zagged, trying to avoid the bull; also referred to as a zig-zag or zigging.